Helen Dickson was born and
South Yorkshire, with her reti
husband. Having moved out o
farmhouse where she raised their two sons, she
now has more time to indulge in her favourite
pastimes. She enjoys being outdoors, travelling,
reading and music. An incurable romantic, she
writes for pleasure. It was a love of history that
drove her to writing historical fiction.

A FAMILY FOR THE JILTED LADY

Helen Dickson

MILLS & BOON

First published in Great Britain 2025
by Mills & Boon, an imprint of HarperCollins*Publishers* Ltd,
1 London Bridge Street, London, SE1 9GF

www.harpercollins.co.uk

HarperCollins*Publishers*, Macken House, 39/40 Mayor Street Upper,
Dublin 1, D01 C9W8, Ireland

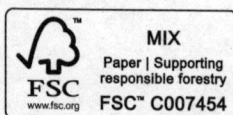

MIX
Paper | Supporting
responsible forestry
FSC™ C007454

This book contains FSC™ certified paper
and other controlled sources to ensure responsible forest management.

For more information visit www.harpercollins.co.uk/green.

Printed and Bound in the UK using 100% Renewable Electricity
at CPI Group (UK) Ltd, Croydon, CR0 4YY

Chapter One

1848

In the days before Nancy's wedding, the guests staying at Aspenthorpe Hall rode and hunted and jaunted off to the nearby village and further afield to explore the country delights. The evenings were filled with sumptuous feasts, brilliant conversation, cards, and for some of the gentlemen, a game of billiards.

It was a beautiful, sunny morning for the wedding. Red and yellow tulips stood to attention in borders and ornate terracotta pots, and the leaves were just coming out on the trees. It had rained earlier, and the air was still drenched with moisture. The ceremony was to be conducted in the thirteenth-century church which stood in its own grounds close to Aspenthorpe Hall in the heart of Oxfordshire. Sir Charles Ryland, Nancy's grandfather, a successful businessman, had purchased the house when its impoverished previous owner had hit on hard times and put the grand old house on the market. There were wedding guests aplenty, and the villagers had conspired amongst themselves to gather together and waited in the grounds of the church to see the beautiful bride and the handsome groom as they came out of the church as man and wife.

They were disappointed, for there was no groom, only a broken-hearted young woman who had been callously cast aside and jilted at the altar.

Having travelled from his home in Berkshire to spend a few days with his close friend Hugh Sutherland, Dominic Blackwell, the Earl of Osborne, was to travel by train to his townhouse in London. Hugh was accompanying him to the railway station in Oxford, just half an hour away. As they passed through a small village, crowds had gathered in the cobbled square and surrounding streets, their eyes focused on the church. There was nothing hostile about the gathering of such a large number of people. In fact, it was quite the opposite. It was joyous with everyone chatting animatedly. Seeing elegant carriages drawn up in front of the church, Dominic assumed there was a wedding. Unable to pass through the throng, the driver was forced to slow the carriage, bringing it to a halt.

Irritated by the delay and in danger of missing his train, Dominic scowled. 'This I could have done without.'

'Calm down,' Hugh said. 'You have plenty of time

to catch the train. It appears there is a wedding—the daughter of one of the wealthiest families in Oxfordshire, which accounts for the large turnout.'

The progress of the open carriage was slow. On seeing the quality of the carriage and assuming them to be members of the wedding party, some people stepped aside to let it through. Coming closer to the church, Dominic observed with little interest. In their wedding finery, a group of guests were gathered outside the church, and in the middle of them was the bride being led towards an empty carriage. She was attired in an ivory gown with a gossamer veil covering her face that did little to hide her features. His interest was finally piqued.

He saw a slender young woman of medium height. Her rich auburn hair was drawn back from her face and covered by her veil, and yet it still managed to look unconfined. Wisps of soft curls peeked out, and he had the strangest urge to reach out to her and put up his hand and smooth them back. Her jaw was strong, clenched at a determined angle, and her whole manner spoke of fearlessness, a fearlessness that told him she was afraid of no one.

She shook off the hands that drew her along. There was defiance and indignation in her manner. Without assistance, she climbed into the waiting carriage, where an elderly lady dabbing her eyes joined her. Looking straight ahead, her head held high and her spine ramrod straight, the young woman didn't acknowledge the crowd, more subdued now as they waited with bated breath for a glimpse of the groom.

Dominic looked towards the church. There didn't appear to be a groom. Judging from the faces of the guests bearing every expression from sadness to sympathy, as they left the square to continue the journey to Oxford, he realised the poor woman had been jilted.

'Who is she?' he enquired of Hugh. 'Do you know her?'

'I know her father, though not well. We meet at local social events on occasion. The lady is Miss Ryland—and quite a character according to the people who know her. She is clever, quick-thinking and sharp-witted. She is also headstrong and apparently rather a challenge for her parents. She is one of six siblings—who tease her unmercifully, by all accounts, but nonetheless they are a close family. She is more beautiful than her sisters, I think, but she always lives for the moment, apart from her charitable works—which are rumoured to be very dear to her heart.'

'How will she take to being jilted at the altar? I imagine it will take some getting over—as it would for any young woman,' Dominic mused.

'As to that, I cannot say. Only time will tell.'

'Indeed it will,' Dominic murmured, already shaking off his brief encounter with the unfortunate bride.

Three years later

Following that disastrous event—a tragic figure, lost in the shadows of the ancient village church, and in the shadows of her own broken dreams, a strong wind had risen on the drive back to Aspenthorpe, whirling away Nancy's memories of the man she would have married and of all she had lost. By the time she'd reached Aspenthorpe and had stopped weeping, something had snapped inside her and triggered a rage that could not be easily calmed.

Thomas had left her for someone who was not unknown to her. He was a handsome charmer, and as a naive eighteen-year-old, she had been flattered by his attentions, her vision so blinded by his character that she'd told herself it was all in her imagination when he'd befriended a pretty, fair-haired young woman. At that time she'd not had one cynical thought in her head, but when Thomas had not turned up for their wedding, her hopes for her future happiness with him had been smashed to smithereens. In the space of twenty-four hours, all his charms had become flaws.

Thomas had made a fool of her, but neither afraid nor diminished, she was determined to pick herself up and contemplate her future. If she was doomed to be a spinster, then so be it, but she was too spirited, too fond of life, and she would not step back into obscurity. Like her sisters, all her life she had dreamed of marrying a man she loved, a man who would love her to the exclusion of all else—a prince charming, to pass the years away within the heart of a loving family, while in reality she had been prepared to give herself to a man who'd neither needed nor wanted her. How weak, how stupid she had been.

But now she was free, free to do as she wished, and she no longer wished to experience any of the things marriage presented. Suddenly the future shone with a brighter light, and she was excited by it. She wanted a purpose in life, to be of use, to make a difference, and on inheriting a legacy from her grandmother when she reached twenty-one, she was provided with the means.

It irritated her when her mother constantly arranged social events to keep her occupied—in the hope that she might find another husband. The day Nancy had been jilted at the altar had affected her mother, as it had almost every other family member. Nancy's misfortune had sadly disillusioned Lady Ryland. The feeling of security that had once existed was gone, and the old glamour and courtesies of the world in which her mother had reared her children were receding into an age gone by. The only way she had of holding on to the past was keeping to the old traditions.

Since the death of Edward, her youngest child, who had passed away after a short but serious illness, her mother no longer visited London, which Nancy could understand. Before Edward's passing, when her father, Sir John Ryland, had been absorbed in his favourite pastimes of hunting, fishing and shooting, and collecting ancient artefacts from around the world, Lady Ryland had stayed for lengthy periods at their house in Belgravia with her three daughters—Nancy, Mary and Georgina—socialising on a grand scale, shopping or visiting the theatre. Since Nancy had been jilted, followed soon after by the loss of Edward, they seldom stayed there anymore. Nancy's father had considered putting the house up for sale, but Nancy and James, his eldest son, who still stayed there on occasion when he was in town, had persuaded him to wait. It was as if the world that existed outside Aspenthorpe had become shadowy and unreal for Nancy's parents.

As the days went by, gradually something of their old selves was restored. Friends and acquaintances began to call at Aspenthorpe once more. Her mother seemed indefatigable in her efforts to entertain. She threw endless dinner parties with a queenly generosity, at which she always excelled and which were always lively, the conversation animated, the food excellent and the wines of the finest quality. Sometimes the guests played billiards or cards after dinner or, during the summer months, spilled out onto the velvety sloping green lawns which surrounded the house.

Nancy loved Aspenthorpe. Standing against a backdrop of fields and moorland, it had been in the previous owners' family since the Middle Ages, and each generation had added bits and pieces to it. The expenditure of such a great house was a formidable sum to Sir John, even with the substantial income he received from his mills and coal mines in the north of the country.

Before her expected marriage to Thomas Marsden, when Nancy wasn't assisting her mother in local charitable works, which was something she enjoyed, she'd spent her days in languid contentment, taking part in the usual activities and gossip with her sisters, picnic parties, riding her favourite horse, tennis, swimming in the river or lounging on the riverbank, watching her brothers, James and David, fishing. James was the oldest of Nancy's four remaining siblings. Already immersed in the family business, he would one day inherit the wonderful green acres of Aspenthorpe. David, the second eldest, was doing his military service.

It was a weekend, and Mary had travelled from Leeds with her husband and their two young daughters to spend a few days. James had a social engagement elsewhere and would join them later. It was good for them all to be together as a family, but it was at these times that Edward's absence was most keenly felt. David managed to get home on occasion, depending on where his regiment was at the time and how much leave he was allowed. Nancy adored all her siblings, but David was very special to her. They had played together, grown up together, and she missed him dreadfully.

The subject of her future was raised when they were gathered around the dining table one evening. Georgina had arrived home after staying with a friend's family in London and was regaling them with tales of what life was like in the metropolis, what tunes were being danced to and the latest fashions. Certain that Georgina's friend was beginning to have a disruptive influence on her, her mother cast her youngest daughter a disapproving glance.

'All this talk of independence and liberation is, to me, anathema in an alien world.'

Nancy sighed, understanding why her mother wished to live within the old order of things. 'Times are changing, Mother. Nothing is the same as it once was,' she said kindly.

'I still think young people should be subjected to more discipline. Young ladies in particular are inclined to too much frivolity these days. You have just reached twenty-one, Nancy. What do you intend doing now? It was a terrible thing that happened to you, my dear, but you cannot dismiss marriage completely from your life. Not all young men are like Thomas Marsden.'

Nancy's hands fell to her lap as she looked at her family. She had nothing but contempt for the institution of marriage that she had once believed would bring her such happiness and fulfilment, but which had ended up promising only misery. Once burnt, one learned to keep away from the flames. 'I don't suppose they are, but I have no intention of finding out. I can think of much worthier things to do with my time than sit around waiting for one to come along.'

'Then what will you do?'

'As to that, I have given it much thought. Now I am able to access the money our grandmother left me, after a great deal of consideration I have decided to open an orphanage—a sort of institute for children.'

A look of despair entered her mother's eyes. 'You have mentioned this before, and you know I am against it. I'm aware of how much you enjoy helping those in need—and it is greatly appreciated, I'm sure—but we are a wealthy family, Nancy, and there is no requirement for you to work. Despite what happened with that wretched Thomas Marsden, I'd hoped you would have found someone else by now.'

'Then I am sorry to disappoint you, Mother,' Nancy said with patience, exchanging a furtive, knowing glance with her younger sister Georgina, who was seated quietly across the table, content, as was her nature, to eat her food and to remain silent and let the conversation take its course.

Where marriage was concerned, Nancy's feelings hadn't changed. She had mixed memories of Thomas Marsden and the times they had spent together, memories of the happiness she had felt at the pleasure and discovery of falling in love. To everyone else, they had seemed an ideal match, both of them beautiful and polished, Nancy with her glossy auburn hair and Thomas dark and always immaculate. The date of their wedding had been pencilled in from the moment they had become betrothed.

Then came the crushing disillusion. Now, three years later, refusing to see herself as a victim had helped her on the path to recovery. The ticking of the clock on the mantelpiece reminded her of time passing, inexorably, relentlessly, and she must grab at opportunity when it came. Her grandmother's legacy had given her a great sense of purpose. A husband was out of the question, but she would not be averse to taking a lover who wanted what she wanted without the ties of matrimony. The thought of living her life without ever knowing the joys and the passion of making love was anathema to her.

'After Thomas jilted me, I no longer want a husband.'

'Do you have any preferences as to where you would like your orphanage?' Sir John asked. 'Please don't look so disapproving, my dear,' he added, glancing at his wife. 'Nancy is in possession of an independence of mind and spirit and a natural confidence that I have long admired. She has opinions on everything, from the education of the less fortunate to how the working class is cruelly exploited by their masters. I am filled with admiration for her decision to stand on her own two feet.'

Nancy gave her father a grateful look, unable to resist the tide of love that swept over her when she met his eyes. She knew he could sense a storm brewing, which always seemed to be the case these days when the subject of her future was raised.

'Yes, as a matter of fact, I do know where I want my orphanage. London, that is where I will open it. I intend going down myself to seek premises I can rent. There's a property in Marylebone which would be conveniently situated for my needs.' She looked at Lady Ryland. 'Please don't worry about me, Mother. I will do well for myself, but not by marrying,' she said, putting down her knife and fork and taking a sip of her wine. 'Besides, I haven't seen any eligible young man beating a path to my door—and I sincerely hope they don't.'

'I suppose you—could consider joining the family business,' Sir John offered tentatively. 'There is always room for one more. James might raise some objections, but I am sure he could be won over.'

Nancy smiled at him. 'Thank you, but no, Father,' she said, a determined light burning in her eyes. 'I intend to go ahead on my own merit. The only drawback to that, however, is that to be a Ryland—to belong to a well-known family—might cause you some embarrassment. Also, those who bring their children to me could either embrace or reject me because of who I am. I don't want to risk it.'

'What are you saying?' asked Lady Ryland.

'I've decided to use your maiden name, Mother—if you will consent, that is. I shall go by the name of Nancy Adams—Mrs Nancy Adams—to avoid any disapproval I will face as a single woman.'

Her mother looked more than a little appalled, shocked and bewildered. 'Why—all this is very irregular, Nancy. I've never heard of such a thing.'

'Perhaps not, but Nancy is right,' said Sir John, firmly in support of his daughter's decision.

'But—how will you explain the fact that you have no husband?'

'I shall tell anyone who asks that I am a widow, that my husband was killed fighting for his country or some such thing.'

'I have no objections to this,' Sir John said. 'If Nancy wants to become successful, then it is essential that she takes on her own identity. The name Ryland is too well-known—especially in the business world. And she could be right. It could prove to be a burden—a risk, even though I do say so myself—to her orphanage's success. Of course you do realise you cannot rely entirely on the money your grandmother left you, so you must look for wealthy benefactors. With my connections, I will do what I can to help you with that. I shall also make a sizeable donation to your cause.'

Nancy beamed at him. 'Thank you, Father. I knew you'd understand. I will need benefactors aplenty if I am to succeed. I will have to furnish the home...' She looked at Lady Ryland. 'There's some old furniture stored in the attics which will never be used—iron bedsteads and chests of drawers. You can help me go through them if you like, Mother.'

'Well,' she said, a softening in her tone which told everyone that she could be brought round. 'I suppose it would be a relief to dispose of some of the things up there. We'll take a look when you have settled on a property.'

Nancy smiled, leaning across the table and squeezing her hand fondly. 'Thank you—and perhaps Georgina would help us, too—give her something useful to do,' she said, glancing at her sister.

'Yes—I would be happy to do that,' Georgina replied. 'It might be fun—trawling through all that stuff. From what I remember, there's enough furniture up there to furnish a dozen houses.'

Nancy sat back in her chair, well satisfied that she would have her family's backing for her venture.

Chapter Two

Five years later

It was the bleating crying of an infant that Nancy heard coming from the upper reaches of the house when she was admitted by a woman she assumed to be the housekeeper. She gave Nancy an edifying look, and Nancy was sure she saw her lower lip curl with distaste, making her feel that she should have used the servant's entrance at the back of the house, not the front door that led into this elegant hall with its black-and-white-tiled floor. The product of years of careful upbringing in a luxurious home and five years at an exclusive academy for young ladies here in London until she had decided to make her own way in life, she wasn't at all fazed by these elegant surroundings.

'I'm Mrs Adams. I've come for the child.'

'You are expected. I'm Mrs Mead, the housekeeper. Lady Jane would like to see you first.'

'Then be so kind as to take me to her.'

The housekeeper nodded. 'Come this way.'

They were halfway across the hall when a woman appeared from one of the rooms, holding a small white fluffy dog in her arms. Seeing Nancy, she put the dog down and crossed the hall with the unshakable confidence and regal bearing that came from living a thoroughly privileged life—rather like her own mother, Nancy thought. The woman regarded her with an attentive, critical expression in her hard and penetrating eyes.

'You must be Mrs Adams,' she said, her voice as cold as her face. 'I am the Dowager Countess Osborne. I expected you before this—an hour ago, to be precise.'

The woman's tone—condescending, authoritative and at the same time lightly contemptuous—made Nancy's hackles rise. The woman's eyes had dropped to her dress, her mouth twisting with distaste when they lighted on the fabric showing beneath her cloak, the front stained from her day's chores with the children, which she hadn't had the time to change. The Countess was wearing a lovely light green gown with a deeper shade of green lace trim on the edges of her elbow-length sleeves, and although it was exceedingly elegant, it did nothing for her tall, slender frame.

Nancy stared into the arrogant face before her, seeing angry pale blue eyes in a fine-boned face, her light brown hair streaked with grey secured in a net at her nape. She might be a woman of note, but after the day Nancy had had at her home for foundling children, she was in no mood to be browbeaten by anyone.

'That is correct, but there was an unfortunate emergency at the institute that needed my attention,' Nancy said without offering a word of apology.

'Well, you're here now, so come this way.'

The Countess set off up the stairs like a ship in full sail. Nancy followed in her wake, the little dog yapping annoyingly at her feet. The woman was a masterpiece of composure. Nancy suspected that nothing ever ruffled her.

She opened the door to one of the rooms on the long landing mounted with impressive portraits of family members past and present, and swept inside. Nancy paused in the doorway, taking a moment to adjust to her surroundings. The curtains were drawn, and it took her eyes a moment to adjust to the gloom. The room was perfume-scented, with an undertone of sickness and medicine. Glass bottles and trinkets littered a dressing table, and mirrors reflecting the room hung on the walls. Her attention was drawn to the bed, where a young woman lay beneath the covers. Her face was a blur in the gloom.

'Don't just stand there,' the Countess chided sharply. 'Come in and close the door.'

It was clear to Nancy that the Countess wanted this whole sorry business over with as quickly as possible.

She did as she was bidden and moved towards the bed. The young woman lying there looked exhausted. Her hands were shaking as she pushed back the covers, her face ashen against the whiteness of the pillows. Her hair was dark, her eyes fixed on Nancy a stunning china blue. She lay in a circle of light, beatifying her face. Moving closer, Nancy looked down at her, keeping a respectful silence. The young woman's eyes were intelligent and despairing. Nancy's heart went out to her.

'Lady Jane,' she said softly, 'I am Mrs Adams from the foundling institute. Do you know why I am here?'

Lady Jane looked at her directly. 'You are here to take my baby away. You will take care of her, won't you? You will see she goes to good and loving people?'

Aware that the future of this young woman and her illegitimate child would have been discussed and decided, Nancy nodded. 'I promise I will do my best. She will be well cared for. When was your daughter born?'

'Earlier today,' the Countess provided. 'It is essential that she is taken into care right away. The child has to be fed.'

'Of course,' Nancy replied curtly. 'I have a wet nurse standing by.' She looked again at Lady Jane. 'There is one thing I must ask you. Her name.'

'Is that necessary?' the Dowager Countess retorted

briskly. 'Surely it is for the people who adopt her to name her.'

'Rose,' said the young woman. 'I want her to be called Rose. This may change when she is adopted, but she will always be Rose to me.'

Nancy smiled down at her. 'Then Rose it is. You have seen your daughter?'

'No, she has not,' the formidable Countess snapped. 'It would not be proper.'

Pain swam in Lady Jane's eyes. 'Mother is right. I couldn't. It would hurt too much—knowing I have to let her go.'

'I understand. It is our policy at the home to keep newborn infants for the first year of their lives, so if your circumstances change and you wish to reclaim her, then—'

'There will be no possibility of that,' the Dowager Countess interrupted. 'When you take her from this house, then she will be gone for good. Now come. Enough talk. I will take you to the child, and then you can go. I will see you receive a generous donation for your institute.'

'For which I am indeed grateful. Funding for the home is always welcome.'

Nancy turned back to Lady Jane. At one point she looked at her directly, to see tears welling in the other woman's eyes. She seemed to say something, but the words were so soft as to be inaudible.

The housekeeper, no doubt browbeaten into secrecy, was holding the swaddled infant. Without ceremony, Nancy took it from her and was then hustled down a narrow flight of stairs that led to the domestic quarters of the house and the back door. Unless she was mistaken, there were also tears in the housekeeper's eyes. There was no sign of servants or footmen. No doubt they had all been given time off before the Countess had bundled her daughter into the house to give birth. The Countess's face was hostile, her heart obviously cold as she faced Nancy.

'You came to me well recommended, Mrs Adams, with the assurance that your home for foundlings is the best there is. I do hope my trust in you is not misplaced. I can rely on your discretion over this matter?'

Nancy looked at her with a bitter twist to her heart. She understood perfectly, although it was clear that forbearance and understanding were not on the list of the Countess's strong points. The moment the Dowager Countess had discovered her unmarried daughter's condition, she would have chosen her strategy immediately. This cold woman could not, would not, allow herself to be socially disadvantaged by Lady Jane's disgrace.

'You can be assured of that. Until the child leaves the institute, I will fulfil my obligation to your daughter and make sure her child is well taken care of. Goodbye, Countess.' She turned away from the other woman's stony face that made no attempt to hide the fact that she was impatient for her to be gone and her illegitimate grandchild along with her.

Holding her bundle tenderly, Nancy left the house, finding herself in a small courtyard with the dimly lit stables beyond. A cold wind had arisen since she had entered the house. She shuddered, relieved to be away from that house and the formidable noblewoman. Taking a moment to look at the infant, she paused, turning back the covering blanket. The child had her eyes closed in slumber, and her rosebud lips formed a pout. She was truly adorable, and the sadness Nancy felt at taking her away from her mother almost overwhelmed her.

Crossing the courtyard, she headed for the gate. Beyond was a lane that would take her back to the road where her carriage was waiting. The sudden appearance of a ghostly apparition out of the stables startled her. Another man followed, shorter in stature. The taller of the two was wearing a redingote, and his hat was pulled well down. Any hope Nancy had of slipping away unseen was banished. Whoever it was had seen her and wasn't about to let her leave without question.

'Wait.' The deep, masculine voice ricocheted off the walls of the enclosed courtyard.

Clutching her bundle to her chest, Nancy stopped and faced him, waiting for him to speak, hoping he would assume her to be one of the servants. He turned to his companion.

'Go on in, Leo. I'll follow shortly.'

In those few seconds, Nancy noticed a good deal about the man who had instructed her to wait. Observing her with steel-blue eyes, he stood tall. Removing his hat, he looked down at her. There was a certain arrogance in the lift of his head. His gaze, uncompromising and intent, settled heavily on hers. There was something powerful in that look, an energy that flowed into her. Indomitable pride, intelligence and hard-bitten strength were etched into every feature of his face. He was clean-shaven, his face slashed with eyebrows more accustomed to frowning than smiling. There was determination in the jut of his chin and in his square jaw.

It was a face that said its owner cared nothing for fools, and in the dark hue of his compelling eyes, silver flecks stirred dangerously like small warning lights. They were watchful and mocking as though he found the world an entertaining place to be, providing it did not interfere with *him*. Fine lines around his unsmiling mouth betrayed a worldly cynicism. His expression was set grimly, and she suspected he did not often smile readily. He would easily dominate the largest gathering without any effort.

'You work here—at this house?' he said.

His voice was deep, his manner harsh. Nancy forgot

her own manners and stared back for as long as she was able, suspecting he was a man diverse and complex, hard-edged and fine-tuned, with many shades to his character and much of it hidden. She was vaguely irritated by the intensity of his inspection, but she refrained from showing her displeasure.

'No, I do not, sir,' she replied crisply.

'Where are you from?'

He didn't ask. He demanded to know. 'I really don't think that's any of your affair,' she retorted.

'Answer me.'

'Or what?' she asked calmly.

His brows drew together. His mouth tightened. Clearly he wasn't used to being answered back.

'This is my house,' he provided. 'I like to know who comes and goes.'

This was different, Nancy thought. He must be Lord Blackwell, the Earl of Osborne. 'I see. Then if you must know I—I was just visiting Mrs Mead.'

'With your child, I see.'

Having promised absolute discretion to the Countess, she nodded. 'Yes.'

'Do you have far to go?'

'Quite a way—on the edge of town.'

'Have a care. The roads are dangerous places to be for lone travellers after dark—especially women.'

Although his manner was still harsh, that first annoyed disdain had vanished. His eyes seemed to assess her, taking in every detail. No longer intimidated, she began to breathe more easily.

'I—I have a carriage waiting for me close to the house. Now, if you will excuse me, I'll be on my way.'

A handkerchief she had been holding dropped from her hand. The gentleman stepped forward.

'Allow me.' He bent to retrieve it and handed it to her.

Nancy took it gratefully. 'Thank you so much. That was careless of me.'

He smiled. 'These things happen.' Bowing his head slightly, he turned and headed towards the house.

Hurrying away, Nancy hoped she would not have the misfortune to meet him again. He wasn't handsome in the classical sense, but with his shock of unruly dark hair, he had the look of a pirate or a highwayman, or even the devil himself. She sensed a wildness in him that surely would terrify even the most experienced of women. He bothered her, bothered her senses. She was determined to put her thoughts aside.

Dominic continued to think of the young woman with a good deal of curiosity and interest as he entered the house. The coach he and Leo, his valet, had travelled in from the railway station had dropped them off at the back of the house. Dominic had paused to await Leo and, letting his attention wander, he'd looked towards the house. His eyes had focused on the door when it was opened and the young woman carrying the infant appeared. She didn't appear to be in any hurry as she stopped to rearrange the blankets swaddling the child.

Remote and slender, she had a purity of profile which had arrested and compelled his eyes. Her devotion to the infant as she smiled and gently touched its cheek seemed absolute. Her auburn hair was haloed in the dying rays of the sun, and he thought, when she lifted her head slightly and continued to gaze down at the child, that her expression of rapturous adoration was like a medieval icon. Intrigued, he had watched her to the point where everything else became a blur around him. At that moment, something had reached out and touched him in half-forgotten obscure places.

At best, Dominic was a fiercely private man, guarded and solitary and accountable to no one. At worst, he was a man with a streak of ruthlessness and an iron control that was almost chilling. He possessed a haughty reserve that was not inviting and set him apart from others in Society, especially the gentler sex.

There had been women in his life and one wife, Sophia, who, after providing him with an heir and thinking of nothing but her own pleasure, had died after a short illness.

Afterwards, he'd taken women to his bed, but he'd been reluctant to let them into his life. His failed marriage to Sophia had impacted him greatly. As a result of her infidelities, he'd mistrusted all women who tried to get too close to him. With a feeling of regret, he thought if Sophia had not deceived him and behaved so shamefully, leaving him with so many bitter memories of his life with her and her ultimate betrayal, then he would have been willing to give his heart another chance.

This ambivalence towards women didn't mean he would never marry again, especially when he could see the benefits to himself. He could be cold and unemotional, but he felt those were the ideal attributes with which to contemplate a second venture into matrimony. He currently had several very good reasons he was considering proposing marriage to a highly suitable American heiress, Elizabeth Wade.

Dominic had no idea what had prompted him to address the young woman just now, except that he wanted to speak to her, to hear her voice. His eyes had been drawn to her bright hair and the fiery tendrils that had escaped the confines of its style and caressed her cheeks and neck. When he'd spoken to her, his gaze had been caught by one particular wispy tress which had come to rest where her neck joined her shoulder, and he'd known an urge to lower his head and place his lips right on that exact spot.

The urge had been so powerful that he'd had to force himself to draw back. He scowled darkly. What the devil was the matter with him? Had it been that long since he'd had a woman? But it wasn't that. In some far corner of his distracted brain, memories stirred, and his pulse gave a beat of recognition. There was something about the way she moved and held her head that seemed vaguely familiar, but he could not for the life of him remember where he might have seen her before. He shrugged, unable to recollect. Perhaps he was mistaken.

Without a second glance, and dismissing the incident from his busy mind, Dominic entered the house by the back door. In the kitchen, which was usually bustling with servants as they went about their work, the quietness surprised him. Leo had already disappeared, probably to the study. Striding into the hall, he paused, feeling an unaccountable air of depression hanging over the house. Looking up, he saw Constance, his stepmother, and Mrs Mead coming down the stairs. They paused, nervously, he thought, clearly taken aback by his arrival. His senses alert, he knew something was wrong. His stepmother's eyes were fixed on him. Her face blanched and her hand lifted to her throat, her mouth tightening into an unattractive line. He walked forward to meet them as they continued to descend the stairs.

His stepmother was not beautiful—handsome would be a better word to describe her. She was tall and had a regal bearing. Dominic remembered a time when she had first married his father. He had been a little afraid of her. He had tried to please and interest her, all to no avail. When he was a youth, she had rarely spoken to him, except to lecture, criticise, instruct or command. Now they had an uneasy relationship—better when they were not in each other's company.

When his half sister Jane was born, Constance had focused all her attention on her. Then her husband, Dominic's father, had been killed when he'd taken a tumble from his horse during a hunt. Dominic had inherited the title and the Osborne estate in Berkshire on his demise. Dominic's grandmother was still alive and lived at Osborne House. His grandmother and Constance did not get on and were unable to reside together in the same place. Constance remained in London unless she was visiting her family in Sussex.

Her blue eyes were narrowed with annoyance now as she gave him a sharp, disapproving glance. 'Dominic—you've taken me by surprise. We didn't expect you to return for another week at least. Your trip to New York was advantageous, I trust?'

Inclining his head slightly, he made no move to approach her. 'I managed to complete my business earlier than expected. I booked an earlier passage on a vessel docking in Liverpool. I did a detour and spent a few days in Oxfordshire visiting Hugh Sutherland. I took the train with Leo from there.'

'And Mark?'

'I have some pressing business to attend to here in London first. It is my intention to go to Berkshire to see my son and my grandmother in a day or so.'

'Welcome home, Lord Blackwell,' Mrs Mead said on a warmer note, having a soft spot for the young master whom she had known since he was a boy. 'Your room is ready for you. You must be fatigued after such a long journey.'

'Yes—I am somewhat—nothing that a stiff drink and some supper won't cure, Mrs Mead. Feed Leo as well, will you? I don't know where he's disappeared to, but he's been complaining of hunger pains for the past two hours.'

'I'll set about it right away.'

'Constance?' he said, indicating with his arm that she should precede him into the drawing room, where she seated herself by the fire, watching as he poured himself a snifter of brandy from the decanter on the sideboard.

'The house is unusually quiet,' he commented, moving closer to her. 'Not a servant in sight.'

'That's because I asked Mrs Mead to give them some time off. I've been down to the country for a few days and only arrived back myself today. The servants will be here in full force tomorrow.'

'And Jane?' After an absence of six months, Dominic was eager to see his sister, whom he adored.

'Jane? Why—she came back with me. She is in her room.'

'I'll go up and see her presently.'

'She—she's in bed I'm afraid—nothing for you to be concerned about. The day before we left Sussex— we were staying with my brother and his wife—she went riding without her cloak and was surprised by the rain—silly girl—and caught a chill. She'll be up and about in a couple of days, but she's best not disturbed.'

Dominic nodded thoughtfully, then spoke in a hard, confident voice. 'I'll have supper and then go up and see her.'

'I would prefer it if you didn't.' She sent him a stern look at the unmistakable edge of intent in his voice. 'But if you must, do not say anything that will upset her, Dominic.'

'I would never do that. It is not my intention to ever upset her,' he said, his words clipped.

There was a silence as Dominic drank his brandy and the Countess continued studying him with that disquieting gaze.

'Will you join me for supper?' he said.

'No. I have already eaten. I take it that since you have arrived earlier than we expected, your business trip was successful.'

'Yes—very. My father would have been pleased with the way things have turned out.'

'Your father!' she exclaimed bitterly. 'I got tired of

telling him to look closer to home to invest his money, coal seeming a likely commodity to bring good returns, but he failed to listen.'

Dominic's features tightened. 'As a matter of fact, he had been considering making investments in the coal industry for some time before his demise. I have made significant investments in the industry that are already proving lucrative—which should please you, Constance. Wealth has always been important to you. Whatever my father did and no matter how much of his time he gave to make you happy, it was never enough for you, was it? He bent over backwards in his endeavours to make you happy, but you were never satisfied. You pushed him relentlessly—always wanting more.'

Getting to her feet, Constance half turned from him. 'Your father—'

'He married you so quickly after my mother's demise as to be almost indecent. He was infatuated with you.'

'Infatuated with my money, you mean.'

'My father was not like that, and you know it.'

'The Chandlers were one of the richest families in Sussex.' She flashed him a look that would silence any man, but not Dominic.

'Not anymore. Your father and brothers were too weak to hold on to it. The Chandler blood has gone to seed, Constance. Accept it and be thankful you married my father. Pity they didn't embrace what they had.'

Constance's face became suffused with rage. 'Why—how dare you besmirch my family? I am your stepmother. How dare you speak to me in this disgraceful manner? I have indulged you overmuch throughout the years I was married to your father. You owe me respect.'

'I owe you nothing, Constance. It is Jane I feel sorry for. How long will it be before you find her a man to marry who fits all your criteria? Whether she likes him or not—forbidden to choose for herself.'

Constance drew herself up with dignified hauteur, resentment gleaming in her eyes. 'Jane? What has Jane to do with anything? You should concentrate on finding yourself another wife, Dominic. What are you—thirty years old? High time you considered settling down. With all your advantages, the woman you marry will indeed be fortunate if she manages to secure you. Have you by any chance popped the question to Miss Wade yet? According to the letters you wrote to Jane from New York, it is what her father is waiting for—and Miss Wade herself, come to that.'

Dominic ignored her sarcasm. '*If* I decide to marry again, I shall do so only when I am ready. As a matter of fact, Elizabeth and her brother Simon sailed with me from New York. Simon has business in London to take care of for his father before moving on to Paris.

I left them in Liverpool to travel to London while I visited Hugh. While in London, they will be staying at Brown's Hotel. I've invited them to lunch tomorrow. If you have no other engagement, Constance, I will introduce you.'

Dominic knew he would have no difficulty in securing Elizabeth Wade if he decided to propose matrimony. Her father, who remained in New York, was a wealthy American. Through his own endeavours, there was a fleet of ships flying his flag and carrying his cargo. He had land and mines of gold and silver that had bought those ships.

A widower with a son and daughter, Mr Wade hadn't passed up the chance to socialise with an earl— British aristocrats had become the husbands of choice for American millionaires' daughters. Elizabeth knew what she wanted. Encouraged from an early age to express herself and fully confident that marriage to her would be advantageous to any man, she left Dominic in no doubt that she found him an attractive prospect. As an American heiress, she enjoyed a freedom of movement and association that was reserved in Europe solely for married women.

Marriage to Elizabeth and the American dollars she would bring with her would go a long way to shoring up Dominic's own finances. He was still feeling the effects of his father's poor financial acumen, but the returns from his own investments in railroad and coal and the like were at last beginning to show significant improvements.

Marriage to Elizabeth would be advantageous in other ways as well as financial. The Blackwells had become thin on the ground. He had one son, Mark, his heir, but he would like more offspring. God forbid anything should happen to Mark, but if it did, then the title was in danger of passing entirely out of the Blackwell family. It had been troubling him for some time.

He had spent years of evasion, trying to avoid a situation such as this, ignoring the whispers and sighs of women eager to shackle him once more. And he had succeeded, believing himself immune to all persuasion, but he could not do so indefinitely. What Sophia had done to him—her betrayal and the tragedy of her death that had come afterwards—still haunted him. When she'd died, he had existed for a time in a state of misery and confusion, despising himself and everyone else who'd tried to get too close. Instead, he had spent many hours with Mark. His young son had been his salvation.

He had deliberately locked the memory of Sophia's infidelities and betrayal away deep inside him, not wanting to look too carefully at it in the light of day, but now he found it rising to the fore like some terrible spectre, trying to snatch him up in its grip once more.

When Dominic finally left New York, he had made no commitment to Elizabeth, and as yet, no understanding had been reached. She was attractive and popular. He did not love her, but making her his wife did not seem such a high price to pay for a lifetime free from financial worry. No sacrifice would be too great if he could restore some of his family's glories and ensure a more stable future for his children. Yet for some reason, still he hesitated in committing himself to Elizabeth.

He helped himself to another snifter of brandy as Mrs Mead came to tell him his supper was waiting for him in the dining room.

'Excuse me, Constance,' he said, striding to the door, where he turned and looked back at her. 'I will see Jane when I've eaten.'

'I told you she is sleeping. It would be better if you waited until she wakes.'

His mind already made up, Dominic ignored her and left the room in search of his supper.

Chapter Three

Dominic adored his half sister. She was small and slender, with rosy dimpled cheeks. Cast in a sweet and gentler mould, she bore only the faintest resemblance to her mother. Unfortunately, Constance's influence had left its mark. Determined that Jane would marry only the best gentleman London Society had to offer, she had instilled discipline in her from an early age, turning her into an obedient, biddable young woman. Her manners were exquisite, and she was skilled in everything a young woman of quality should be. Her mother had taught her how to pout prettily and sit poised and straight-backed, her hands folded in her lap in total submission.

Dominic entered Jane's room quietly, immediately struck by an aura of illness in the dimly lit room. Crossing the carpet to the bed, he stood and looked down at his sister, feeling an abiding love for her welling in his heart. She looked so very young and vulnerable and small in the huge bed, her hands fidgeting with the sheet in front of her. Her eyes were closed, her hair braided and draped over her shoulder, her skin flushed. She was in an agitated state, turning her head on the pillow and muttering as if in some kind of delirium about a child, pleading with someone to help her.

Alarmed, feeling that whatever it was that ailed her was more serious than a chill as her mother claimed, gently he placed the back of his hand on her forehead. It felt hotter than was normal.

Jane's eyes flickered open. They glanced about the room, coming to rest on him. She managed to offer a weak smile. 'Why, Dominic!' she breathed. 'Is it really you? You've been gone so long I thought you were never coming home. Have you come to help me? What a wonderful surprise.'

Reaching out and taking her hand, he bent over to place a kiss on her brow. 'I finished my business earlier than I thought. I did not know you were ill. Had I known, I would have come home immediately to take care of you. What ails you, Jane? Your mother tells me you have a chill, but I suspect it is more than that. Has the physician been to see you?'

Closing her eyes, she shook her head. 'Mother didn't think it was necessary,' she whispered, 'and as you know, she is always right. I—I will be better in a few days. Please don't worry about me.'

'But I do worry about you, Jane. All the time.'

'Have you seen Mark?'

'Not yet. I'll be going to Berkshire shortly. I'm hoping you will come with me.'

'Yes—of course. I would like that. It's so long since I last saw my dear nephew.'

'Too long, Jane, but we have to get you better first. Now I'm home, I shall have Dr Stevens come to look at you.' When he saw she was about to protest, he silenced her with a gentle finger across her lips and sat on the bed facing her, holding her hand. 'Don't argue. I insist.'

'Please don't,' she whispered, her eyes fluttering closed as if talking was too much for her. 'I-I'm over the worst.'

'What did you mean when you asked if I have come to help you? How, Jane? How can I help you?'

'Bless you, Dominic. Bless you—but you can't help me,' she murmured faintly, her eyes fluttering open once more, settling on his face. She tried raising her hand to touch his cheek, but it was as if she had no strength. 'No one can. I don't want to worry you. But don't look so anxious,' she breathed softly. 'I'm going to be all right… Mama says so…'

Seeing a tear run from the corner of her eye, Dominic wiped it away with his thumb. He was full of remorse that he had not been with her, and resentment towards his stepmother that she was treating Jane's illness so lightly when it was clear she was really unwell. 'You are upset. Tell me, Jane. Tell me what is wrong with you?'

'Mama told you. It is just a chill.' She closed her eyes, drawing a deep breath and expelling it slowly before continuing. 'Please don't argue with Mama. You know how cross she gets when you question her.'

'I'll deal with her as I think fit. But tell me, Jane. When did you arrive in London?'

'Yesterday—early evening. Why? Is it important.'

'No, but I cannot for the life of me work out why the servants have all been given time off when you need looking after.'

'Mrs Mead is here, and my every need is taken care of.'

'I don't doubt that. There's a great deal of good in Mrs Mead. She has shown nothing but kindness to us both over the years.'

'Yes—she has…' Jane sighed.

Dominic could see that she was becoming visibly weaker and felt alarmed. Leaving her to sleep, he sought out Leo and sent him to Dr Stevens to ask him to come immediately. He returned to his sister to await the man's coming. Constance was outside the room. Her face was white and strained, as if she had been waiting for him in wretched suspension. Dominic looked at her with the cold, speculating expression of a long-standing opponent and wondered not for the first time what had attracted his father to this temperamental, difficult woman with sharp eyes and a vicious temper. He could still feel the anger and every second of his helpless fury when she had treated her husband's death as nothing more than an everyday occurrence—casting him off as one would a nuisance that had blighted her life.

'What have you done?' she said, her tone sharp.

'Something that should have been done as soon as you arrived in London. I've sent Leo to ask Dr Stevens to attend Jane. She is weak and feverish. He will examine her and give her medication.'

'I told you, Dominic, she has nothing more serious than a chill. Jane will be better after a good night's sleep. I do wish you would listen to me and not trouble Dr Stevens.'

'I have listened to you, Constance—far too many times, and do not always like what you have to say. I will sit with her until Dr Stevens arrives.' On the point of opening the door, he turned and looked at her. 'Why are you so against Dr Stevens seeing her? You are usually so fastidious over her health that it baffles me why you would not want the doctor to see her. Is there something I should know, Constance?' His question seemed to unnerve her, which increased his curiosity as to why she was behaving so strangely. 'What is it you aren't telling me?'

Stepping away from him, avoiding his penetrating

gaze, she said, 'Nothing, there is nothing I have to tell you. I am Jane's mother. I know what is best for her.'

'Do you, Constance? I don't think so. Otherwise you would have sent for Dr Stevens without having to be told,' he said icily. 'Perhaps you would like to be present when he examines her.'

'Of course.' On that note, she turned and left him.

Dominic vacated Jane's room when Dr Stevens, a small, elderly man who had been the family's physician since Dominic had been a boy, arrived. Constance bustled into the room and closed the door. Dominic waited, pacing the landing. After a while, Dr Stevens came out, followed by an apprehensive-looking Constance.

'Well?' Dominic asked. 'Is Jane very ill?' He walked beside the physician, noting how he had avoided looking at Constance.

Not until Dr Stevens was in the hall did he answer Dominic's question. 'No, Lord Blackwell. I wouldn't say that she is ill in the ordinary sense.'

Dominic frowned. 'Explain to me what you mean by that.'

Dr Stevens looked at him directly. 'Your sister has a fever brought on by childbirth. She has had a child—sometime within the last twenty-four hours, I would say.'

'You cannot know that,' Constance retorted.

'But I do,' the doctor contradicted her. 'When I examined her chest, the evidence was all too clear. She is lactating, my lord.'

Rendered silent, Dominic looked at the physician with blind incredulity. 'A child? My sister has given birth to a child? For the love of God, tell me you are mistaken,' he demanded, grinding the words between clenched teeth.

'I am not mistaken. I can only hope the child is well. Perhaps I should take a look at it before I leave.'

Dominic turned his furious gaze on Constance. 'Constance? What have you to say about this? Is this true—that Jane has...'

Constance stared at him hard, then nodded. 'Yes—yes, it is. The child is not here.'

'Then where in God's name is it?'

'You must realise that Jane couldn't keep it. It had to go. I have placed her with a woman—a Mrs Adams, who will look after her.'

'A girl? Jane has a daughter?'

'Yes.'

'And this is the true reason why there are no servants—no one except Mrs Mead to bear witness to Jane's childbirth.'

'I thought it was for the best. The infant is being well cared for. I do not wish it any harm. I just wish it had never been born. You must understand that it cannot be kept in the family. The shame and the scandal would be too much.'

'For you, maybe, Constance, but not for Jane.' Dominic glanced at the physician, who was looking most embarrassed at being party to this family dispute. 'How is Jane?'

'She will recover in a few days. She does have a fever, and I've left some medication which should alleviate the symptoms. Should the fever get any worse, then send for me. Otherwise I will call on her tomorrow. Oh,' he said as he half turned away. 'I am acquainted with Mrs Adams. She runs a home for abandoned babies and destitute children—a splendid job she does. I am often called to the home when any of the children are ailing. You can be assured that the child will be well cared for.'

'Thank you. That's good to know,' Dominic said, showing him to the door. Then he turned and walked back to where Constance stood, defiance in every line of her body. He was known to be a hard man, a stubborn, iron-willed man, but he was immensely shaken by what Dr Stevens had divulged. 'What a callous and heartless individual you are, Constance,' he ground out, his eyes alive with some dreadful emotion he was unable to conceal. 'I am disgusted by your behaviour. It's beyond belief.'

'Are you, Dominic? Are you really? Think about it. Would you really raise a bastard child as a Blackwell?'

'It is Jane's child—and yes, yes I would—I will. Who is the father? Where is he?'

'As to that, I cannot say. Jane refuses to divulge his name.'

'Then she must be persuaded to tell us. The man must be made to face up to his responsibility. It is clear I have been away far too long. When the child has been brought back and Jane is better, there will be questions to ask, but at this moment all I can think of is getting the child home. Where can I find this Mrs Adams's establishment?'

Constance was horrified. 'You cannot mean to bring her here—to this house?'

'It is where she belongs. Now, where is she, Constance?'

Constance backed away from him. 'I can see there's no talking to you when you are in this mood, Dominic.'

'You're damned right there isn't,' he said, his face hard with contempt. 'Where is Mrs Adams?'

Constance raised her head and gave him a venomous look. 'I am not obliged to tell you.'

Dominic's eyes narrowed dangerously. 'Be assured that I shall find Jane's baby—with or without your help.'

Taking a deep breath, Constance gave in. 'You will find her at Mrs Adams's foundling home in Marylebone. I'm not sure of the exact location.'

'The woman,' he said, suddenly remembering the woman he had seen earlier.

'Woman? What woman might that be?'

'I saw a woman leaving the house when I arrived. She was carrying a child—Jane's daughter, I presume.'

'Yes, it would be.'

His face tightened, and his eyes hardened. 'Then I will find her. You can count on that, Constance. No doubt you paid the woman to take her away.'

'I made a donation to her foundling home—a generous donation, I might add. Despite her being illegitimate, I do want what is best for the child.'

'That child is your granddaughter, Constance. What is best for her is to be with Jane—her mother. Has Jane rejected the child?'

'I don't know how she feels, but she knew she could not possibly keep it.'

'Because it will affect you and your standing in Society. That is why, isn't it, Constance? Let's face it. You do not care what happens to the child as long as it is out of sight.'

Constance merely glared at him and returned to Jane's room. Dominic raked his fingers through his hair. The devil in him stirred and stretched, then settled to contemplate this latest challenge. Dear Lord! What a mess. Since there was a child that Constance had so callously abandoned, he could not in all decency turn his back on it.

Dominic hadn't known what to expect of Mrs Adams's establishment for abandoned children, and seeing the large, square-built building with a pillared entrance in its own walled grounds, well situated and with outbuildings to the rear, manicured gardens on either side and warm light glowing from the windows, he was pleasantly surprised.

He was admitted into a large entrance hall by a woman he thought to be in her mid-thirties. Wearing a white apron over her dark blue dress, she went to see if Mrs Adams was available, leaving him to assess his surroundings. He was struck by how pristine everything looked, how the few pieces of furniture gleamed along with the floor. Cooking smells permeated the air, and indistinct voices floated from the rest of the house, somebody opening and shutting doors.

The woman who had admitted him led him into what he presumed was Mrs Adams's office and told him to wait, that Mrs Adams would be with him shortly. After five minutes of waiting and growing impatient to glimpse the woman at his home earlier, he went back out into the hall. Seeing a room across from Mrs Adams's office and hearing voices coming through the partly open door, he crossed towards it, peering inside without entering the room. Unaware of his presence, Mrs Adams was speaking to a young woman dressed in plain black garb—he assumed she was one of the staff.

But it was on Mrs Adams that his gaze settled. He looked at her intently, startled once more by her beauty. Her eyes were open wide, warm and wonderfully expressive in her heart-shaped, strikingly lovely face, her skin creamy, flawless and glowing with health, with an aureole of auburn hair pinned about her head.

Backing away from the doorway, he returned to her office, strangely content to wait.

Tired after an exceptionally busy day, Nancy was more than ready to put her feet up. She kept a full staff of women with Betty Shaw in charge when she herself was absent. Nancy lived in two comfortable rooms at the top of the house, which had once belonged to a well-to-do family. The attics were originally built to house the butler and servants of the house. Sometimes, when she wanted some peace and quiet away from the home, she went to stay in the family house in Belgravia. She'd also had her horse brought to London and rode him most mornings in Hyde Park. If she couldn't spare the time, then the groom she employed to take care of her two carriage horses exercised him.

Georgina, whose marriage ceremony was planned shortly at Aspenthorpe, which Nancy would make time to attend, often came to stay, and the two would catch up on family gossip. A sadness hung like a shroud over the family at this time. David had gone with his regiment to fight in the Crimea but, as was the case with hundreds of other young men, he hadn't come back. Everyone was devastated.

Nancy didn't know the details of what had happened to him. It was enough for her to know he would never come back. It was six months since he had been reported missing, believed dead. Nothing had been heard since, and everyone suspected the worst, that he had indeed been killed in battle.

She had just been checking on the two infants that had been brought in earlier and instructing a member of her staff on what needed doing, when Betty had told her that she had a visitor waiting to see her, and no, he hadn't given his name. Curious as to who it could be, she removed her apron and entered her office. On recognising the gentleman standing near her desk, the same one she had encountered on leaving the Blackwell residence earlier, and remembering how his mere presence had affected her, she hesitated before closing the door and approached him, desperately trying to crush the apprehension that seeing him again stirred inside her.

His presence seemed to fill the whole room. She felt drawn to him as if by some overwhelming magnetic force, and for an instant, a restlessness awoke inside her. She experienced a feeling of strange unease. He had a look she saw rarely these days—the complete indifference of inherited position. It was something that could not be acquired or even reproduced. It had to develop over time.

Not as dishevelled as he was on their previous encounter, his dark hair was brushed back from his brow, his blue eyes the colour of smoke. He had a long, aquiline nose, and his eyelids were heavy, drooping low, giving him a lazy, sleepy look. Attired in a dark green jacket and pristine neck linen, tall and lithe, he moved with the confident ease of a man well assured of his place in the world and completely unconcerned about the world's perception of him.

Struggling to remain calm and composed and pinning a smile to her face, she said, 'Lord Blackwell. This is a surprise.'

'I imagine it is—and not a very pleasant one, I'll wager,' he replied in clipped tones.

'We'll have to see about that. What can I do for you?'

'I am here to collect the child I saw you taking away from my house earlier—the child you passed off as your own.'

Meeting his hard gaze, Nancy was aware that an atmosphere of disturbing, inexplicable hostility had entered the room that until a moment before had been filled with early evening quiet. So, she thought, he remembered her. She could tell from the tone of his voice that he recalled the woman he had met at his house, dressed in practical work clothes—plain and soiled in places from the children she had nursed that day. She observed him calmly while experiencing a general feeling of unease. Her cheeks grew hot, and a tremor passed through her now she was face-to-face with him once more.

He was tall with broad shoulders, his powerful body suggesting a steely strength he might employ mercilessly to achieve his ends. His dark features augmented that impression, and there was an undeniable combination of power and authority she found intriguing. He was the kind of man she had often dreamed a perfect lover would be, the nights they would spend together holding a thousand exceptional and unexpected pleasures for them both. But she could not allow herself to become caught up in a romantic dream. Her emotions would be torn asunder, and she would find no solace anywhere.

Folding her hands sedately in front of her, giving no indication of the intense feelings he had aroused within her, she looked at her visitor squarely. 'Collect, Lord Blackwell? She is not a parcel you expect to be delivered. As for passing her off as my own, it was necessary at the time. Do you have a letter from Lady Jane to clarify your intention to remove the infant from these premises?'

'No, I do not.'

'Then I'm afraid I cannot oblige you, sir.'

'I insist that you do. You are Mrs Adams?'

'I am.'

'And this establishment is yours?'

'It is—although it is funded by some extremely notable people.'

'I imagine it is—my stepmother, the Dowager Countess, being one of them, apparently. Now, will you please go and get my sister's child, and I will take her home.'

'Believe me, Lord Blackwell, I would dearly like to hand her back to Lady Jane, but I promised I would take care of her child. Until I have her permission to return her, the child must remain here. She is being well cared for and at present is with the wet nurse, being fed.'

'I do not doubt the care you administer to the children here, Mrs Adams, which is highly commendable and worthwhile, but if you refuse to hand her over to me, then you do realise I could have the child removed by force.'

An icy tremor of alarm trickled its way down Nancy's spine. Her heart skipped a beat as she met Lord Blackwell's eyes, seeing something she did not care for glowing in their depths. 'I do so hope it will not come to that, and that something can be arranged.'

Lord Blackwell raised his head haughtily. 'It will, if my wishes are not granted. I insist on seeing her.'

'Lady Jane knows you are here?'

'No.'

Nancy could feel a gathering of concentration, like a shadow entering the room, as though dark forces of will were being directly focused on her. 'Then I'm afraid I cannot allow you to have her.'

Without taking his intimidating eyes from her face, Lord Blackwell moved closer to her, towering over her. 'Are you saying you forbid it?'

Flinching from the sting in his tone, Nancy took a step back. Averting her eyes, feeling uncomfortable beneath his much too penetrating, enquiring gaze, sensing the atmosphere between them suddenly changing in a subtle kind of way. In that warm, tastefully furnished room, all reality seemed to have been suspended, leaving her to hang in the numbing vacuum of her own uncertainty.

'Yes,' she said in answer to his question. 'It's the way we do things. It is necessary to have rules and to abide by those rules. I gave my word to your sister that I would take care of her child. I ask you to respect that and not to pressure me, my lord.'

Lord Blackwell shook his head with a rueful smile. 'I do respect it, Mrs Adams, and I quite understand why it is necessary in an establishment such as this to have rules. But rules are made to be broken on occasion—when necessity arises,' he said softly, his gaze languidly sweeping over her, his eyes settling on the gentle swell of her breasts straining beneath the fabric of her dress, measuring, lingering, a slow smile curving his lips.

The soft sincerity in his voice, the liquid tone of it, rippled over Nancy's skin like a gentle caress and took her breath away. Behind the words, she detected an intractable force, coercing, seducing, and she was almost drawn in by it, but then she remembered his purpose for being there. Inhaling a long, shaking breath and choosing her words with great care in the hope of preserving the strength she needed to withstand this arrogant lord, she said firmly, 'You have got it wrong. You have misunderstood me completely, and if you had listened to what I have been saying instead of getting into a temper, you'd have heard me say that when you have Lady Jane's permission, you can see her—or return her to your sister with her written confirmation that this is what she wants.'

One eyebrow lifted in sardonic, arrogant amusement. 'I am not deaf, Mrs Adams. I heard perfectly what you were saying. But I think you take your position too seriously—that you see yourself as some kind of saviour of the children you admit to your establishment. Ah,' he said when fire, flame-hot and sure, appeared in her eyes, 'I appear to have touched a nerve. I see you also have a temper.'

'Hasn't everyone, Lord Blackwell?'

Nancy could feel the anger begin somewhere in her breast, a hard knot just where her heart lay. Having admitted him into the home with nothing but good intentions, she found his harsh manner and egotistical attitude outrageous. She also felt a dreadful resentment that he should feel he had the right to speak to her as though she were nothing and no one at all. But she kept her temper subdued, which she found, as the moments passed, to be reasserting itself. It was there, simmering beneath her outward calm.

Stiffening her spine, she raised her head defiantly. 'I do lose my temper, and I am hurt just as easily as anyone else. Not until afterwards do I remember and try to understand why the person who made me lose my temper might have belittled me in such a way. I run a clean, disease-free house which offers a place—a shelter, if you like—where children in need can come and live. Not only is it a refuge where children can mend their injuries and recover their strength, there is also a qualified medical man who comes on a regular basis to treat them if need be. I have a caring, clean and reliable staff who have permanent, full-time employment. We do also have some volunteers who come to tend the children free of charge. Not all the children we accept have a family or anyone to love and take care of them, Lord Blackwell. Many babies and children we take in would perish in the gutter without establishments such as this.'

As she took a deep breath, her eyes changed from their usually warm shade of amber to spark with fire. There was a spot of colour at each cheekbone, and her mouth was finely drawn with determination. 'When I opened this home, my intentions were honourable and completely honest. I did not expect to have them flung back in my face.'

Lord Blackwell's expression softened. 'It was remiss of me to question your good intentions, Mrs Adams. I do apologise most sincerely. I am not usually so unmannerly, and I realise I spoke to you most unfairly. Is there a Mr Adams?'

Taken unawares by his question, Nancy faltered. 'No—no, there is no longer a Mr Adams—not that it is any of your concern.'

'You may not consider the question important, but it is to me. Since my sister has entrusted her daughter to someone I know nothing about, it is perfectly natural that I want to know everything there is to know about you.'

He stared at her, one black brow raised interrogatively. There was a direct challenge in his eyes, which Nancy found disturbing. She could sense the sleeping animal within him begin to stir. Her thoughts were thrown into chaos, for she had not expected such an uncompromising response to her hasty remark.

'I do not wish to offend you,' Lord Blackwell went on, 'but I do not know you, so how can I be certain I can trust you with my sister's child?—although I have to admit Dr Stevens spoke highly of you when he came to see Jane.'

'What exactly do you fear?' she asked sharply. 'That

I might abuse her, that I am not equal to the task of caring for her?'

'I am naturally apprehensive. If you were in my place, wouldn't you want some indication of my good faith?'

'Yes, I would,' she conceded, 'but you must forgive me if I appear to resent having my good intentions questioned.'

Seemingly contrite, he moved away from her. 'I apologise. I meant no offence. I've been in New York for some considerable time. On returning home today and discovering what happened to my sister, I'm sure you can understand my shock on learning she has given birth to a child. I realise the importance of your work—of the good you do for those less fortunate— but my concern for my sister and her daughter is paramount to me.'

In a more compassionate tone, Nancy said, 'I do understand how shocked you would have been on learning of Lady Jane's condition, Lord Blackwell, and I'm sorry I cannot help you just now—but there are set rules. I truly cannot ignore them.' It was not her place to pry into the personal affairs of the women who gave up their children, and certainly not with this tall, powerful man looming in front of her, his closeness making her heart do strange things.

'If you must know, I'm finding this whole affair most difficult to navigate,' he retorted, rubbing the muscles at the back of his neck. 'My sister has presented me with a delicate situation that has to be dealt with right away. I have no choice but to step in. The child is my kin and must be taken back to where she belongs—which is the reason I am here now, and to see what kind of establishment my stepmother banished the child to.'

'I assure you this home is well-run with only the best women to care for the children.'

'Forgive me for being blunt, but there are some cruel people in this world, Mrs Adams, people who would think nothing of using children for their own disgusting ends.'

'I am well aware of that, Lord Blackwell, which was one of the reasons why I established this institute—for disadvantaged children and abandoned babies. May I make a suggestion?'

'Please do.'

'I could bring her back to you myself in the morning, if that is agreeable to you? It will give you time to speak with your sister—and to find a wet nurse for the infant should you need one.'

'You would do that?'

'Of course. I would be glad to. My sole concern is for the child, and I also believe her place to be with her mother. Although I realise how this situation might concern Lady Jane's mother.'

He nodded. 'My stepmother cannot see further

than her own ends. It concerns her more what Society thinks of her—how the stigma of having an illegitimate granddaughter will affect her, rather than caring for the emotional well-being of my sister and her child.' He moved closer to her. 'I imagine you would abhor such behaviour, that such trivial matters should be set aside in favour of an abandoned child.'

'Absolutely, Lord Blackwell, but since we did not meet until today, I had no idea you had any picture of me in your mind. I fail to see how you've had the time to form any opinion of me at all.'

'Do you intend on taking in other people's children forever?'

Nancy paused and contemplated his question. 'It is worthwhile. It's hard work, but it gives me enormous satisfaction knowing the children who come here are safe and looked after and when the time is right are well placed to make their own way eventually.'

He nodded thoughtfully. 'Well said, Mrs Adams, but you must have other matters of interest.'

Nancy sighed. 'There are many things that interest me. I would also like to travel the world—to see all the exotic places of interest I read about—but that is just a dream. I'm sure it will pass.'

Lord Blackwell did not laugh. 'There is nothing wrong with having dreams and longings. We'd be nowhere without them.'

'But in the end, I have to be realistic. I can't see my

situation changing dramatically in the foreseeable future. This is the real world—my world, a world I have created for myself, for as long as I want it to be.'

'Forgive me if I appear surprised. You are an attractive young woman, Mrs Adams. Does your family agree with what you do?'

'They do not object, exactly. My mother is of a different opinion, but my father is supportive of what I do. My work is often hard and intense and keeps me away from home for long periods, but I take pride in what I have achieved—that even the children who come here for a short time go away with full bellies and, if they are lucky, a pair of boots, even though I know that in all probability they will sell them for a few pennies when they are back on the streets. A great many of them are orphans. Others are unwanted, having been turned out by parents who have too many mouths to feed already, and others have been sold to chimney sweeps and the like for a few shillings. The children who come to us have nothing—and very little hope. Someone has to watch out for them.'

'And you think you can make a difference to their lives?'

'A few of them, yes. Sadly, we cannot house them all.'

'There are always the workhouses—and the charity schools—and the hospitals for those who are injured.'

'The workhouses are appalling places, but better

than living on the streets. It's a sad world for the underprivileged, Lord Blackwell. Are you aware that out of all the people in London who die, almost half of them are children? Isn't that terrible?'

'I was not aware of it—although I have to admit that I've never had reason to think of it until now. This is the first time I've had anything to do with destitute children.'

Nancy looked him straight in the eye. 'I am not proud, Lord Blackwell, just determined to carry on what I started five years ago, and if you or anyone else can find fault with that, then I am sorry for you.'

'On the contrary, Mrs Adams, I can find no fault with that. You speak brave words. Such sentiments are highly commendable and admirable to say the least.'

Beneath his steady gaze, Nancy could feel his eyes on her as she moved towards the door. His manner was all consideration and regard as he made a study of her person with a strange sort of intensity she could not define. He was studying her with those strongly marked eyebrows slightly raised. His gaze was penetrating, and she felt the full force of it as her heart rate increased.

It was with some amusement that she looked back at him. 'My lord, you are studying me most intently— as if I were some artefact. Or maybe I have a smut on my nose? Is that it?'

Lord Blackwell strode across the carpet towards

her. His eyelids lowered as his gaze passed over her. 'Your nose is perfect,' he replied softly. 'I'm trying to read your expression. And as for studying you as if you were an artefact, do not be offended. Artefacts are rare and mysterious things, intriguing and often difficult to interpret. It is not unusual that incorrect conclusions are made about them.' He smiled. 'You are not only beautiful and clever but mysterious also.'

What was he saying? Nancy wondered. That he did not think of her as a servant? 'You consider me to be a mystery, Lord Blackwell? If so, I assure you I have never thought of myself as either secretive or mysterious. I am no great mystery at all.'

Lord Blackwell looked at her as if she were of the utmost importance. 'I am merely trying to work out what kind of person you are.' He smiled again. 'Allow me to give you a word of advice. Be careful what you express with your eyes, Mrs Adams. They are far too eloquent. Being a man of the world, I am quick to interpret their language. I may know very little concerning your background, but in the brief time we have been acquainted, I have come to understand a great deal about you as a person—and who can say? Maybe after tomorrow, when you return my sister's child, I may know a good deal more.'

Nancy opened the door to indicate their meeting was at an end. 'I am what you see, my lord—nothing more or less than that. Now, if you will excuse me, I have work to do—babies to feed, children to get to bed.'

He nodded, stepping past her into the hall. 'Then I will bid you good-night. I can depend on you bringing the child to my sister in the morning?'

'Of course. That is what I said I'd do. Good night, Lord Blackwell.'

Nancy watched him leave, a troubled look in her eyes. Within the space of the short time of their meeting, Lord Blackwell had awakened in her an emotion she had never before experienced. She was not quite sure what it was nor how it had come upon her so suddenly, only it moved strongly inside her. But she had no desire to examine it, and him, in close detail. Yet she could not deny that he was the first and only male since Thomas who had aroused even the smallest interest in her—not having had the time or the opportunity to entertain taking a lover as she had initially intended. In the beginning, all her efforts had been directed toward the opening of her establishment with a hundred and one things to do every day. But of late, and with a little more time on her hands, she was often beset with loneliness. She looked forward to when her mother and sisters came to London and she could catch up on the gossip from home.

Thinking of Lord Blackwell, she strongly suspected he was a complex man who would be as elusive as smoke, a man who could break the heart of the woman who loved him. She crossed to the mirror hanging above the fireplace, contemplating her features. She was deeply disturbed by what Lord Blackwell had said as she tried to see what he saw in her. He had said she was beautiful. Was she? Somehow the wide, lustrous eyes staring back at her looked alien to her, but determinedly she plunged her gaze into their depths.

And suddenly, like a will-o'-the-wisp, it seemed that someone else gazed out at her, someone almost childlike in her innocence, but at the same time seductive—a temptress who seemed to grow from a tiny seed in a recess of her personality, a seed that had lain dormant in fertile soil until this moment. But she vanished as quickly as she appeared, too shy, too coy to be caught, but far too real to deny.

She sighed wistfully, continuing to study her face. Lord Blackwell had cast some magical enchantment over her. His dominance was accomplished in the moments when there had been a softening in his character rather than by force, and she instinctively sensed that once she succumbed to the mesmeric potency of his personality, she would then be wholly at his mercy.

Chapter Four

Climbing into his carriage and ordering the driver to head for home, Dominic's thoughts lingered on the young woman he had just left. Mrs Adams didn't seem to be the warmest and most welcoming young woman—at least, that was the impression she'd initially given him. And yet she was wholly herself—a rarity, which came as a surprise to him. He could not recall ever seeing another woman who resembled her.

If ever he had discounted the possibility that a woman's features could be flawless, then he was swiftly coming to the conclusion that if Mrs Adams belonged in Society, she would set the standard by which all other women would have to be judged, at least in his mind.

If her face wasn't at the very least perfect, it came as close to being so as he was able to bear. He'd noted that several feathery curls had escaped their tight confines at her temples and in front of her ears, lending a charming softness to the hairstyle. In contrast to her auburn tresses, her peach-like skin seemed more fetching by far than the complexion of any other ladies of his acquaintance. A faint rosy hue had adorned her cheeks, and her soft, winsomely curved lips had pursed intriguingly when she had chastised him. As for her large, silkily lashed, warm amber eyes, their appeal was so strong that he had to mentally shake himself free of their spell even now.

Mulling over their conversation about destitute children, he scowled. Mrs Adams also had an annoying tendency to prick his conscience and to make him feel inadequate in some way, which he was beginning to find irritating. Not for the first time, the thought that he had seen her somewhere before came to him, that she seemed familiar, but for the life of him, he could not remember where.

With the child in her arms, Nancy arrived at Lord Blackwell's house the following morning as promised. She was met by Mrs Mead, who showed her into a high-ceilinged library. Lord Blackwell was seated at a desk with papers strewn over its surface. When she entered, he pushed back his chair and strode towards her. Immediately there was a resurgence in her of that unnerving awareness of his vitality and magnetism that had affected her the night before.

'So, here you are as promised, Mrs Adams?'

'And with the child, Lord Blackwell. She is unsettled, though. You have secured a wet nurse for her?'

'I have one standing by if needed, but it would appear my sister would prefer to feed the child herself. As she is still not completely well, I have tried to dissuade her, but she is adamant. Getting my sister to do anything she doesn't agree with is like piloting a ship into a harbour. It needs a steady hand on the tiller.'

'I see,' Nancy said, pleasantly surprised. 'Please don't be concerned. My navigational skills are quite exceptional, and in this instance, your sister and I are sailing in the same direction. She is doing right by her daughter.'

He stared at her with surprise. 'She is? Well, Mrs Adams, my knowledge concerning the intimate matters of raising a child is rather limited, so for the present, I will bow to your judgement. But I make no secret of the fact that I would prefer her to make use of the nurse. There is no need for her to—to...' He waved a hand in the direction of the child.

'To what, Lord Blackwell?'

'Women in Jane's position do not generally nurse their own children.'

Nancy took a moment to study him. It was clear that his sister feeding her own child was confusing to Lord Blackwell. Likely he hadn't ever seen a woman with a baby at her breast. In fact, she wondered if he had any experience of babies at all. She surmised that a man with no experience of fatherhood would react like this. 'Then they should. The closeness of nursing her own baby creates a special bond between a mother and her child,' she said, keeping her voice light.

'I have yet to be convinced of that.'

Nancy noted an underlying bitterness to his words—or was it regret?—which made her wonder if perhaps he knew more about raising a child than he cared to admit, and that it had not been a pleasurable experience. 'Would you like to be introduced to your niece, Lord Blackwell, before I take her to her mother?'

With his hands thrust deep into his trouser pockets, the rigidity of his spine and the set of his broad shoulders telling her he would rather not, he took a cursory glance at the child when Nancy turned the covers back from the infant's crumpled up little face. Then, his expression unchanged, he stepped back. 'She looks very well, I suppose, but at this age, they are somewhat uninteresting.'

'I disagree.'

'You do?'

'Babies are so vulnerable, totally dependent on others. It's interesting to watch them grow and develop personalities as the weeks and months pass.'

'You seem to know all about it, Mrs Adams. You have children of your own, perhaps?'

'No,' she replied, lowering her eyes.

'Mrs Mead will take you upstairs,' he said abruptly, turning from her. 'Jane is impatient to see her child.'

Nancy smiled at his back, wishing he would turn and really look at his niece.

The room smelled of fresh flowers arranged beautifully in a vase on the dresser. Jane was lying beneath the covers on her bed, washed and freshly clothed. On seeing Nancy, she pulled herself up in the bed. Nancy approached slowly, smiling at the young woman whose eyes were fixed on the squirming bundle in her arms.

'My baby,' she whispered, holding out her arms for her daughter. 'My darling Rose.'

'How are you feeling, Lady Jane?' Nancy enquired. 'Better, I hope?'

'Oh, yes. Much better now Dominic is home. When he found out about the baby, much to Mama's dismay, he immediately insisted that Rose be brought home— where she belongs, he said.'

'And I am sure your brother is right. A baby belongs with its mother.'

'Even though the circumstances are not ideal, and I will feel my mother's displeasure for years to come.'

'I sincerely hope not.' Nancy gently placed the baby in Lady Jane's arms. 'I have been told that you wish to nurse Rose yourself.'

'Yes, oh, yes, of course I do. My breasts hurt. It will be a relief to feed her. Mrs Mead will help me with any problems I might have. Mama has taken to her room, having no wish to be present at my reunion with my daughter.' Lady Jane pulled away the soft blanket in which her daughter was wrapped and looked at her with complete absorption and adoration, placing a soft kiss on her brow. 'She is beautiful, don't you agree, Mrs Adams?—the most beautiful girl in the world.'

Nancy beamed. 'She is indeed a beautiful baby.'

'Just think,' Lady Jane whispered, 'when you took her away last night, I truly thought I would never see her again. Yet here we are. What a wonderful moment this is—but, oh—it is not as happy as it should be. She is beautiful and would certainly have been a papa's girl. But that cannot be.'

Nancy heard the catch in her voice and saw that her eyes were swimming with tears. 'He—he doesn't know he has a daughter?'

Lady Jane shook her head, striking the tears away with the back of her hand. 'He—he is dead. Sadly, he will never know about her.'

Nancy's heart went out to her. She wondered at the identity of the young man Lady Jane had lost her heart and virtue to, but it was not her place to pry. It would be no simple matter for her to raise a child out of wedlock, even with her brother's support. 'I am so sorry to hear that,' Nancy said sincerely. 'Your daughter needs feeding, Lady Jane. Would you like me to assist you—or would you prefer Mrs Mead?'

'No—please show me,' Lady Jane said, pulling apart her nightdress to expose her milk-engorged breasts. 'See,' she said unabashedly, 'I have enough milk to feed two babies.'

Half an hour later, baby Rose lay in Lady Jane's arms, happily replete. Mrs Mead came in and, after acknowledging Nancy, began fussing about Lady Jane and the infant, informing the young mother that the nursery was ready to receive her child and a nurse to take care of her. Nancy got up from where she was sitting beside the bed.

'I must leave you now. I'm sure you will get on just fine with Rose, Lady Jane—with Mrs Mead to help you.'

'Oh, yes, you can count on me,' Mrs Mead said, beaming broadly and gently touching Rose's delicately flushed cheek.

'You—you will come and see me again, won't you, Mrs Adams?' Lady Jane said.

Nancy smiled. 'You know where I am if you should need me, Lady Jane.'

Nancy let herself out, meeting the Dowager Countess on the landing, her little dog fussing around her skirts.

'Ah, Mrs Adams,' she said curtly. 'You brought the child back, I presume.'

'I did, Countess, on the orders of Lord Blackwell.

He was most anxious that the child be reunited with her mother. Lady Jane is delighted with her.'

'I expect she is. My stepson will soon realise his mistake. Only time will tell if my daughter has done the right thing when she fails to make a good marriage due to this day's work.'

Having no wish to become involved in a conversation that did not concern her, Nancy headed for the stairs. She had done her best with the child, and now she could leave the family to acclimatise to Lady Jane's situation. 'Excuse me, Countess. I have a carriage waiting to take me back to the home.'

'How is Jane?' Lord Blackwell asked, coming up behind the dowager.

'She will be fine. I believe Dr Stevens is to call on her sometime today. Have him take a look at the child—although I don't think there is anything to be concerned about. Rose has been fed and is sleeping like the proverbial babe.'

'And the wet nurse?'

'Unless something drastic occurs that prevents your sister from nursing her child—which I am sure it won't—then I would discharge her.'

'Thank you for all you have done. You won't go unrewarded. I shall see to that.'

'The Countess has already been most generous in making a donation to the institute, but more funds are always welcome. We couldn't manage without the fundraisers and benefactors. The children who come to us have to be fed and clothed—most of which are donated to us—and if they are sick or injured, we patch them up as best we can.'

'Even though some of them are criminals, unci-vilised and riddled with vermin and diseases they might pass on to you?' the Dowager Countess re-marked with a distasteful twist to her lips.

'Of course, and since those are exactly the kind of children who come to us, we have all the more rea-son to try and make their young lives more bearable. Times are hard just now, and the number of deprived children is never-ending, but we do have plans to raise more funds to enable us to find other premises and hopefully found another orphanage.'

'Are you that successful in your fundraising?' Lord Blackwell asked.

'Sometimes. You see, I make it my business to know the names of wealthy people I can approach for monetary contributions.' She smiled when she saw his eyes register surprise. 'You must think me terribly mercenary to go around trying to extract money from people like I do, but it's because I—and the good peo-ple who work for me—care so much for the children.'

'You are that hungry for their money?'

'Oh, yes—and I am not afraid or ashamed to say so.'

'Really?' the Countess remarked coldly. 'Just re-member that greed is a terrible thing, Mrs Adams.'

'I'm not a greedy person, not for myself. Only for the children. Money means nothing to me, but I have to agree that it is a useful commodity, and a few pennies can be the difference between life and death to a starving child.'

'That may be so,' the Countess snapped, 'but for a young lady to tout for money by herself is highly irregular, I would have thought. It is a dangerous game you play.'

Nancy gave her a hard stare. 'Try telling that to the children, Countess. Now, please excuse me, but I must be getting back.'

Nancy proceeded to make her way down the wide carpeted staircase. She tried her best to avoid the Countess's dog trying to get her attention. And then it happened. The dog disappeared beneath her skirts. Unable to retain her balance when it got between her feet, she slipped. Down she hurtled, hitting her head on the balustrade and landing at the bottom of the stairs in an undignified heap.

Immediately Lord Blackwell was looming over her, holding out his hand, only to withdraw it when the dog appeared from beneath her skirts. Scooping it up, he held it out for his stepmother to take it from him.

'That damned dog, Constance. It will be the death of someone one of these days. I've told you time and again to keep it in your room.'

The Countess took the dog from him, holding it close to her chest as if it were the dog that was injured.

'Are you all right?' he asked Nancy.

Raising her tousled head, Nancy slowly brought herself to a sitting position. She tried to bring the world back into focus. Lord Blackwell was on one knee beside her, looking at her with concern. 'I—I think so—but don't be too hard on the dog. I—I should have looked where I was going.'

'Nonsense,' he said sharply. 'That dog is always getting under one's feet.'

'Well—if you're not injured, Mrs Adams, I'll go and shut Bella in my room where she can't do any more mischief.'

On that note, the Countess went back up the stairs, leaving Nancy alone with Lord Blackwell, totally oblivious to the footman and a female servant who had rushed to assist her.

'Here, let me help you to your feet,' Lord Blackwell said, standing up and taking her elbow.

With an effort, Nancy struggled to stand up, pushing back her hair, wincing when she put weight on her right leg, her head spinning. 'I—I think I may have twisted my knee,' she said when a pain shot through it. Reaching out, she grasped Lord Blackwell's arm to support herself. 'I—I'm sorry,' she managed to whisper, unable to sustain her weight. 'I—I don't feel at all well…'

'Mrs Adams?'

The voice was concerned. Lord Blackwell was speaking to her. She forced her eyes open and blinked, trying to focus, but her vision was blurry. The floor lurched and pitched beneath her, and she swayed like a person who has had a drop too much to drink. A terrible dizziness assailed her. Putting her hand to her head, she crumpled to the carpet again.

Nancy was disconcerted but eternally grateful when strong arms scooped her up.

Entering the drawing room in his arms, Nancy tilted her head back and met Lord Blackwell's eyes, almost on a level with her own, eyes that were warm and danced as though he found their closeness and isolation vastly entertaining. Any antipathy she had felt towards him seemed to melt in the most curious way, for she found herself quite intrigued by this confounding man. Conscious that he held her tightly against his hard frame, his arms firmly fixed about her, she continued to stare at him.

Dominic was not a man of such iron control that he could resist looking down at Mrs Adams's feminine form. Noticing things like how her gown clung to her round curves so provocatively, concealing the bountiful treasures beneath, gave him a clear sense of pleasurable torture. Now she was so close he could feel her warmth, smell the sweet scent of her body. The colour on her cheeks was gloriously high. Her eyes were sparkling like twin amber orbs. They were the most brilliant eyes Dominic had ever seen, of a hue so bright they seemed lit from within.

Fixing his eyes on her slightly open mouth, her lips so luscious they begged to be kissed, sent heat searing into his loins. Why did he feel this explosion of passion for her? How could this one woman make him lose his mind in such a way? It dawned on him as he looked down into her face upturned to his that he wanted to place his mouth on hers more than anything else. When he had lifted her up, his one desire had been to aid her discomfort, but in that moment, another kind of desire, far more potent and primitive, swelled inside him, one he wanted to savour and enjoy.

Lowering his mouth to hers, he succumbed to the impulse that had been tormenting him and kissed her long and deep, yet he was gentle and undemanding, feeling the softness of her lips beneath his. His arms tightened, pressing the contours of her body to his, and he almost lost his head entirely when he felt her lips open under his and she kissed him back. After several seconds which seemed like an eternity, Dominic raised his head and tenderly gazed down into her melting amber eyes. The woman in his arms affected him like a heady wine. He saw in her warm, open face that she was struggling to release herself from the trancelike state induced by his kiss.

'I wonder,' he murmured.

'What?' she breathed.

'If you are as guileless as you appear to be.'

She smiled, a smile that was as relaxed as a child at play and as pure as spring water. 'I don't think so. I do have a tendency towards disobedience and defiance.'

His eyes narrowed, studying her with quiet intensity. 'You're a most perverse young woman, that's for sure. You didn't mind my kiss?'

'I think it's a little late in the day to protect my honour—so no, I did not mind in the slightest. Now, I think you should put me down on your sofa before you drop me into another undignified heap on your carpet.'

This he did and swiftly disappeared to have a word with Dr Stevens who had just arrived.

Seated on a green-and-cream-striped sofa, Nancy took a moment to dwell on what had just happened between them. In that moment, held in his arms, she had felt inexorably drawn to him. She already wanted to taste his kisses again—and more, knowing she would be unable to resist the rising desire in her that begged for fulfilment. And therein lay Lord Blackwell's appeal. Yet the warm emotions he had aroused in her also caused her some unease. Where he was concerned, to keep her sanity intact, she had already decided to keep him at arm's length, but things had changed. Was that all it had taken for him to kiss her? She was furious with herself for having succumbed so easily and foolishly to his charms. She had let herself be mindlessly borne away on a rush of fleeting passion!

A maid entered carrying a tray, which she placed on a small table, her round young face lit by a cheerful smile.

'Well, Mrs Adams, feeling better, are you? You gave us a rare fright, you did, especially His Lordship.'

'Yes,' Nancy managed to say. 'I'm feeling much better...'

'Lucy, Mrs Adams. My name is Lucy.'

'Lucy, and I'm sorry to have been so much trouble.'

'Nay, don't say that. You've been no trouble, and it wasn't your fault you fell down the stairs. The Countess's little dog gets everywhere, she does—always getting under everyone's feet. Dr Stevens has arrived to see Lady Jane. Lord Blackwell's asked him to also take a look at you when he comes down.'

'There's no need—really. I'm fine.'

Lucy poured her a cup of tea and handed it to her. 'His Lordship insists. You can drink it while you wait for the doctor.'

'Thank you for the tea, Lucy,' she murmured, taking a sip of the warm beverage, the memory of her undignified tumble down the stairs returning in all its humiliating clarity. She felt a deep resentment towards the selfish Countess whose carelessness with her dog had brought her downfall.

Scarcely had Lucy left the room when Lord Blackwell strode in with Dr Stevens. Placing her cup on the tray, she allowed the elderly doctor to examine her knee. Telling her there was no damage done, that she had simply twisted it in her fall, he prescribed rest and left.

'I trust you really are feeling better?' Lord Blackwell said, looking down at her with concern.

'Yes, thank you. I'm sorry to be so much trouble, but I must leave. I have a carriage waiting for me.'

'I know. I made the decision to send it back to the institute. My carriage is at your disposal when you are ready to leave. But please don't be in a hurry. You didn't mind me asking Dr Stevens to take a look at you?'

'Of course not. That was thoughtful of you.'

'Nonsense. He arrived at a fortuitous time to see Jane. You hit your head when you fell—you'll have a bruise later. How does it feel?'

'I have a slight headache—nothing to worry about.'

'You will have to rest your knee for a few days.'

'That is no easy matter—with so much to do— although it does feel a little less sore now. I apologise for the inconvenience I must have caused, but I really should be getting back.'

An easy smile curved his lips. 'Not before you're ready. We don't want a relapse. You gave us all quite a fright.'

'And I must have looked a sight,' she said, returning his smile. 'Although probably no worse than I normally look after a full day caring for the children.'

'Now you are being ridiculous and do yourself a grave injustice,' Lord Blackwell remarked. 'I marvel at the courage you display under such duress.'

Gingerly Nancy tried standing, wincing slightly when she put her full weight on her damaged knee. 'You really shouldn't have sent my carriage away. I am sure you are a busy man, my lord. I hate to trouble you.'

'It's no trouble at all. After all, it would not have happened had my stepmother kept that wretched dog of hers under control.'

Nancy attempted a step. It was a mistake. He was too close, and with the sofa behind her, she could not retreat. He looked straight into her eyes, overwhelming her with the sheer force of his personality. She felt as if she had been stripped naked by the unexpected intimacy of that brief contact and their kiss earlier. She struggled to appear calm, but her cheeks burned with embarrassment. He smiled, and she knew he'd read her perfectly.

'I was about to say don't get up,' he murmured, his voice as smooth as silk. 'You don't have to hurry away. You have suffered an injury to your head which could lead to concussion—and you will need to rest your knee. There is a room made ready. You are welcome to remain until you are fully recovered.'

'Thank you, but I wouldn't dream of it. I must get back. I have staff to take care of my needs. I think I can make it to the door.'

'Sit down and wait until I have the carriage brought round—unless you would like me to carry you into the hall? It would be my pleasure.'

'I'm sure it would—but since you are not to be trusted to keep your hands to yourself, I will wait here.' She sank down onto the sofa once more, reproaching herself for acting foolishly. Surely she was far too sensible to be overawed by an illustrious lord, however handsome he was?

He glanced at her, a mischievous twist to his lips, and she felt her cooling cheeks begin to burn again. A glint of amusement flickered in his intelligent eyes, almost as if he had guessed what she was thinking. Nancy waited until he had left the room before feeling herself relax. What sort of person was he, she wondered, this man she had not known existed until yesterday? His kindness and concern had been exemplary—but the kiss had almost been her undoing.

What she had done for Lady Jane was becoming

more complicated than she had ever anticipated. Not only did she have her work to contend with, she also had to find a way of dealing with her own irrational attraction to Lady Jane's brother. She couldn't believe he had aroused such a strong response within her—no one since Thomas had achieved that.

With the carriage waiting to take Mrs Adams back to the home, Dominic entered the room to find her sitting where he had left her on the edge of the sofa. He was reminded of a bird about to take flight. He observed her for a moment, strangely touched by her concern for his sister. He looked at her as if seeing her for the first time. She possessed the animal grace of a young thoroughbred, and a femininity that touched a chord hidden deep inside him. He looked at the thick wealth of her hair, knotted at her nape, which displayed to perfection the long, slender column of her throat and the sharp, stubborn angle of her chin, which in turn was softened by the amber colour of her large eyes and the sensuous beauty of her face.

There was nothing right in what he was thinking about her. She had done her duty by his sister, and common decency dictated that he must not forget that—difficult as it might be. He must keep his distance mentally and physically, and he must not think about her in any personal way. But the kiss had changed things between them. He suspected that she was very much her own person—but he would have also been surprised to learn that she was a woman who socialised with some of the best families in England.

'How are you feeling now?' Lord Blackwell asked.

'Better,' Nancy replied, getting to her feet. 'I can manage to walk out to the carriage. How is Lady Jane? Have you looked in on her?'

'I have, and she's positively glowing with motherhood. Her mother told her of your tumble, and she has expressed a desire to see you before you leave. She won't be pacified until you show yourself—if you can make it back up the stairs.'

'Yes—I'm sure I can,' she replied, taking a few steps across the carpet, relieved that her knee wasn't so bad after all. 'I'll go up and see her, and then I'll be on my way.'

Lord Blackwell followed her up the stairs and into his sister's room. Nancy glanced at the Dowager Countess hovering across the room and was relieved the dog was nowhere in sight. Jane smiled when she saw Nancy, shuffling higher up the bed. Rose was in the crib beside her.

'Mrs Adams, Mama told me of your tumble. I do hope you are not hurt.'

'No. Just a bump on the head and a bit of a twist to my knee. Nothing to be concerned about. I am unhurt, truly.'

'Then I am glad to hear it. Mama said you tripped over her dog.'

'Yes,' Nancy said, avoiding the Countess's eyes, 'something like that.'

'See,' Lady Jane said, leaning over and peering into the crib. 'Rose is sleeping. She is so pretty—do you not agree, Dominic? You have barely looked at her since she came back.' She gave her brother hovering at the bottom of the bed an anxious look. 'Why, Dominic? None of this is Rose's fault.'

'I agree. I put the blame wholly on the man who seduced you—which we will speak about later. Mrs Adams has to leave now, Jane.'

Taken aback by her brother's sombre tone, Jane reached out and took Nancy's hand.

'Must you leave?' she asked.

'Yes, she must,' her brother insisted. 'I will accompany her, and when I return, we can talk, Jane. Come, Mrs Adams. I have the carriage waiting. I'll accompany you back to the institute.'

'There really is no need,' she said, letting go of Jane's hand. 'I can manage quite well on my own.'

'I wouldn't hear of it.'

After bidding the two women a hasty goodbye, Nancy allowed Lord Blackwell to usher her down to the hall. Reaching the step on the stairs on which she had stumbled, he put out his hand and took her arm, just as two visitors were being admitted. Nancy heard him utter a soft curse beneath his breath, which told her that perhaps they were not exactly welcome, but his displeasure lasted only a moment, and then he was striding across the hall to welcome them. After shaking the gentleman's hand—a tall, good-looking man with pale blond hair—he turned to the young woman and placed a light kiss on her cheek.

'I trust you had a pleasant journey down to London?'

'Yes,' the gentleman replied, handing his hat and gloves to a hovering footman. 'As you know, it's Elizabeth's first time in England, so the journey from Liverpool enabled her to see something of the country.'

Feeling very much out of place and not wishing to intrude, Nancy stood some distance away, reluctant to put herself forward. The lady made the exquisite picture of fashionable sophistication. With her dark hair perfectly coiffed beneath a plume of tantalising white feathers, and a fitted, high-necked jacket of quilted dark green satin that hugged her body and accentuated the full swell of her breasts, this woman's appearance was dramatic and could not be faulted. She was not beautiful, or even pretty, but alarmingly arresting.

Watching her, for some reason she could not define just then, Nancy was both resentful and fascinated, seeing the woman move as close as she could to Lord Blackwell with a possessiveness accorded to someone who was intimate with him. Suddenly, she felt strangely inadequate, knowing at that moment she could not compete with the fascination of this woman. She felt vulnerable and gauche.

Turning, Lord Blackwell held out his hand for her to come forward.

'Allow me to introduce you to Mrs Adams. Mrs Adams, this is Simon Wade and his sister, Elizabeth, from New York.'

Miss Wade bowed her head like a queen bestowing a regal favour upon a lesser mortal before she brought her eyes back to Nancy, settling a frosty smile on her in a cool, exacting way. Impersonally her green eyes raked her with a single withering glance, noting her plain attire with a look of distaste that was only a shade away from insolence. Nancy knew the woman had decided there and then that she was as poor as a church mouse and had no social credentials to recommend her. Immediately a wall of antipathy seemed to spring up between them.

'I'm pleased to meet you, Mrs Adams,' Miss Wade said, although Nancy didn't believe it for one minute. In that intense moment, surrounded by the opulence of Lord Blackwell's house, Nancy felt some emotion from Miss Wade pressing in on her, squeezing her with icy, inflexible fingers. The woman was striking, secure in her own strength and sure of her own incomparable worth.

'I'm pleased to meet you, Miss Wade—you too, Mr

Wade.' Looking directly at the stranger, she saw he was an attractive man with sultry features and dangerously hooded eyes, and he exuded all the confidence of a conceited charmer.

'Mrs Adams has been visiting my sister, Jane,' Lord Blackwell provided.

'You are Lady Jane's governess?' Miss Wade asked.

Lord Blackwell laughed. 'My sister is a little old for a governess, Elizabeth. No, Mrs Adams was just paying a call.'

'So you are a friend of Lady Jane?' Miss Wade commented wryly and with a practised smile, giving Nancy a flash of white teeth from between her parted lips.

There were hidden connotations behind the smile, and Nancy was not quite sure how to read them. There was nothing like a smile to confuse a foe or charm a friend, and Nancy's lips curved graciously. 'I am an acquaintance,' she replied pleasantly, self-consciously tucking a stray curl behind her ear. In Miss Wade's eyes, she might resemble a pauper, but she had no wish to look as dishevelled as one into the bargain.

Miss Wade gave Nancy a look which suggested that her presence devalued the occasion—no doubt pondering what the world was coming to when the upper classes entertained their servants.

'And your husband?' Miss Wade asked.

'I am a widow.'

'I'm sorry to hear that,' Mr Wade said, his voice as smooth and seductive as the softest silk, his eyes absorbing every detail of her face and figure. 'You live in London, Mrs Adams?'

'For most of the time, yes. I run a home for destitute children and abandoned infants.'

Miss Wade gave her an arch look. 'Really? Goodness! I cannot imagine anything worse than having hordes of children about one's feet.'

If Miss Wade hoped to see a flicker of emotion pass across Nancy's face, she was disappointed, for Nancy continued to smile. 'Your conjecture is quite wrong, I assure you. I enjoy what I do. It is extremely rewarding in many ways.'

'Do you live with family here in London?' Mr Wade asked.

'No. My parents are country folk.'

'And your father?'

'Is a businessman—and a collector of antiquities—of which he never tires.'

'Really?' Miss Wade replied, giving her another arch look, seemingly unimpressed. The full red smile never wavered, but her eyes were cold. Everything about her was precise and impeccable. 'How very odd. And does he travel for these antiquities?'

'He has done—in the past. But not anymore.'

'Has he been to New York?'

'He has—*we* have, as a family—some years ago

now.' If Miss Wade was surprised by this, along with Lord Blackwell, she did not show it.

'And did he find anything to his liking in New York?'

'No. Nothing at all. He much prefers Europe and Asia for the things that interest him most.' Nancy managed to retain a cool and unruffled expression as she watched Miss Wade's diamond earrings flash against her cheeks.

'Good Lord!' Mr Wade said. Lifting a quizzing glass to his eye, he trained it upon Nancy and boldly inspected her once more. 'I can't believe you were in New York and we never met. I would have remembered for sure.'

Miss Wade gave him a withering look. 'And you are sure of that, are you, Simon?—I very much doubt it.'

'Enough, you two,' Lord Blackwell said, giving each of his visitors a tight smile. 'You're being rather outrageous and are embarrassing Mrs Adams.'

Nancy's eyes narrowed, and anger stirred inside her. She looked in vain for some trace of softness in Elizabeth Wade, but the American woman was as cold and hard as the marble floor on which she stood. 'Think nothing of it, Lord Blackwell. Now, if you will excuse me, I have things to do.'

'Mrs Adams was on the point of leaving when you arrived,' Lord Blackwell said, seemingly bemused by the conversation between her and Miss Wade.

Nancy could see he was unsure of what to do next since he had told her he would accompany her back to the institute, and yet now it would appear rude to leave his guests. Reading his mind, Nancy said, 'Please—don't concern yourself with me, Lord Blackwell. I'm capable of taking myself home.'

'I'm aware of that, but I insist that a footman accompanies you.' He beckoned to the hovering footman. 'Accompany Mrs Adams, will you? See she gets home safely.'

Glad to be gone, Nancy nodded to Lord Blackwell's guests. 'It's been pleasant meeting you. Please excuse me.'

'By all means,' said Miss Wade haughtily. 'We do not wish to keep you from your work, Mrs Adams.'

Nancy looked her straight in the eye, having made up her mind that she did not like Mr Wade or his sister. 'You won't do that. Goodbye.'

She followed the footman out to the waiting carriage, but not before she overheard Miss Wade remark that Lord Blackwell's sister should be more particular who she invited to the house, and that people like her should never enter a gentleman's house by the front door, unless, of course, she didn't know any better.

Making herself comfortable, Nancy leaned her head back on the soft upholstery and closed her eyes, glad to be gone from that house and all the people in it, hoping she would never have the misfortune of seeing any of them again—in particular Miss Elizabeth Wade. She knew their types—had she not met such people when she had been in New York? Endowment from birth with financial provision made them the superior beings they so obviously thought themselves to be. They possessed also the glorious belief that they were unique in the world.

Nancy was disconcerted at being subjected for the first time in her life to a situation like this, to being denigrated by such poor specimens as Mr Wade and his sister, and she felt a surge of resentment—in particular toward Miss Elizabeth Wade, that she was having fun at her expense. She had met people like this in the past, but that was before she had left home, and they had therefore been on equal terms.

Chapter Five

It was early evening the following day when Dominic found his way to the institute to see Mrs Adams. Despite his experience with the opposite sex, he wasn't familiar with women of her class. He'd made a point not to be, but this one intrigued him. He was curious. Beneath the severe and plain façade she presented to the world, she was a beautiful young woman, and he wondered why such an attractive woman would want to dedicate her life to caring for underprivileged children.

He was a shrewd and rational man, a man of breeding and style who understood his motivations and knew his goals. He prided himself on his good sense not to be swayed by emotion or flights of fancy, so it came as a shock that he wanted to know more about Mrs Adams—and that was the moment he realised what was happening. He, the proud and distinguished Lord Dominic Blackwell, who kept London alive with gossip when he was in town, was afraid of the effect that this woman was having on him. Thinking of her soft mouth, he felt a hunger stirring inside him he found difficult to control. He had experienced the warmth of holding her in his arms and the exquisite pleasure she had made him feel. He had tasted the sweetness of her mouth, and when he recalled the way she had enthusiastically responded, it made him want to feast on the entire banquet, and making love to her seemed plausible.

When she had left the house, knowing there was no reason for them to meet again now she had brought Jane's infant home, completely out of the blue he'd felt a surge of admiration for the young woman who had not been daunted by Elizabeth and had given him an insight into her life. The sweet wild essence of her shone like a rare jewel, and without warning, he felt hot desire pulsating to life within him—unexpected and unwelcome. He had to see her again. From the moment he had laid eyes on her, he had tried not to think of her, tried to resist the way his thoughts had so frequently turned to her as he tried to focus on Jane and her predicament and his potential relation-ship with Elizabeth, knowing how dangerous those feelings were to him.

Before he had met Mrs Adams, he had been con-templating proposing marriage to Elizabeth, but not any longer. He was incredibly relieved he had done nothing to suggest to her that he had ever had marriage in mind.

At the institute, he was admitted by one of the women who worked there. When he asked to see Mrs Adams, he was told she had retired for the night. As if sensing he was not going away until he had seen Mrs Adams, she left him to enquire if she would see him.

Feeling tired after a busy day, Nancy took her time getting ready for bed. After slipping off her shoes, she pulled the pins from her hair and shook it loose so that it cascaded down past her shoulders like a lustrous veil dancing with auburn lights. Seating herself close to one of the windows, she looked out as darkness began to descend. It was the hour when fashionable people usually left their homes to visit the theatre or some Society event.

She loved going to the theatre when her mother came to town with Georgina. She would shed her workaday clothes and accompany them to the opera or a play. Afterwards she would stay over at their house in Belgravia to catch up on family news and hear what was happening in and around Aspenthorpe.

It would have been her brother David's birthday tomorrow. She muttered a prayer to suppress the deep-rooted emotions that surged up every time she thought of her brother. The feelings of loss and sadness came in equal measure, threatening to overwhelm her.

When she had woken this morning, she had hoped that work would take her mind off David, but it hadn't. She'd thought of him constantly, and she had not been able to dispel his image from her mind.

Open on her desk was a letter from her mother reminding her of Georgina's wedding the following week and that she expected Nancy to go home for the occasion. She wrote that she could understand how difficult this would be for Nancy and that it would bring back unpleasant memories of the time when Thomas Marsden had jilted her at the altar. Yes, Nancy thought, her mother was right, but she could not be absent from her sister's wedding. Not all men were like Thomas, and she didn't imagine for one moment that Georgina's betrothed—a quiet, likeable young man—would do something so wicked as to leave her standing at the altar in the same church that had been the venue for her own wedding.

Not yet ready to go to bed, she opened a book and began to read. After half an hour, unable to stop thinking of David, she was about to put the book aside when there was a soft tap on the door. After walking through the sitting room, she opened the door. It was Betty who stood there. When she was told a gentleman by the name of Lord Blackwell was down below and wanted to see her, it crossed Nancy's mind to refuse, but on second thought, she told Betty to show him up.

Straightening her skirts, she waited. At the sound

of his footsteps on the landing outside the door, she experienced a rush of feeling, a bittersweet joy. When she admitted him into her private quarters, she knew her cheeks were flushed, for she was in no proper state to receive visitors. And now, confronted by him as he stood in the doorway, all her senses were alert. She was conscious of her own inadequacy—of her plain, faded, stained grey dress that no elegant lady would ever wear, of her loose, tangled hair and bare feet.

Lord Blackwell cocked a brow. 'I know it's late, and you can send me away if you wish, but can I come in?'

She took a deep breath, trying to stifle her rising embarrassment. She could refuse to admit him, but the truth was that his visit might concern Lady Jane. She could see no harm in letting him in.

'Yes, of course.' Opening the door wide, she stood aside for him to pass.

'Thank you. Forgive me if I intrude. I won't stay long.'

Dominic was thinking that she looked almost demure, but he suspected there was nothing demure about Mrs Adams. She swept back her abundant hair—the colour of a flaming sunset—framing her high, clear forehead. He found himself wondering how it would feel to run his fingers through its soft tresses. He was drawn to her eyes with their dark curling lashes, which were the most exquisite thing about her face.

At that moment, there was a defencelessness about her. He felt a softening to his heart. It was a tenderness, a sudden liking without a feeling of desire for her, and he felt a strange urge to protect her from all life's ills. Her face mirrored her confusion on being caught unawares. With her hair tumbling about her shoulders and her small bare feet exposed beneath the hem of her skirts, she looked much younger and more innocent than she had appeared to him on their previous meetings, and at that moment, she seemed as childlike as his sister. She raised her eyes, and he saw there was a sad, brooding look in them. Dominic was struck by the mournful look on her face.

'Why are you here, Lord Blackwell? Your sister has her child back where she belongs, so I cannot for the life of me imagine why you have come to see me at this hour.'

With a mixture of languor and self-assurance, absently moving further into the room, he let his gaze sweep over her in a contemplative way. 'When you left the house yesterday, I didn't get the opportunity to say goodbye properly and to thank you for what you have done for Jane.'

'There is no need, Lord Blackwell. I was merely doing my job. Taking in abandoned children is what I do, and if I get the chance to return them to their rightful home—and their mother—then it makes it all worthwhile.'

'Come, now, it is more than that.'

Moving to stand before the hearth, where a fire glowed in the iron grate, her face was half-turned away from him. All he could see was the curve of her cheekbone and the long, silky flutter of her dark lashes. Her face was composed when she turned her head slightly, and he saw that her eyes were now clear and untroubled. In fact, she looked as she usually did, unapproachable and detached from those about her. Her lack of self-consciousness and vanity were extraordinary to him. His dead wife and Elizabeth considered every detail of themselves from their perfect coiffures down to their well-shod feet. Dominic was mystified by her cool reserve. Her face was set in a mould of stiff politeness.

'No, that's it, Lord Blackwell. Your sister is a charming young lady,' she said crisply. 'Where she is concerned, I did what was asked of me—you see, I take my responsibilities seriously. You and Miss Wade may not approve of me and what I do, but be assured that I am not out to hurt Lady Jane in any way.'

'Ah. So, you overheard what Elizabeth said as you were leaving, in which case I can see some form of apology is in order.'

'It is not for you to apologise for Miss Wade's rude

remark. Only she can do that, but it has to be sincerely meant.'

'Of course. I understand that. However, since you mention it, I did not say that I don't approve of you. On the contrary. I have nothing but respect for you and the work you do. Although what my opinions are concerning you has no bearing on the case. My paramount concern is my sister's happiness and well-being.'

'Which is as it should be. She is going to need you for what lies ahead.'

'I do not need reminding of my duty, Mrs Adams— although I cannot help but think Simon Wade and his sister arrived at an inopportune moment.'

'It doesn't matter to me. I dare say the properly reared young ladies of her acquaintance would be horrified and fall into a swoon at being introduced to someone like me leaving a gentleman's house by the front door. I might not have been born with blue blood in my veins and all the privileges that come with it, but I have a loving family and have learned much. My life has been enriched by them. Yes, along with my siblings, I have been to many places and seen things good and bad, but I would not change a thing. It is not where a person comes from that matters. It's who a person is inside that counts.'

Dominic stared at the proud, tempestuous young woman in silent, cool composure. Her words reverberated around the room, ricocheting off the walls and hitting him with all the brutal impact of a battering ram, but it failed to pierce the armour of his reserve, and not a flicker of emotion registered on his impassive features.

'That, Mrs Adams, was quite an outburst. Have you finished?'

Pausing to take a restorative breath, Mrs Adams finally said, 'Yes, I have—and I am quite sure that in no time at all, Miss Wade will have forgotten all about the ordinary, uninteresting woman she met at your house.'

Something flared in Dominic's intense gaze, and he managed a faintly crooked smile, his eyes lingering on the soft contours of her mouth. 'That is not how others see you. There is certainly nothing ordinary or uninteresting about you, Mrs Adams. Take my word for it,' he said softly. 'You may always appear self-assured—but I suspect that beneath your cool façade, hidden fires burn.'

Hot colour flooded Mrs Adams's face, and she suddenly seemed bemused. He was looking at her intensely. She lowered her gaze, averting her eyes, as if trying to shake off the effect he was beginning to have on her.

'You should not say such things. You seem to forget that you are almost a stranger to me—as I am to you.'

Dominic sighed. 'Forget? How can I forget when you remind me of it whenever we find ourselves together? Not by word, I admit, but by your manner. How can I forget when we shared such a kiss?' With trembling fingers, she swept a stray lock of hair from her face, an innocent gesture that made his blood run hot. 'I don't remember hearing you object to it at the time. You cannot deny that there is an attraction between us.' He moved closer to her, looking at her and cocking one elegantly shaped brow. His eyes captured hers against her will, holding them imprisoned and challenging her to deny it.

Shaking her head slowly, she stepped back. 'It has to be this way. The kiss took me by surprise. I was injured—my head as well as my knee,' she reminded him. 'You took advantage of that fact.'

'You were not so badly injured that you did not know what was happening when you responded so eagerly to me. What is it you want, Mrs Adams? It has to be more than what you have now.'

'I confess that what my heart yearns for goes against everything I deem honourable,' she murmured, her voice trembling.

Crossing his arms, Dominic leant his hip on the arm of a chair and calmly looked at her in impassive silence before saying in a voice that was as soft as velvet, 'And what does your heart yearn for, Nancy Adams? Tell me.'

Drowning in the seduction of his gaze, she shook her head slowly. 'I can't.'

Her reply brought a curve to his lips. 'My dear Mrs Adams—you are transparent. I read you well. I know what it is you want.'

'No, you do not. I ask you to forget the kiss. You must.'

He looked at her thoughtfully for a moment, touched by her innocence, for that was how she seemed to him at that moment, even though she was a widow and would have known the intimate touch of a man. He was so desperate to have her, to bury himself in her, that he could feel his control slipping like gossamer threads under too much strain.

Standing upright, he shifted his gaze to the fire, watching in contemplation as the flames took hold of a log. 'Do I have a choice? You are an extremely fascinating woman. You intrigue me.'

'And you are a man of the world, my lord. I decided to make my own way in life a long time ago. What you see within these walls is what I have achieved— what I am. Speaking to me like this, you must realise you are making it very difficult for me.'

Cool and remote, feeling a stirring of admiration for this unusual young woman who spoke her mind with such force, Dominic studied her for a moment, as though trying to discern something. Her eyes were a warm amber. She had fine-textured skin the colour of fresh cream. There were tiny lines at the corners of her eyes that told him she was a woman who smiled often.

But she did not smile at him.

He already knew she was a widow. She had also disclosed her father was a businessman and that as a family, they had been to New York. The more he found out about her, the more intrigued he became. It was curiosity about her that had brought him here tonight. His instinct detected untapped depths of passion in her that sent silent signals instantly recognisable to an experienced male.

The impact of these signals brought a smouldering glow to his eyes. How deeply was she mourning her husband? What had he been like? Had he aroused the pleasures and sensations of a loving wife? If he, Dominic, had a mind to, it would surely not be too difficult a task to demolish her uncertainty and have her melting with desire in his arms. Briefly, the idea of conquering her appealed to his sardonic sense of humour—if that was what he wanted, which he didn't. The idea of seducing a woman for his own gratification was unthinkable. He was not like that, and he never would be. Where Mrs Adams was concerned, he must remember that for him, because of the position she held, she was untouchable. When he had entered the room, he had felt a sadness about her. It was still there.

'Forgive me, Mrs Adams, but I cannot help observing that you do not seem yourself this evening. If you are unwell after your fall, or if there is something troubling you and you would like a sympathetic ear, then I am at your disposal. I am a good listener—or so I have been told.' His seriousness brought a smile to her lips.

'It is nothing to be concerned about, I assure you, and I am quite well, if a little tired. There are many demands on my time, and it's been a busy day.' She sighed. 'It's just memories—that's all. Before you arrived, I—I was thinking about my brother, you see. After completing his military training, he was sent to Crimea to fight the Russians. He—he was reported missing, believed killed, a few months ago.'

With deep understanding, Dominic nodded gravely. 'I see. I'm sorry. It is natural that you should mourn him.'

'It is just that—well—tomorrow would have been his birthday.'

Dominic saw her eyes filling with tears, and she turned away quickly, no doubt ashamed of herself for showing her emotions. With an effort, he restrained himself from moving closer.

'If he was alive, I am sure we would have heard something by now. If he is dead, then I know nothing will ever bring him back. I will have to get used to not having him around, but it's not that simple when you've been so close to someone all your life. Usually I'm all right, but with tomorrow being his birthday... Do you understand what I mean?'

'Yes, I do,' he answered, beginning to feel a trifle envious of this deceased brother of hers for being able to evoke such devotion in her. 'The trouble with life, Mrs Adams, is that it is never what we expect, and in many cases, that could be a blessing. When you lose someone close—in war or in peace—you have to carry on, however painful that is at first. It is something you have to do. You and your brother must have been very close.'

'Yes, we were. I have another brother, James, much older, but David, the brother who is missing, was just one year and two days older than me. I remember the last time we celebrated our birthdays together. He was eighteen and I was seventeen. We had a party at home. It was such a happy occasion. I'll never forget it.'

'Your family must have been a consolation to you when he was reported missing.'

'No. Oddly enough, they seemed to clam up after that. No one wanted to talk about it—especially my mother.'

'But you did?'

'Yes, very much.'

'The war in Crimea has claimed many lives. Few families with husbands and sons in the military who were out there remain untouched by it.'

'You speak as if you too have a loss to bear.'

Dominic's eyes darkened. 'I do, but not through war. I lost my wife several years ago, leaving me with a son, Mark. My mother was killed in a riding accident when I was a youth, and my father died hunting. I still find it hard to think about.'

'I'm so sorry. I shouldn't have told you about my brother. By doing so, I have reminded you of your own losses, which must be painful for you.'

'Yes, something like that, but of course I still have Mark, whom I love dearly. And I tell myself that when my father went on to marry Constance, even though I couldn't take to her, something good came out of my mother's loss—Jane.'

'Jane is a delightful young woman, and I am glad to hear you have a close relationship with your son—but one can never forget those we have loved and lost...' Her lips trembled, and she put up her fingers to still them, turning away.

She seemed engulfed by a great sadness—being reminded of the loss of her brother and probably her husband, too—making him wonder once more about his demise and how deeply she had loved him. Dominic watched her, his eyes travelling admiringly over her gracefully bowed head. As he studied the pure line of her profile in the dwindling light, his fingers touched her arm lightly. She turned back to him, composed now. Her gaze was compelling, and he knew, by some miraculous communication from her mesmeric eyes, that she was thinking of his touch. Neither of them spoke, but something passed between them that they both fully understood.

Mrs Adams lowered her gaze, and Dominic looked away, deeply aware that if he remained in this room alone with her, cloaked in the secret intimacy of the warmth and accumulating shadows, he was very much in danger of overstepping the invisible barrier they had erected and taking her in his arms.

'I should go,' he said, not wishing to disturb the harmony which had sprung up between them, and yet at the same time not wishing to embarrass her by creating a situation they might both regret later—one which could have a disastrous effect on them both. Moving to the door, he opened it and looked back at her. 'Tomorrow I'm travelling to Berkshire to see Mark. I last saw him before I went to America. I will be staying overnight and returning to London in two days.'

'He—he will have missed you, I'm sure—being away for so long.'

He nodded, and his eyes softened. 'And I him. You said you were tired—which is hardly surprising after the day you've had. Get some rest. Good night, Mrs Adams.'

Without moving, Nancy watched him go. She stared at the closed door for a long time, wondering what had brought him to the home to see her. He hadn't said, although he had been concerned that she might be suffering after-effects from her tumble down his stairs. She thought of how he had looked when he had appeared in the doorway, having noticed that his dark hair had been brushed smoothly back from his forehead and gleamed in the orange glow from the lamp and the firelight. When he had left, his lips had been curved in a slight smile, which was something she was beginning to recognise but was too afraid to analyse, knowing it would be sure to lead to complications between them.

Her mind dwelt with wonder on the compassion she had seen in his eyes, his voice devoid of mockery when she had told him about David, and the consolation his closeness had brought her. But most of all, her mind dwelt on his wife and how devastated he must have been when she died, leaving him to raise their son alone.

Three days later, Nancy went downstairs, fully expecting to spend another busy day with the children, only to find an enormous exotic bouquet of pink and white roses had just been delivered. They smelled divine. Believing the flowers to be from her family, she asked one of the servants to put them in a vase and to display them on the round table in the hall. In a hurry to get on with her work, she slipped the sealed note accompanying them into her pocket. It wasn't until later, when another bouquet of mixed flowers was delivered and she saw that this one was from her family, that she took the note from her pocket to read that the first bouquet had been sent by Lord Blackwell, wishing her a happy birthday.

Totally bemused as to why he would send her flowers and wondering what he was about, she took the first delivery into her office and asked for the second delivery to be put on display in the hall instead.

It was midday when Lord Blackwell arrived in a carriage driven by himself. She was working in the office when he was admitted. He was casually dressed in a dark blue jacket and dove-grey trousers and she caught the scent of pine, which she would always associate with him.

She stood up when he came in, placing her pen carefully on the desk. 'Lord Blackwell! You take me by surprise. I must thank you for the flowers, but there really was no need for you to go to so much trouble.'

'Nonsense. It's your birthday. One cannot let it pass without some form of gift. You like the flowers?'

'Why—I—yes, of course. They're beautiful. But—how did you know?'

'You told me. Two days after your brother's, if I remember correctly. One doesn't have to be a genius to work it out.'

'But—you shouldn't...'

'If you won't accept the flowers as a gift from me

for your birthday, then please accept them as a token of my thanks and appreciation for what you have done for Jane. Besides, you gave me pleasure in your company the other night—however brief—which I enjoyed. Do not deny me the pleasure of giving you something in return.'

Nancy smiled, looking once again at the flowers standing on her desk before returning her gaze to his. He was completely relaxed, his smile creasing the corners of his eyes and softening his rather severe features. 'Very well. Thank you. I appreciate your gift. Did you manage to see your son?'

'Yes. It was good to see him. He was glad to see me too, although I think he was more interested in the gifts I brought him from New York. I got back to London last night.'

'I'm glad you had a successful journey. Now, if you will excuse me, I have work to do.'

'You mean you are turning me out already?' he asked with mock severity.

'I am merely pointing out that I am an extremely busy woman, and I was trying to make my books balance when you came in.'

'I know you are always up to your eyes in work, which is why I think today you should take some time off and come for a drive with me. The sun is shining, and it would be a shame to waste it. I'm sure you have earned some time off for relaxation. I am also sure you will be pleased to learn that there is not a child or a column of figures on the itinerary.'

Nancy stared at him in astonishment. 'I couldn't possibly.'

'Yes, you can. I thought we might take a drive onto the heath. We will admire the scenery and shop if you have a mind to—and stroll by the pond. Mrs Mead has also prepared a picnic basket for us, so you cannot possibly refuse since you would be in danger of hurting her feelings. You don't expect me to eat it alone, do you, Mrs Adams?'

'No—I—of course not.'

'I can think of nothing more desirable than to spend the afternoon in your company. It's not as though either of us is attached to someone else. You are an extremely attractive and desirable woman, Mrs Adams.'

'Come now, my lord,' Nancy said, her voice under control—almost thoughtfully calm as she replied. 'Isn't that what every gentleman says to a lady he's just propositioned?'

Lord Blackwell gave a lift to one eyebrow and laughed. 'Wit as well as beauty,' he said softly. 'I like that. So, what do you say? Does my offer appeal to you? Nothing would please me more.'

At first Nancy hesitated at the thought of spending the whole afternoon alone with him, without the protective shell her position always gave her, but her hesitation only lasted a moment. She could not deny that she was tired, and it would be nice to relax for a while in his company. She couldn't remember the last time she had done anything for pleasure—and it was her birthday, after all. A drive onto the heath would make a pleasant change. Only she was becoming aware that her attraction towards Lord Blackwell deepened every time they were together, causing her to hesitate for a moment, but when he favoured her with such a charming, engaging smile, she found it impossible to refuse his offer and melted a little, returning his smile. His very look made it plain to her that he desired her unashamedly, and in her present confused state, she was ready to find comfort in any kind of positive feeling.

'You are extremely persuasive, Lord Blackwell.'

'I know. Does that mean you'll accept?'

'Yes,' she said softly, looking into his eyes, unaccountably certain that he would be hurt if she refused. 'How can I possibly refuse? But you will have to wait while I change into something more suitable.'

'Of course—but don't take too long. Patience is not one of my virtues.'

Nancy laughed, heading for the door. 'You mean you have others?' she quipped, going out before he had time to reply.

Attired in a floral print day dress and matching jacket that hugged her small waist and a face-framing bonnet, Nancy met Lord Blackwell in the hall. For a moment, as his eyes took in this change in her, his expression was one of admiration.

'Well now, Mrs Adams, you look quite delightful. Shall we go?'

Knowing the flowers and the arrival of Lord Blackwell and her sudden declaration that she was going for a drive with him would arouse speculation and gossip among the staff, and aware of their curious glances peeping through the windows as she sat in the carriage beside her escort, she merely smiled, determined to enjoy the ride.

The day was pleasantly warm, the sun shining down out of a clear blue sky as Lord Blackwell drove towards Hampstead Heath. As Nancy relaxed against the comfortable upholstery, she sighed with deep contentment. They were quiet for the most part as he negotiated the traffic, and when they conversed, it was of nothing in particular.

They picnicked on the grassy bank of the pond beneath a large willow tree. As Lord Blackwell handed her a glass of wine, their fingers brushed together, and she realised how close he was to her, smiling into her eyes with that slightly mocking, secretive smile of his.

Each of them was becoming increasingly aware of the strong intensity of feeling developing between them, and Nancy was filled with a sudden glow not unknown to her, which she had often experienced with Thomas, and now with Lord Blackwell. He was very much aware of her as a woman—this she knew by the sensuous manner in which he regarded her, and on occasion by the very tone of his voice when he spoke to her and the look in his eyes. She knew she was in danger of falling hopelessly under his spell, but whatever happened, she must not give way to recklessness with him.

The more they were together, the more she was in danger of becoming overwhelmed by him. She would have to be careful—she could not afford to become involved with him in any way unless it concerned Lady Jane, and as far as she was concerned, that matter was now closed. If she wanted to keep her sanity intact, then that was how it must remain.

It was eight years since she had been jilted, and she had vowed then that she would not go down that path again, never allow a man to dominate her feelings, her emotions and her life—but a love affair? Now, she thought, beginning to assess their situation in a whole new light, that was a different matter entirely, and she couldn't deny that it did hold some appeal. It had for some time.

Slowly they ate the delicious food Mrs Mead had packed for them, which was more like a feast, the chicken and ham, cheese and fresh fruit washed down with a delicious white wine.

The afternoon passed in a wondrous warm haze.

They discussed many things—in fact, Nancy had never talked so much. The conversation stimulated her imagination. She was excited by it.

Lord Blackwell, having removed his jacket and with his white shirt open at the throat, stretched his lean body lazily out on the grass. He looked to where she sat close to him, completely at her ease, her face slightly pink from the effects of the wine and the warmth of the sun. They talked and were silent, comfortable to be in each other's company, content to sit in the shade of the willow and watch others stroll by.

'It's good to see you so relaxed. Are you glad you came?' he asked.

She sighed. 'Very much. Thank you for bringing me here. It was just what I needed.'

'Then we'll do it again. You'll have to add it to your list of social events.'

She smiled, sitting up, not committing herself to anything where he was concerned. 'I don't have a list of social events. For a long time now, my social life has been at a standstill. Sometimes when my mother and sisters come to town, we visit the theatre. Otherwise all my efforts have been concentrated on running the institute.'

'That is a shame. Everyone has to have time away from their work.'

'It's not such a chore for me. I enjoy my work—although I shall have a week-long break when I go home for my sister's wedding. I have much to do—to plan for, since I will have my time taken up with organising a fundraising garden fête when I get back.'

'And where is the location of this fundraising event?'

'I haven't decided. I've had a couple of offers from benefactors to use their gardens here in London, so it will be pretty central for everyone who would like to come along. The institute holds one every year, and it always proves to be a lucrative event, with invitations going out to several people of note.'

'Then I hope you do well.'

'Thank you. It looks promising, and attendance will be good, providing the weather is fine.'

Nancy looked at him, admiring his clean-cut profile and strong body as he leaned across to fill her glass, even though it was still half-full. The warm sun had turned his skin a wonderful shade of olive. He caught her eye and found her studying him. She flushed, and he smiled. Not for the first time, her thoughts turned to the beautiful Elizabeth Wade. She had clung to his side with a possessiveness accorded to a betrothed or a wife. Was their relationship a close one? she wondered.

'We mustn't be too late leaving,' she said, feeling vulnerable suddenly, taking another sip of her wine in an attempt to hide the confusion he was creating with her emotions. She felt a quiver of alarm, more so when she realised it was not of him she was afraid, but this situation. She should have declined his invitation to come to the heath, but it was too late now. 'I like to help settle the children down and feed the ones that cannot feed themselves.'

'We'll leave when you've finished your wine, but there's no immediate hurry.' He was silent for a moment, studying her, before he next spoke. 'What happened to your husband, Mrs Adams? How long were you married?'

Thrown completely off balance, Nancy stared at him. 'My husband? Oh—I—no, we—we weren't together very long. Do—do you mind—but—I prefer not to discuss that particular matter.'

He looked at her hard for a moment, then glanced away. 'I'm sorry if it upsets you. I didn't mean to pry.'

'There's no need to be—sorry, I mean. Perhaps some other time.'

He nodded. 'As you wish. You know, when I first saw you, I had the strangest feeling that I had seen you before, but for the life of me, I could not think where.'

Sudden panic caused Nancy's heart to skip a beat, but somehow she managed to remain calm and keep smiling. She certainly couldn't remember seeing him before, but if he had chanced to see her at a social event somewhere, then it would have been before she had opened the home. She certainly would have remembered if they had ever been introduced.

'I very much doubt it. I can't recall meeting you. You must be mistaken—perhaps someone else with a likeness to me. I—think I would have remembered you if we had met.'

Chapter Six

Having eaten and drunk a couple of glasses of wine, Nancy was engulfed in a dull kind of lethargy, breathing in the warm, sweet-scented air. Lord Blackwell was watering the two carriage horses. Taking advantage of his absence, she lay back on the soft grass. Apart from the birds, everything around her was peaceful and silent. There wasn't even a breeze to stir the occasional leaf.

She sighed, looking up at the sun glancing off the tips of the leaves on the upper branches of the trees, feeling a peace and contentment wash over her—like a whisper, an excited expectancy of things to come. She smiled for no reason, wondering if this sudden feeling of elation and happiness warming her heart had been brought about by her companion. It was against her better judgement that she allowed her thoughts to wander idly along these lines—until she heard the sound of his light tread on the grass beside her.

Opening her eyes, she squinted up at him, shading

her eyes from the glare of the sun. 'Are the horses all right?' she enquired.

'Yes—well watered,' he replied softly, sitting on the grass beside her and falling in with her mood. 'What are you thinking?' he asked, his voice very low and quiet.

'Oh,' she sighed, thinking how wonderfully attractive he looked, 'just how peaceful everything is—and how lovely the heath looks at this time of day.'

Lord Blackwell smiled the self-satisfied smile of a conspirator who was hoping the peace and intimacy of the moment would continue.

'Although I must say,' Nancy said, smiling up at him, 'that if we have many more spring days as warm as this heralding a particularly hot summer, when London stifles in the heat, then I shall begin to wish I were in the countryside with cooling breezes.'

'You do have a point. Now come along,' he said, taking her hand and helping her to her feet. 'I'll get you back to the institute.'

Returning to Mayfair having left Mrs Adams at the home, Dominic thought about the afternoon they had spent together. After she removed her bonnet, her hair had shone in the light and shade beneath the rich foliage of the trees. The sun was going down when they had walked back to the carriage, and a luminous haze had begun to settle over the heath, lengthening the shadows of the trees.

He'd been deeply troubled as he watched her, for he was continuing to see her as an extremely desirable woman. Surprisingly, there was no joy in this discovery. With hindsight, he now knew it was a situation he should have tried to avoid. That she shared his own feelings he knew without being told, but these feelings must be repressed for the time being. He wanted nothing between them to threaten her single-minded independence, which was clearly so important to her, so matters would continue very much the same. But should their relationship change and become anything deeper, then there was a strong possibility that he would lose her altogether. They stood on the brink of passion, neither of them daring to overstep the mark.

Aspenthorpe was in a state of upheaval over Georgina's forthcoming marriage to the son of a lord from Wessex. When Nancy arrived, guests from all over the country were already beginning to fill the vacant rooms that had been prepared for the occasion.

Georgina was panicking that they weren't going to be ready on time, but her mother, being her usual efficient and well-organised self, was adamant that nothing could possibly go wrong. As Nancy was the chief bridesmaid, her mother had ordered the dress to be made to her daughter's measurements in her absence—and she'd lost no time in letting her know it had been a nuisance and that she should have been at Aspenthorpe, on hand for the seamstress and to help with the preparations for her sister's wedding.

It was no use Nancy going over the old argument that as she had responsibilities which took up most of her time, she could not just come home whenever her mother ordered her to, so she just sighed submissively and said, 'Yes, Mother.'

Unlike Nancy, who had battled to get her own way to win her freedom from the monotonous routine of upper-class family life, Georgina was quite different. She was content with a quiet country life, passionately interested in country pursuits, and was happy to help her mother with the local fundraising charities.

It was the most spectacular Society wedding the area had seen in a long time, covered by newspaper reporters, with crowds of excited people standing in the roads around the church to watch wealthy people from the business world and some aristocratic guests arrive in their luxury carriages drawn by splendid horses and liveried footmen in front. Then came the groom followed by the bridesmaids and at last the radiant bride on the arm of her proud father.

Georgina was calm and happy—the perfect bride, everyone said. After the ceremony, a splendid reception was held at Aspenthorpe. No expense had been spared on the food and Georgina's elaborate trousseau. After the endless speeches had been made and toasts to the happy couple drunk, the guests began to dwindle, and once again the house slowly returned to normal.

Remembering her own wedding day, bitter memories she would rather forget came to the fore for Nancy. She'd been disappointed, embarrassed and hurt when Tom hadn't turned up for their wedding, sending nothing afterwards but a short note of apology and a tawdry explanation that he was in love with someone else. Encumbered by her emotions, even though she was happy for her sister, she put on a brave face and endured Georgina's day, impatient to be back in London.

The day of the garden fête arrived. Lord and Lady Lambert, who made regular donations to the institute, had generously put their house and extensive gardens at Nancy's disposal. It was a pleasantly warm day, and the sun was shining. The event had been well advertised, and booths overflowing with all kinds of merchandise were presided over by volunteers and staff from the institute. Several older children, excited to be involved in this fun event, worked beside them.

The fête always attracted a crowd of fashionable visitors. Ladies protected their delicate complexions from the enquiring rays of the sun beneath fancy parasols, pausing to gossip to friends and acquaintances while the gentlemen escaped and headed for a marquee selling liquid refreshment. When the fête ended, there would be several worse for wear!

It was always hard work preparing for the event with extra care and attention to detail. Objects of beauty and interest had been donated and were to be auctioned off later—which was the highlight of the day. A flower stall decked with intoxicating blooms was inundated with young couples, the gentlemen purchasing single red roses to be presented to their blushing partners. There was an archery range, and there were pedlars of lotions and potions. Inside a colourful tent, an elderly lady presided at a table before her a crystal ball. She was dressed in a voluminous red-and-gold gown. Shining gold dangled from her ears, her arms, neck and fingers jangling with a colourful array of jewellery and beads. Her black hair was piled atop her head. For anyone who stepped over her threshold and crossed her palm with silver, eager to be told what their future held and later to laughingly analyse and dissect her forecast, her gaze was penetrating, as if her dark stare could read their souls.

The gardens were bursting at the seams with people, and a carnival atmosphere prevailed. All were in high spirits, the air alive with a cacophony of voices. Poised and outwardly calm, inside Nancy was alert, her nerves stretched tight as she went from one stall to the next to make sure everything was proceeding as it should. She was attired in a cream sprigged day dress with a cerise sash and a cream narrow-brimmed hat with velvet streamers to match the sash.

She smiled when Jeremy Lambert, Lord and Lady Lambert's youngest son approached her. He was always happy to see her and had often invited her to accompany him to the theatre or a soirée, but she had always declined, making it quite plain that, fond though she was of him as a friend, that was all it was. Along with her determination to avoid any kind of serious relationship, she had stressed that her work was too important to her at this point in time to become entangled with anyone emotionally. With that he'd had to be content.

'May I say how delightful you are looking, Mrs Adams? I can't tell you how happy I was when Mama told me you had agreed to hold the fête here.'

A dashing and flamboyant young man with fair hair and brown eyes, Jeremy was always amenable and polite. He had the kind of pedigree Nancy's mother would approve of, and she would be more than happy if Nancy were to take him back to Aspenthorpe.

'Which she has done for the past two years—for which I am extremely grateful. Although I think I have you to thank for putting in a good word.'

He grinned. 'Well—I always look forward to it. I'm delighted to see you again. I wanted Mama to open up the gardens to you again in the hope that you hadn't forgotten me.'

'I will never forget you, Jeremy,' she said, laughing, warming to his natural charm and easy manner.

'Well, that's something, I suppose.' His grin was impudent as he subjected her to a long, lingering gaze. 'I've had a look round. I must congratulate you. You seem to have thought of everything. Only one thing is missing.'

'And what is that?'

'There is nowhere to dance.'

'You can't have everything, Jeremy.'

'I'm beginning to realise that. I dance well, Mrs Adams, and would have asked you to partner me had there been a dance floor.'

'I don't doubt you are a superb dancer. Perhaps another time.'

'I'll hold you to that. The fête has got off to a good start. You must be pleased.'

'I am. Thank goodness the weather has favoured us.' Her gaze seized on her employee Amy. She frowned. Laughter and frivolity surrounded that young lady wherever she went. She was a good, enthusiastic worker, and the children at the institute adored her, but there were times when she needed to curb her exuberant behaviour. She was in high spirits behind her stall. Nancy suspected she had already visited the marquee with her young man and imbibed something more inebriating than lemonade. 'If you will excuse me, Jeremy, I must have a word with one of my workers.'

'Of course. To compensate for the lack of a dance floor, and since I can't persuade you to accompany me to an evening at the theatre, unwilling as I am to pass up an opportunity for your company, can I persuade you to join me later for a drink?'

'Yes—thank you. I think I shall be in need of some refreshment by then.'

As he sauntered off, Nancy turned her attention to Amy.

Not in the mood for wandering around a garden fête, it was with reluctance that Dominic had agreed to escort Elizabeth and Simon to this one. Once through the gates, Elizabeth's gaze taking in the bustling throng and declaring how very quaint it all looked, she insisted that they take a turn of the stalls to investigate what was on sale.

When Elizabeth paused at a stall selling bric-a-brac, Dominic's eyes did a slow sweep of the grounds and came to rest on a woman in the company of a gentleman Dominic recognised as Jeremy Lambert. He looked away, but his gaze was soon drawn back to the woman, slender and lissom and lovely. Recognition flowed across his face and pleasure lit his eyes, followed by pure masculine admiration as his gaze drifted over Mrs Adams. Pressing business had consumed him for the past month, and now, on seeing her again, he realised just how much he had missed her.

He remembered how she had told him about the fête she was to hold to raise funds for her institute, but it had slipped his mind.

The effect of seeing her was overwhelming. Desire hit him with such unexpected force that for a brief moment, he could not move. His stare was one of admiration that paid homage to her striking beauty. Seeing her away from the institute, attired in her sprigged summer gown, she was different. An inner excitement touched her cheeks with the flush of a delicate pink rose. It added a special sparkle to her eyes, and a smile hovered at the corners of her mouth. He sensed a change in her, an extra quality that set her apart from the realms of physical attractiveness. It made her seem more alive than he had ever seen her.

Gazing on her unforgettable face made his heart ache. Never had he seen her look so provocatively lovely, so regal, so glamourous and bewitching. His gaze shifted to Jeremy Lambert, who was looking down at her upturned face like a hungry fox staring into a hen coop. He was totally unprepared for the effect this had on him and could not for the life of him understand why it should infuriate him so much, but of all the males in London, why did she have to draw the attention of Jeremy Lambert?

He didn't like to see other men coveting her, to watch the admiration and appreciation in young Lambert's eyes as they devoured her. He guessed the other man's thoughts were not so very different from his own, and he despised him for it. For the first time in his life, he experienced an acute feeling of irrepressible jealousy that twisted his gut and caught him completely unawares.

When she moved away from young Lambert, he was tempted to go to her, but Elizabeth, unaware of where his attention was riveted, put a hand on his arm and guided him in the opposite direction.

After speaking firmly to Amy, who was contrite and promised she would behave with more decorum, Nancy was approached by Betty.

'You've had a word with Amy I see.'

'Yes, Betty. She's harmless enough, but I don't want her slipping off to meet that young man of hers. I have no one to cover her stall.'

'Don't you worry. I'll keep an eye on her.' Some distance away, Betty had noticed Lord Blackwell. 'Don't look now, but Lord Blackwell is here. He's looking at you as if you're fit to eat. He seems more interested in you than he does the lady he's with.'

Nancy's breath suddenly caught, and she was unprepared for the joyful thrust to her heart. All her senses came alive. Slowly she dared to look across the crowded lawn. There were so many people it was difficult to know where to look at first, but then she saw him, her eyes drawn to his like a magnet. The gentleman was indeed Lord Blackwell. He looked so poised, so debonair. A slow half smile curved his lips as he met her gaze across the distance that separated them. Images rushed unbidden into her mind, prompting memories of a spring day and a drive onto the heath, of an exciting firm-bodied man with fingers that had touched her own when he had handed her a glass of wine.

'My goodness!' Betty said, clearly impressed. 'He's handsome, I'll say that for him. I wish a man would look at me like that.'

Nancy's gaze slid to the woman at his side, tall and beautiful and with scarlet lips. She was exquisitely dressed in a gown of seagull-grey silk belted with jade-green velvet, her elaborate hat covering her sleek hair, curled feather fronds sweeping from left to right lying in the brim. Nancy instantly recognised Elizabeth Wade and her brother, but she had no intention of approaching them. Miss Wade laughed, her laughter as light as a balloon sailing up into the sky, and something decidedly unpleasant entered Nancy's heart. If she were to analyse it, she knew she would discover it was something akin to jealousy.

On seeing Nancy, Miss Wade's eyes narrowed, and she placed a gloved hand possessively on Lord Blackwell's arm, whispering something in his ear and drawing him away.

Determined not to allow seeing him to affect her

work, Nancy turned away, but as the afternoon wore on, she could not help her eyes straying back to them, which annoyed her even more.

The fête was drawing to a close, all the objects at the auction had come under the auctioneer's hammer, and people began to disperse. Nancy helped with packing up the stock that remained unsold and would be taken back to the institute. The day had been a success, and she was well pleased with the tidy profit that would be ploughed into the institute.

Jeremy, determined not to let her escape before she had joined him for a drink at the marquee, came to find her and whisked her away to sample the spiced wine and to eat some early strawberries. Unfortunately, the strawberries were all gone, but she found herself sipping the spiced wine, which was delicious.

Some of the gentlemen and ladies still lingered round the marquee, several in jubilant spirits after an afternoon of overindulgence. Nancy smiled. When Jeremy excused himself and turned to speak to someone, Nancy closed her eyes and sighed, lifting her face to a warm breeze scented with cooked food and woodsmoke.

'A penny for your thoughts, Mrs Adams.'

The voice was rich and deep. Turning her head, she felt heat suffuse her cheeks as her body trembled into life, awakening her thoughts. Just a few feet away, Lord Blackwell was watching her.

'I was just gathering my thoughts before I head back to the institute, my lord.'

'Has it been a successful fête?'

'Yes—although I won't know quite how successful until later when everything has been totted up.'

He moved closer. Nothing was more obvious to Nancy at that moment than his eyes. They immediately took in every detail of her appearance. The greatest compliment he bestowed on her was to smile admiringly.

'You look lovely,' he said. 'I saw you earlier. I'm glad to know my memory of the occasion of our previous encounter on the heath is not at fault.'

Hot colour washed over Nancy once again. 'It was a lovely day—thank you. Have you enjoyed the fête?' she asked politely, glancing with disapproval at Amy, who was in the middle of a rather raucous group of revellers.

'I have to confess it is not my usual idea of entertainment, but Elizabeth and her brother thought it would be—interesting, having nothing like it in New York. I'm glad you enjoyed our outing on the heath. We should do it again.'

Seeing Miss Wade heading towards them out of the corner of her eye, Nancy stared at him. For one awful moment, she was seized with a passionate dislike for the other woman. She was clearly very well acquainted with Lord Blackwell. How well? Not for the first time, she wondered what Miss Wade was to him. Nancy was tired, and suspicion was doing all kinds of things to her self-esteem at that moment. She told herself angrily she was being oversensitive to read so much into it, but if the woman was either Lord Blackwell's intended or his mistress, then Nancy should not be going anywhere with him—and he should know better than to ask, unless he was playing her for a fool.

'We should? Are you sure that would be wise, Lord Blackwell?' she said crossly, looking meaningfully at Miss Wade as she advanced on them. 'I would have thought one woman at a time would be enough for any man.' Elizabeth Wade slid into position by his side, her condescending eyes passing insolently over Nancy as if she were a bad smell. Nancy stepped back, her anger at such rudeness mounting. She gave Miss Wade a tight, equally condescending smile, the devil rising up inside her. 'It is kind of you to ask me to go out with you, Lord Blackwell, but I must refuse. However, I'm sure Miss Wade would like you to show her the delights of Hampstead Heath—if you have not already done so. Excuse me. I appear to have a situation developing that needs my attention.'

Nancy was not aware of the anger flaring in Lord Blackwell's eyes as she strode to where several young people clustered around the marquee. Amy's young man appeared with a bottle of sparkling wine, his fingers placed over the uncorked neck as he proceeded to shake it vigorously. Amy collapsed against him in a fit of uncontrollable giggles while everyone else whooped with laughter and moved out of range of the expected shower of wine.

He released his finger after a final vigorous shake, sending a fizzing, frothy fountain out in front of him. Unfortunately, at that moment, people were beginning to leave the marquee, and two of them were the recipients of the young man's spurting wine.

Behind the stream of liquid, buoyed up by the excitement of the moment and unable to focus properly, the young man had no notion of the havoc he had caused. Amy, who had been laughing at his harmless antics, suddenly caught sight of her employer. Her laughter stopped, the smile becoming frozen on her lips. The laughter from everyone turned to gasps.

The woman who had taken the full blast of the sparkling wine was absolutely livid, her face as white as paper. Elizabeth Wade looked down at her dress in horror, the seagull-grey creation soaked, the bodice clinging to her body like a second skin, outlining all the contours beneath it.

There was a complete hush as everyone exchanged uneasy glances. Observing the ruin to her dress, Lord Blackwell stood beside her with a dangerous calm.

Nancy quickly gathered herself and went to Amy.

'You silly girl, Amy. I told you not to leave your stall. You should know better than to behave with such complete abandon.'

'You—you know this—this person,' Miss Wade uttered scathingly.

'This young woman works for me at the institute. I'm certain she and her friend meant no harm.'

'No harm?' Miss Wade seethed. 'Look at me.'

The softening emotion Dominic had felt on seeing Mrs Adams had vanished when she'd thrown her harsh parting words at him and Elizabeth. In its place was something steel-hard. Fury boiled inside him. What in God's name had got into her? What was she playing at? Why had she turned on him when he had nothing but good intentions where she was concerned? He'd been aware of what he was doing when he'd taken her to the heath that day, but now he was beginning to realise that it was madness to encourage what he was feeling. After what he'd experienced with Sophia, he understood the strategy of moving with caution.

His eyes swept over the high-spirited group frozen into immobility, with varying degrees of criticism. Of them all, he singled out Nancy, his expression now icy enough to make hell freeze over.

Fully aware of the catastrophe he had caused, the young man went puce with horror, quickly stepping forward to apologise. 'I say, I'm most awfully sorry,' he said, taking his handkerchief from his pocket and offering it to Elizabeth in an awkward gesture to mop up some of the liquid. 'I—I didn't see you.'

Angrily Elizabeth knocked his hand away. 'That was obvious,' she flared. 'You fool. How dare you? Look at my dress. It's totally ruined.'

'Well—you'll soon dry in this heat,' said the young man, which did little to comfort Elizabeth as he made a desperate endeavour to make light of the situation. In fact, his tactless attempt to do so only seemed to increase her ire.

Drawing a steadying breath, Mrs Adams stepped forward in a vain attempt to retrieve the situation. 'I must apologise for the young man's over-exuberance.'

Dominic's eyes were impervious when they looked at her. 'I should think so. Of all the irresponsible things to do. One would only expect such immature behaviour from children.'

Mrs Adams met his gaze, hot colour of indignation highlighted on her cheeks. 'Kindly have the courtesy to hear me out,' she said coldly. 'As you can see, the unfortunate incident happened in just a harmless moment of fun.'

'Then let us be thankful not everyone here was as irresponsible as your—your friends, otherwise we would all be awash with whatever was in the bottle,' Dominic ground out.

'Then it is a pity you did not partake of some your-self, Lord Blackwell, for I am certain it would have put you in better humour,' Mrs Adams uttered caus-tically.

He arched his brows when he met her defiant gaze. 'Really,' he drawled. 'I make no apology for my hu-mour. It seems to me there has been enough wine drunk in this vicinity to compensate for the rest of us.'

Mrs Adams lost her carefully controlled temper at his refusal to accept their apology. Her eyes spar-kled with outrage. 'You really are quite insufferable, and I am very sorry I ever tried to apologise to you.' She looked at Elizabeth beside him, who was visibly shaking with anger. 'I do hope your journey back to your destination won't be too uncomfortable,' she said stonily. 'And this young man was right. The day is unusually warm, so I'm sure the heat will soon dry your dress.'

When Lord Blackwell and Miss Wade went to join her brother waiting in the carriage in the gravel drive-way, high spirits were restored, the incident forgot-ten—by all but Nancy. She turned to Amy, who had the grace to look contrite.

'Amy—go and help with the packing up. I'll speak to you later.'

With a sullen glance at her young man, Amy walked away to resume her duties, leaving Nancy to say her goodbyes to Jeremy and Lord and Lady Lambert.

* * *

Had Mrs Adams but known the unfortunate truth—
that initially Dominic had seen the funny side of the
incident—her anger might not have been so acute.

On seeing the high and mighty self-assurance
which Elizabeth was in possession of at all times
stripped away in such a comical fashion, Dominic had
had to restrain an impulse not to laugh. Ever since
he had left Mark at Osbourne Hall, he was impatient
to return. Striving to get urgent business done that
kept him in London, he had not felt like laughing in
days, and now, unfortunately, was not the time. To
have done so would have provoked Elizabeth to further anger at the humiliation heaped on her by the
young revellers.

That had been Dominic's first reaction to the incident, but it had changed quite dramatically, for the
rush of resentment he had experienced when Mrs
Adams had quickly sprung to the defence of her employee and the young man was quite ridiculous. Contrary to what Mrs Adams thought, he did understand
the reasons for their exuberance.

Unfortunately, his anger had been sparked when she
had thrown the remark about Hampstead Heath at both
himself and Elizabeth. At the time, he had wondered
at the reason, but now he was beginning to think the
underlying cause of her sudden ire might have more
to do with Elizabeth than anything he had said. Was

it possible that she was jealous of Elizabeth? Immediately he was contrite. He had given her no reason to be. But he was determined to get to the bottom of it. Whatever the reason, the argument had made a light-hearted situation unpleasant and awkward, which he now deeply regretted.

Chapter Seven

When Jane was fully recovered from childbirth, Dominic questioned her again regarding the father of her child. He had tried to draw her out on the subject several times now, but she'd remained resolutely tight-lipped. It was midday, and she was in the drawing room with Constance. He had told them both that he wanted to speak to them, that it was about time she disclosed the identity of Rose's father.

From where she sat, Jane nervously watched him enter the room and sit opposite. Constance sat beside her on the sofa.

'I should tell you that I shall be travelling to Berkshire shortly to see Grandmother,' Dominic told them. 'Now you are recovered and Rose is thriving, I think it's best that you come with me, Jane. Some country air and time spent with Grandmother will do you good.' He looked at his stepmother. 'I trust you have no objections, Constance?'

'No, I have not. I agree. Some time away from Lon-

don will do her no harm. Of course, I shall not be going with her.'

'I would not expect you to, Constance. You and my grandmother are hardly the best of friends.'

'No, you are correct. She never forgave me for marrying your father.'

'That's between you and her. But she is extremely fond of Jane and will enjoy having her stay for a while. I've written to her explaining about Rose. I have yet to hear about her reaction.'

'When do you intend leaving?'

'In a couple of weeks. She's giving a weekend house party. I told her we would be present.' Crossing his legs and steepling his fingers in front of his face, he looked at his sister. 'Now, Jane, I think it's about time you told us more about this individual who seduced you. The matter is more serious than you appear to realise. It will affect your whole future.'

'Please don't say that. You make what we did sound so sordid. He didn't seduce me. I—I loved him so much, you see—I still do,' she finished quietly.

'You were barely seventeen years old,' Dominic said, trying to remain calm.

'And why did I not see it?' her mother said, her expression hard and accusing when she looked at her daughter. 'Where did these—these clandestine meetings take place? Out of consideration for your weakened state after giving birth, I have not pressured you on the subject, but now, enough is enough. I demand to know, Jane.'

Jane looked down at her hands resting in her lap, her fingers twisting a handkerchief. 'Very well—I will tell you. It was when I went with you, Mama, to stay with friends in Oxfordshire. We met when I was out riding. He—he lived close by, you see. We met again when we came to London. His—his family have a house in Belgravia.'

'How did you manage to meet him? As far as I was aware, you were chaperoned whenever you left the house—is that not so, Constance,' Dominic said, casting his stepmother an accusing eye.

'Yes—at least, that is what I thought. Of course, now we will have to consider how we deal with this. Who will marry her now—with a bastard child?'

'Oh, I'm sure you'll do your utmost to find someone, Constance,' Dominic ground out, 'unless the man in question steps forward and faces up to his responsibility.'

'Please don't blame Mama. It wasn't her fault. We—we met in secret. I'm so sorry to have deceived you, Mama—you too, Dominic—but he was a soldier about to leave for the Crimea.'

'And his name?'

'There is no point pursuing this, Dominic. He—is dead.'

Dominic paused. 'And how do you know this?'

'I—I read about it in the papers. There are frequent

accounts of what is happening over there. Apparently he was reported missing, believed killed in action,' she said quietly, lowering her eyes, but not before Dominic had seen her pain. He instantly softened.

'I'm so sorry, Jane,' he said gently. 'That's most unfortunate. Please tell me his name—for the sake of your child if nothing else. It is important that she grows up knowing who her father was.'

'David—his name was David,' Jane relented after a moment.

'And his family? They should be notified that they have a grandchild to remember their son by, don't you think?'

'I—I suppose so. I hadn't thought...'

'His name, Jane,' Dominic persisted.

'Ryland,' she said quietly, lowering her head. 'His name was David Ryland. His family live in Oxfordshire—at Aspenthorpe Hall.'

Dominic got to his feet. 'Ryland? I have heard of the family. Sir John Ryland is one of the wealthiest men in the country. It would be too much of a coincidence for there to be two families with that name in Oxfordshire. I shall make a point of writing to him before travelling to Oxford to see him. You can count on it.'

Jane nodded. 'Yes,' she whispered. 'I thought you might.'

Dawn had broken when Nancy let herself out of a back door and left the institute, crossing the yard to the stables with a spring in her step. She wore a tweed jacket over a plain dark green woollen skirt and a hat clamped to her head, her hair secured at her nape by a green ribbon. Robert, the groom, was already leading Archie, her rather fine dark brown stallion with a white blaze, out of one of the stalls.

She crossed towards them, running her hand over Archie's coat, which rippled like satin beneath her glove. The horse whinnied and nuzzled her with affection, blowing warm breath onto her cheek.

'Thank you for saddling him up, Robert.'

'Would you like me to come with you, ma'am?'

'I'll be all right. Don't worry about me. After a good gallop in the park, I'll be back in no time at all.'

When she rode into the park, the sun was beginning to rise in a line of crimson on the horizon. As she urged Archie into a gallop, the trees passed by in a haze, her horse whipping up grass in its wake. The tall trees cast long blue shadows over the park, which was sparkling with early morning dew. The air was fresh and exhilarating, and Nancy breathed it in deep, delighting in the feel of the horse moving beneath her. Nothing could compete with the thrill of riding a fast, capable horse.

She followed a narrow path through a thicket. As she emerged, the path turned. She pulled up to a halt when she suddenly found herself confronted by another horse and rider. Taken unawares, her horse reared, which caused her to slip almost gracefully from the saddle into a ditch.

Unhurt, still holding her whip, she sat for a moment to recover from the shock before struggling to sit up. Her horse, recovered from the surprise, bent its head, blinking its dark eyes and nuzzling her shoulder with its velvety nostrils, its rich, dark coat shining in the shadows of the trees.

Nancy knew she should be annoyed with Archie, but she couldn't. It wasn't his fault that another horse should suddenly appear in front of them. As she was about to get to her feet and climb out of the ditch, aware that the other rider had dismounted from his own horse, she looked up to find him looking down at her, hands on hips. Her eyes opened wide in amazement. It was none other than Lord Blackwell. At that moment, she wished the ground would open and swallow her up, but there was no escape.

'Well, well, Mrs Adams. You are the last person I expected to bump into—literally, it would seem.'

Nancy gazed up at him, so surprised at seeing him that she was unable to get a word out. What she was not expecting was the sudden quickening of her heart when she looked up at him, the look of recognition and cynical amusement in his eyes. His buff-coloured breeches fitted him to perfection, and there was not a crease in his dark green jacket, which emphasised his lean, muscular body. His cravat was smooth and snowy white, highlighting his incredibly handsome face. She met his gaze unwillingly, with growing annoyance that he should be here to witness her calamity.

'Don't just stand there. Have the goodness to help me up, will you?'

'Have you always been accident-prone?' he said sardonically, taking her hand and hauling her out of the ditch. 'First it was a fall down my stairs, and now a tumble into a ditch. Where next, I wonder?'

Nancy stiffened her spine when she remembered the unpleasantness of their last meeting at the fête and her anger when he'd suggested another outing on the heath when he was obviously paying court to Elizabeth Wade. Her eyes clouded suddenly, her mouth becoming set in a hard line. 'And of all people,' she said, brushing the bits of grass from her skirts, '*you* have to turn up.'

'And, it would seem, right on cue. You're having a spot of trouble with your horse.'

'Nothing I can't deal with,' she snapped ungraciously.

'I'm sure you're more than capable of dealing with most things, but I doubt even you could have controlled a horse that collided with another at the speed you were riding. Are you all right? Are you hurt?'

'No,' she replied, touched by his concern. 'Perhaps a little shaken at first, but that's all. I haven't fallen off a horse since I was a child.'

'If you hadn't careened out of the thicket like that, it would never have happened,' he said, with no hint of an apology.

Nancy stared at him incredulously, for she was convinced the accident was not entirely her fault. 'Me?' she gasped.

'Yes. Who else?'

'It was not entirely my fault,' she voiced aloud, suddenly furious at having all the blame shoved onto her. 'You are not entirely blameless. I was not riding at speed. I was forced to pull my horse to a halt when you appeared out of nowhere. The thicket is dense. How was I to know you were there?'

Lord Blackwell looked at her, a strong slant to his jaw and his voice like steel. 'I might have known you would try and shelve the blame. I would expect nothing else from—'

'A woman! Is that what you were about to say?' Her antagonist must have been aware of the storm that swept through her as she faced him, resolute, defiant, her small chin thrust forward. She favoured him with a glance of biting contempt. 'There is nothing wrong with the way I ride. I will have you know that I was sitting on a horse before I could walk. I am an extremely competent horsewoman and resent anyone who says otherwise.'

'Nevertheless, the fact remains that you fell from

your horse. There is a chance that you might have hit your head—'

'There is nothing wrong with my head,' she stated firmly.

'If you say so.' He shrugged, seeming to give the unfortunate incident no more concern. 'However, I think I should escort you back to the institute—to make sure you arrive in one piece.'

'I am able to find my own way back,' Nancy said tersely.

'Nevertheless, I insist,' he said in a smooth tone which told her he would brook no nonsense. 'Being a gentleman—which you are at liberty to dispute, if you wish—I cannot leave you to ride home alone. Come now, Mrs Adams. You cannot deny me my act of chivalry.'

In spite of her annoyance over his behaviour just now and on their previous encounter, Nancy found herself smiling at him.

'Ah—you see—you can smile. You should do it more often. Anger does not become you.'

'Far be it from me to object to any chivalrous inclinations you may have, my lord, so it seems I will have to accept.'

'Thank goodness. Now come along.'

Forced to admit defeat, Nancy placed her foot in his linked hands and hoisted herself onto her horse. For a moment, there was silence between them as they rode their horses slowly side by side, which Nancy was the first to break. Meeting his gaze squarely as he cast her a sidelong glance, she took a deep breath.

'Thank you for helping me out of the ditch, my lord.'

The merest ghost of a smile touched his mouth. 'I might have been tempted to ride off through the thicket and not bothered to stop, but I am not so un-gallant. It would seem that apologies are the order of the day,' he said softly, fixing his eyes ahead of them.

Nancy looked across at him in some surprise. 'Why? Are you saying you admit the accident was your fault, after all?'

'Let's agree that we were both at fault for that. I was talking about my lack of self-control when we met at the fête. It was inexcusable,' he said, making a ges-ture of self-reproach. 'I was not at my best that day.'

'Evidently.'

'I do improve on acquaintance, I assure you,' he murmured, his eyes twinkling wickedly at her.

'Probably—and I suppose the same could be said of rattlesnakes and suchlike—but that does not mean one has to like them. However,' she said, smiling again de-spite herself, 'your lack of self-control was not unrea-sonable. Had someone soaked me in sparkling wine, I would likely have behaved exactly the same as Miss Wade. She had cause to be angry.'

Lord Blackwell smiled across at her, a singularly

attractive smile that took Nancy unawares and had an unsettling effect on her.

'It is good of you to say so.' After another moment of silence, on a more serious note, he said, 'Tell me, why were you so angry with me before that? For what reason? Had it anything to do with Elizabeth, by any chance?'

Nancy glanced at him. 'Am I mistaken in thinking you and Miss Wade are—are...'

'Are what, Mrs Adams? Tell me.'

'Her manner is such that I assume she is your—your...intended—or perhaps even your mistress.'

His brows rose at her plain speaking. 'Elizabeth is not my intended—nor is she my mistress, as you so charmingly put it. To set your mind at ease, she is the daughter of a business friend of mine. Nothing more than that. Be assured that you have nothing to worry about where she is concerned. I've made no commitment to her, nor do I intend to.'

'No? Then perhaps you should inform her of that, because when a woman sidles up to a man the way she does to you, then that is where she wants to stay. I suspect she fully expects to become the next Countess Osborne.'

'Then she is going to be disappointed. Elizabeth wanted to see Europe, so she accompanied Simon, who came here on business for his father. The three of us met in New York and became better acquainted on board ship—nothing more than that. They will be leaving London shortly. Simon has business in France before they return to America. Our paths may not pass again for many years, if ever.' The harsh lines of his face had dissolved into an unexpectedly charming smile, and his gaze rested on her upturned face. 'There is only one woman I have eyes for just now, and she is right here. You intrigue me, Mrs Adams.'

She looked at him sharply. 'I do? In what way?'

'There are few ladies of my acquaintance who voice their opinions in so forthright a manner as you.'

Now it was Nancy's turn to be surprised. 'Then I can only assume that your experience with the female sex is somewhat limited, Lord Blackwell.' A gleam of suppressed laughter lit his eyes, and Nancy supposed that her remark about his inexperience with women had not been taken in the way she had intended. 'However, you are right. I do tend to speak my mind, but I do not see that as a failing.'

Lord Blackwell arched a sleek black brow in amusement when his gaze met hers. 'And to add to that attribute, the cut and thrust of your tongue are sharper and deadlier than any rapier,' he drawled.

'I'm glad you've noticed,' Nancy replied with an impudent smile and a delicate lift to her brows.

Lord Blackwell lost the battle to suppress his smile. 'You have spirit, I have to give you that. I can see your impression of me is far from favourable. On our last encounter concerning a bottle of wine, you accused me of being outrageous and insufferable.'

'Do you admit it?'

'Some of what you said hit the nail on the head. I am also noted for my obstinacy.'

'And do you agree that you can be a touch overbearing at times?'

'Only a touch?'

'Well, perhaps a little more than a touch.'

Nancy caught Lord Blackwell's blue gaze that seemed to slice the air between them, warning her not to overstep the mark. She met his eyes calmly, with a defiant lift of her chin. 'And you have no need of a sword to put anyone in their place. You can accomplish as much with just your eyes as you can with the point of a sword. I swear you could slay a man at twenty paces.'

'And you, my dear Mrs Adams, have the unique distinction of putting my back up.' He smiled across at her indulgently. 'You must forgive me my failings. The ladies of my acquaintance are usually more languishing than combative. I can be quite charming, you know.'

Nancy favoured him with a mocking glance. 'Is that so?'

'Most ladies do find me charming and pleasant—and some actually enjoy my company. I'm confident you would agree if you got to know me better.'

There was no room along the narrow path they were traversing to move out of his way when, with casual self-assurance, he nudged his horse closer to her own, his gaze sweeping over her in an appraising way. She found herself staring at him, momentarily captivated. The lazy, dazzling smile he bestowed on her transformed his face. It was the most wonderful smile she had ever seen, full of provocative charm. Oh, yes, she thought, feeling her heart do a little somersault, when he smiled like that and spoke in a soft-as-honey voice and looked at a woman from under those drooping lids, he could make a feral cat lie down and purr. She found hot colour washing her cheeks under his close scrutiny, and she chastised herself for that betrayal.

Lord Blackwell saw it and smiled infuriatingly. 'Do I unsettle you, Mrs Adams?' he asked with a slight lift to his eyebrows.

'You don't unsettle me in the least,' she lied, trying to keep her tone light.

'Come now, you're blushing,' he taunted gently.

'I am not.' Her unease was growing by the second, but she tried not to show it, attempting to maintain a façade of uninterest and indifference.

'Yes, you are. Your cheeks are as pink as my grandmother's roses in the gardens at Osborne House.'

'Good gracious,' Nancy laughed. 'If that's the kind of melodramatic nonsense you engage in with the ladies of your acquaintance, I am surprised they don't vomit.'

'I assure you they don't.'

'No—well—perhaps if they're all vacuous young ladies unable to see farther than your impeccable credentials, they wouldn't, would they?'

Astounded by her reply, Lord Blackwell threw back his head and burst out laughing. 'No,' he replied when he was able to speak, 'they wouldn't dare. Now, will you accede to my request and lower your weapons and agree to a truce?'

'Very well,' she agreed, bestowing on him a broad smile, looking at him from beneath the thick fringe of her lashes. 'I hate arguing—however, my sword may be sheathed, Lord Blackwell, but please remember that it is still there and every bit as sharp and lethal.'

Lord Blackwell's lips curled with wry amusement. 'It will make the play between us all the more exciting.'

Nancy gave him a smile that was utterly devastating, and she was certain she glimpsed approval lurking in those inscrutable blue eyes.

'I recall you saying that your father is a businessman,' Lord Blackwell said after a brief silence. 'Your horse is a splendid animal and you ride very well, and the dress you wore for the fête was of fine quality, which tells me you come from a prosperous family—and yet you work for a living.'

'I don't have to—it is by choice that I do so. I have been involved in charitable work from an early age. I bought the premises for my institute out of a legacy left to me by my grandmother.'

Lord Blackwell nodded. 'I see. Then that explains it. Were you brought up in London?'

'No. Oxfordshire—which is where my parents still live.'

'And your horse?' He grinned. 'Don't tell me. You paid for it out of your grandmother's legacy.'

Nancy laughed lightly. 'Something like that.'

'Your grandmother must have been a wealthy lady.'

'Yes—she was. She was quite rich.'

'What was she like—your grandmother?'

'Oh—small and wrinkled—with white hair. Isn't everyone's grandmother?'

'No. Mine is quite different,' he said, smiling. 'She is a formidable old lady, her mind as agile as it was in her youth. In fact, she has insisted I visit Osborne House to attend her weekend house party next week. I intended going anyway—to spend some time with Mark. Would you care to accompany me?'

Surprised by his invitation, she slowed her horse and looked at him. 'A house party? You would take me to your grandmother's house party? What on earth for?'

He met her gaze. 'Why would I not take you? I like being in your company. It will give us an opportunity

to get to know each other better. Besides, my grandmother is always desirous of seeing a new face.'

'But—I can't possibly come.'

'Why can't you? It would give me the greatest of
pleasure.'

'I hardly think it would be seemly. I work for my
living. I feel quite sure your grandmother's other
guests would be very perturbed if I were to appear.'

'I shouldn't think that would bother you, Mrs
Adams. Besides, like you, my grandmother is heavily involved in charity work. You would have much to
talk about. She might even donate to your institute.'

'Donations are always welcome. It's my escort I'm
having trouble with,' she shot back.

Lord Blackwell's lips twitched with ill-suppressed
amusement. 'Dear me, you do have an aversion to
me, don't you, Mrs Adams? I find any preconceived
ideas you might have about me being something of a
scoundrel rather insulting. Maybe you see me as some
kind of threat.'

'I do not consider you as much a threat as an inconvenience.'

Laughter twinkled in his eyes. 'I can see how confused you must be. It is a wholly perplexing prob-
lem you have there, and it is clearly up to me to put
things right.'

Nancy's cheeks became flushed with indignation.
'Are you laughing at me, Lord Blackwell?'

'Heaven forbid, I wouldn't dare. I want to become better acquainted with you. Now, what do you say? Will you come with me to Berkshire? I will even say please if that will persuade you.'

Nancy did not want to be persuaded. She did not want to become better acquainted with him—or did she? She did find him terribly attractive, and she always enjoyed being in his company. And then there was that kiss…which she refused to think about just then. The memory of it always set her senses soaring. Still, if it was true what he said about his grandmother and her charity work, if it meant another subscription to the institute, then that would be a good reason for accepting his invitation.

When Lord Blackwell saw her hesitate, he smiled. 'Come, Mrs Adams. The decision shouldn't be too hard for you to make. Your reticence only heightens my determination to persuade you. I am also willing to donate to your institute—but I might change my mind about the size of my donation. The amount will be considerably smaller than it would be if you were to accompany me to Berkshire. Should your colleagues at the institute find out, they would never forgive you.'

Quite unexpectedly, Nancy smiled pleasantly, and she was satisfied to see that he almost reeled under the impact. Her eyes contained sparkles of light, and the soft rose tinting her cheeks deepened. Her lips parted over even white teeth that shone, and a small dimple appeared in her cheek. Her smile widened, and so did the dimple.

'I suppose I could accept your invitation—purely for the sake of civility and the institute, you understand.'

'And a generous donation,' he was quick to point out.

'Of course—but this sounds very much like blackmail to me, my lord.'

'*You* might say that,' he murmured softly. 'I would prefer to call it persuasion.'

'Very well. I am persuaded. I surrender—but just for the one night. It's a busy time at work. Betty is very capable, but I don't want to be away too long.'

Having reached the institute and ridden round the back to the stables, Lord Blackwell dismounted. Holding out his arms, he assisted her to dismount. He did not move away when her feet touched the ground.

'I was hoping you'd accept,' he said quietly. 'If we continue in this fashion, Mrs Adams, we might even become friends.'

'I would advise you not to place any wagers on that, Lord Blackwell.'

Taking her gloved hand in his, he raised it to his lips. 'I might be tempted,' he said, with more meaning than she realised. 'I am not averse to the odd gamble now and then.'

Nancy's eyes were level with his broad, muscular

shoulders. Every inch of his tall frame positively radiated raw power and leashed sensuality; he excited her in every way, which caused her to once again remember her vow not to succumb to any man's wiles. And yet the thought of taking a lover—which she had set aside since she was always so busy—returned. She just knew Lord Blackwell would make the perfect lover. How could she claim disinterest in the man when his mere presence could so effectually stir her senses? Lifting her gaze to his handsome features, she met his knowing eyes, seeing something relentless and challenging.

'Has there been no one to spark your interest since the demise of your husband, Mrs Adams?'

'No. I have my work, which is important to me.'

'And you would allow nothing to interfere with that? Not even love?' he murmured softly, his gaze capturing hers.

'Absolutely not.'

'Why? Are you afraid of love?'

She averted her eyes. 'No, it just hasn't happened.'

He gave her a sceptical glance. 'Now, why is it that I don't believe you?'

'Whether it is true or not, I would not admit something of such a personal nature to you.'

'Mrs Adams, as a woman, you are truly unique.'

Nancy looked at him warily. 'You are not trying to seduce me by any chance, are you, Lord Blackwell?'

'Would you allow me to seduce you, Mrs Adams?'

In spite of the fact that his eyes were touching her like she had never been touched before, Nancy gave him a defiant look. 'Now you're mocking me.'

'I wouldn't dream of it. You are far too clever to mock.'

'Tell me, Lord Blackwell, do you always get what you want?' she asked.

'Usually,' he replied. 'Perhaps because I'm totally selfish, some would say arrogant and a complete scoundrel—or so I've been told by those who know me. It's the way I am, you see—having people pander to my smallest needs, to gratify my every whim.'

Nancy slanted him an arched glance. How could she remain at odds with this man when he smiled that engaging smile? It was no longer possible. Her lips curved in a smile of her own. 'What you really mean is that you were a spoilt child. Still,' she quipped, 'you're a male, so I would expect no less. You really are a rogue, Lord Blackwell.'

He grinned. 'I admit it. What I need is an attractive, patient and extremely tolerant young woman to take me in hand, to make me see the error of my ways and reform me.'

'Then I wish you luck with finding her. Intolerance and impatience have always been two of my failings, but there must be a female somewhere who will fall for a silken tongue and be willing to expend so much energy, time and effort on such an unenviable task. Try Miss Wade. She does seem taken with you. One cannot help but notice it. Now, I really must go inside.'

'Very well,' he said, releasing her hand and mounting his horse with perfect ease, his black riding boots gleaming like glass. Looking down at her, he smiled. 'Jane is to travel with us. She will be taking Rose. We'll take the train from Paddington. I'll make all the arrangements and inform you of the time we are to depart. You will come?'

'Yes, I will come. I look forward to seeing Jane and Rose. Thank you for asking me.'

Both Nancy and Dominic would have been surprised to know that on leaving the park, their presence had been duly noted. Miss Wade had drawn her horse beneath the concealing foliage of the trees to avoid being seen and to await her brother, and had observed through narrowed eyes the sight of Dominic riding in the park with a woman who was now attired considerably better than the last time she'd seen her.

Something in Dominic's heart moved and softened as he paused a moment to watch Mrs Adams hurry into the institute. Where she was concerned, nothing made sense.

Nancy Adams was unlike anyone he had ever met. She was different, a phenomenon. He sensed a goodness in her, something special, sensitive—something worth pursuing. She had been married before, so she must be familiar with the emotions, the feelings that a woman usually experienced with her husband. And yet there was also something untapped inside her that not even she was aware of—passion buried deep. What would happen if she allowed it all to come out?

Chapter Eight

Nancy dressed with special care in a light blue travelling dress with a short matching jacket for the journey to Berkshire. She arrived at Paddington Station at nine o'clock to find Lord Blackwell and Jane had already arrived. Rose was being carried by her nursemaid, who was to accompany them. Lord Blackwell was dressed immaculately in dove-grey trousers and a fine worsted bottle-green coat, his pristine white shirt contrasting sharply with his dark hair. Jane welcomed her warmly.

The station was noisy with the influx of passengers who were waiting for their trains. Their train was already at the platform. Accompanied by a porter who had taken charge of their luggage, Lord Blackwell led the way to the first-class compartments, taking Nancy's hand to assist her to climb aboard. The gesture was unexpected, and Nancy quivered in response. His stare homed in on her as though he, too, had felt the shock of electricity that bolted through her when they touched, and Nancy's heart skipped a beat. Her cheeks coloured as she turned her head away and took her seat beside Jane in their compartment.

When they were all settled, Nancy focused her attention out of the window as, with a cloud of smoke and soot and a hiss of steam, the train pulled out of the station. She loved travelling by train. These new locomotives never failed to amaze her. After a frenzy of investment and speculation during the previous decade, which had stimulated the coal and iron industries, the railway network was growing rapidly. When travelling to Aspenthorpe, Nancy always looked forward to the journey. It was fast and efficient, thanks to the steam locomotive.

They were met at the station by the Blackwells' open carriage. Jane made herself comfortable beside her brother while Nancy sat beside the nursemaid holding Rose. The infant had cried frequently on the train, no doubt unsettled by the noise. Thankfully she was sleeping now.

The final leg of their journey offered a spectacular taste of the countryside. The trees were dressed in their finest and in all shades of green, the hawthorn hedgerows heavy with sweet-smelling white blossom. Pretty villages and honey-stoned cottages were tucked away in the folds of the gently rolling hills.

'We're close to Osborne House now, Mrs Adams,'

Jane informed her. 'It's a lovely old house. It's been in the family for generations, isn't that so, Dominic?'

He nodded. 'Longer than I care to remember. The upkeep of it certainly hits the pockets.'

'And is this where you live when not in town?'

'It is my ancestral home and where I was raised. On my father's demise, I inherited the estate and the earldom. My grandmother, who no longer travels to London, still lives there.'

'And you say she is heavily involved in charitable works.'

'Absolutely. She is passionate about the welfare of others—especially children. Along with others, she tries to make a difference to their lives. It is important to her. So you see, Mrs Adams, you have a lot in common.'

'She must be an impressive lady. I look forward to meeting her.'

The coach passed through tall gates, then travelled along a curved drive. There was no sign of the house as they passed through splendid parkland where a herd of red deer paused in their eating to observe the coach. At a bend in the drive, the hall came into view, a welcoming, red brick mansion, lovingly preserved for centuries. Built in pleasing symmetry, it stood in perfect harmony against a backdrop of woods and parkland with laurels and rhododendrons and tall dark firs overshadowing ponds where water lilies strove to bloom in the gentle shade. The house stood like a brooding sentinel, the many windows reflecting the sunlight. Wide steps with ornate pillars on either side led to double mahogany doors.

'My goodness. How right you are, Jane. What a beautiful house,' Nancy said without taking her eyes off the impressive building. Its elegant beauty expressed power and pride, and she was touched by its timeless splendour. 'Is it very old?'

Lord Blackwell smiled at the dazed expression of disbelief on her face. 'I'm afraid it is,' he said, preferring to watch her myriad of expressions rather than the approaching house. 'Built during Tudor times, the structure remains unaltered.'

'And all those windows,' she murmured, watching the sun's rays glint off the glass.

'People were enthusiastic for enormous windows in those days,' he replied.

'I know.' Aspenthorpe Hall had its fair share of windows. 'That's because glass was very expensive. It became a status symbol. People used it in great quantities to show how wealthy they were. Your ancestors must have been very rich.'

'They were. The first Earl of Osborne was a powerful politician and a trusted adviser to Queen Elizabeth.'

'Really?' Nancy said, impressed. 'And did she ever visit Osborne House?'

'Frequently. She liked living at her subjects' expense. I intend having considerable alterations and improvements made in the future. I have an architect drawing up plans at present. I'm happy to see we've arrived before the hordes descend on us for the weekend. It will change dramatically when they do.'

As soon as Nancy entered the house, she was greeted with unaffected warmth. She felt this was a house where courtesy and mutual affection ruled in perfect harmony. The Blackwells lived in a style of elegance she was accustomed to.

Lord Blackwell's grandmother came to welcome them in the hall. Nancy stood back while she spoke to her grandson and granddaughter. Attired in a deep rose dress with her white hair carefully coifed, she was in her eighties and as sprightly as a woman half her age. She radiated kindness and gentility that was immediately endearing to anyone who met her, but according to Lord Blackwell, when she had a mind to be, she could be awe-inspiring.

On the train, Lord Blackwell had mentioned that he'd written to their grandmother and explained the situation regarding Jane, so she was prepared when her granddaughter arrived with a baby in her arms. She admired Rose, who was still sleeping.

'She's a lovely child—but then, I would expect nothing less with you as her mother, Jane. We'll go into the ins and outs of how it all came about later.

I've ordered a light lunch to be served. We can talk while we eat. I'm sure you must be ready for something after your journey.'

'I'll eat later if you don't mind, Grandmama,' Jane said, hovering in the doorway with the nursemaid holding Rose. 'Rose has been fractious during the journey. I would like to see her settled.'

'Very well, dear. I'll have something sent up. The nursery has been prepared, although it's been a long time since a baby was in there.'

Nancy had just enough time to admire the wealth of elaborate wood and plasterwork before being ushered into a small room leading off from the hall.

'I don't expect the guests to arrive until mid-afternoon,' Lady Blackwell said. 'Everything is ready for the weekend. Come and sit down.'

Over a collation of cold meats and salad, they conversed easily. When Dominic mentioned Nancy's work and the institute, his grandmother was all attention.

'How interesting. You have your own premises?'

'I do. The institute is conveniently placed to give easy access for those in need—mainly young children and babies, of which there are so many. There's a sorry lack of places for them to go.'

'I couldn't agree more. But—forgive me for saying this, but aren't you a little young to be in charge of so many children?'

'I don't think so. I am passionate about what I do, although I have to admit it is hard work.' She smiled. 'I don't do it all by myself. I have a well-run establishment with responsible and caring staff to look after the children.'

'And you take children of all ages?'

'We do. The babies stay with us for the first year of their lives. Sometimes the mothers reclaim them. If not, then they are adopted into families we consider suitable. We do our best to find situations for the older children where they can work and hopefully learn a trade.'

'And your institute is funded by donations?'

'Yes, but we raise money in other ways too—fêtes, markets—anything to help with the upkeep.'

'I am impressed, Mrs Adams. And is Mr Adams involved in the institute, too?'

'Mrs Adams is a widow, Grandmother,' Lord Blackwell provided.

'Oh, I see. My condolences, my dear. Well, I will look forward to having a serious discussion about your charity work before you return to London. Since my husband died and the family are all occupied with other things, I find I have too much time on my hands. I would like to hear more about your institute. We might be able to help each other.'

Nancy smiled. 'Yes, I would like that.'

'That's all very well, Grandmother,' Lord Blackwell said, 'but don't forget that Mrs Adams is here to socialise, not to work.'

'And I must remind you, Lord Blackwell,' Nancy remarked smartly, 'that I accepted your invitation to meet your grandmother because I was interested in hearing about her charity work. Socialising is secondary to that.'

'Well said, Mrs Adams,' Lady Blackwell told her with amusement, 'but you must enjoy your stay with us. Remember that you are a woman first.'

Nancy smiled. 'I will keep what you say in mind—although I have to get back to London tomorrow.'

'I'm sorry to hear that. I was hoping you would be staying the whole weekend. But I do understand that you are a busy young lady. I must say that when Dominic wrote and told me he would be bringing an acquaintance along—a lady, no less—I did wonder if he was contemplating settling down to married life again at long last,' she said, casting a look of disapproval at her grandson. 'Mark is looking forward to seeing you, Dominic. My grandson is a widower, Mrs Adams, who happily dotes on his son. I believe Mark is down by the lake with his fishing rod. You will meet him presently.'

'I look forward to it,' Nancy said.

Having finished eating, Lord Blackwell pushed back his chair and got to his feet. 'If you will excuse me, I will go and find him—and in answer to your query, Grandmother, I promise that when I do decide to settle down, you will be the first to know.'

Later, as the guests began to arrive, knowing Lord Blackwell would be occupied receiving them and feeling the need of some fresh air after the journey, Nancy slipped out of the French windows that led onto the terrace. Going down a flight of shallow steps to the extensive gardens, she followed the paths that meandered through the well-kept beds of flowers in full bloom, adding a vivid splash of colour. Seeing a lake beyond the gardens, she headed towards it. A slight breeze blew over the water, and she stood on the edge to watch the ducks swimming and diving on the sparkling surface.

She stood a while, admiring the view. It was a large lake surrounded by tall trees with a boathouse on the other side. Turning her head, she looked towards a small landing platform that reached out over the water. A young boy was sitting there fishing with his trousers rolled up to his knees and his bare feet dangling in the water, a little black dog stretched out by his side. This must be Mark. Nancy walked towards him. About six years old, he sported a shock of dark brown curls. Having felt a tug on the end of his line, he began happily winding it in, smiling broadly when he saw a reasonable-sized trout wriggling on the end.

When she climbed onto the landing stage, on seeing Nancy, he stopped smiling and gave her a direct look. He seemed to be assessing her, and when his eyes ceased to regard her so seriously, a smile tugged at the corners of his mouth. She noted that he bore a striking resemblance to Lord Blackwell. The dog got to its feet to welcome the newcomer, its tail wagging frantically. Bending down, she stroked its fluffy head and ears before turning her attention to the boy.

'Hello. You're in luck.'

'Yes—it's a beauty, don't you think? Do you like to fish?'

'I do,' she replied truthfully. 'Although I must confess that I'm not very good at it and have never caught anything very big. Whenever I went fishing with my brothers, I rarely caught anything. Do you enjoy fishing?'

Carefully taking the fish off the hook, the boy placed it in a bucket beside him before looking at her again. 'Yes, I do. I'm quite good at it. My father keeps the lake well stocked with pike and carp and trout.' He glanced at the dog when it began jumping up at Nancy in an attempt to get her attention.

'Floss, sit down,' he ordered. The dog immediately did as she was told but did not take her expectant eyes off Nancy, clearly hoping for another pat.

'She's a sweet dog—and very obedient.'

'Not always. I've tried training her, but she gets overexcited when she meets somebody new.'

'What are you going to do with the fish?'

'I take them to Mrs Jenkinson—she's the cook. She'll cook them for tea. My name is Mark, by the way.'

'I'm pleased to meet you, Mark. I'm Mrs Adams.' Nancy studied him closely. 'I know you are Lord Blackwell's son.'

He nodded, getting to his feet and picking up his bucket. 'He's been away—to America. It's a long way away—across the Atlantic Ocean. I'd like to go there one day. I wish he'd taken me with him.' He looked up at her. 'I'm going back now.'

'What about your shoes?'

'I don't have any.'

'But—you might hurt your feet.'

'No, I won't. I never wear them when I go down to the lake to fish—only in winter. Then, that's a different matter.'

'Doesn't your father mind you coming down here by yourself?'

'No—not really. I know not to go onto the lake.'

'Do you mind if I walk back with you?'

'Of course not. Are you one of Great-Grandma-ma's guests?'

'Yes—although I've travelled from London with Lady Jane and your father.'

Suddenly the boy's eyes lit up, and his lips broke into a broad smile. 'I know Aunt Jane is here. I must go and see her—it's ages since she's been here.' He took a few hurried steps away from her before remembering his manners and turning to look back at her. 'I'm sorry. Will you be able to find your own way to the house?'

Nancy laughed. 'Of course. Hurry along.'

Deep in thought, Nancy made her way back to the house. Mark was a lovely boy. Lord Blackwell had told her that his wife had died several years ago. She wondered why he didn't talk about her. Perhaps her death had been so traumatic, and he had loved her so much, that it was too difficult for him to discuss.

Arriving back at the house, taking a moment to relax in one of the chairs on the terrace while it was quiet, she made herself comfortable and breathed in the clear air, closing her eyes to enjoy this moment of peace.

'Why, Mrs Adams,' a clear voice rang out. 'What a surprise seeing you here.'

With a sickening jolt, recognising Miss Wade's voice and resenting the intrusion, Nancy's heart sank. Had Lord Blackwell told her Miss Wade had been invited as well, then she would have declined his invitation. Opening her eyes, she pinned a slight smile on her lips. She would do her best to be amenable even though she disliked the American woman intensely. Miss Wade, who was accompanied by her brother—

who didn't come high in her estimation either—sat in one of the empty chairs across from her. Mr Wade, appearing to be in good spirits, sat beside her, crossing his long legs out in front of him, his eyes assessing Nancy, grinning a wolfish smile. He was the very picture of the kind of man her mother had taught her to steer clear of.

'Lord Blackwell invited me. I was merely taking a moment's respite.'

Miss Wade was elegantly dressed in a grey travelling skirt with a short green jacket. A hint of rouge reddened her lips. Her austere gaze settled on Nancy in a cool, exacting way. Impersonally her eyes raked her from head to foot in a single withering glance. Clearly she had not forgotten their previous encounter, Nancy thought, when Amy's young man had soaked her dress in sparkling wine. She clearly resented Nancy's presence here at Osborne Hall.

'How delightful to see you again,' Miss Wade said with a practised, condescending smile.

'We've only just arrived,' Simon Wade said. 'Are you here for the weekend?'

'I shall be leaving tomorrow.'

'It was generous of Dominic to invite us. Did you travel from London alone, Mrs Adams?'

'No. I accompanied Lord Blackwell and his sister.'

'We have yet to meet his sister—a charming girl, according to her mother.'

'Yes, she is.'

'It's such a novelty for us to visit a proper stately home in England. Dominic's grandmother has several interesting things planned to keep us occupied. Are you to join the ride into the village tomorrow morning?'

'Probably. I haven't made up my mind. And you, Miss Wade? Will you be riding along with the rest?'

'Oh, yes. Wouldn't miss it. I enjoy riding when I get the chance. Dominic has told us he has some splendid horses in his stable. I believe you have some good fox-hunting areas in England. I'd like to be here for the hunting season.'

'The season is from the end of October to early April, so I'm afraid you're too late.'

'That's a pity. So that leaves several months when hunts are not actively killing wildlife. Do you hunt, Mrs Adams?'

'No. I enjoy riding, but I am averse to killing animals for sport.'

'I couldn't agree more,' Simon Wade said. 'I could never see the point in it.'

'Nevertheless, I am rather envious,' Miss Wade remarked. 'Does your father keep horses?'

'Yes—a few,' Nancy replied, curious as to what had prompted Miss Wade to ask the question. 'Why do you ask?'

Miss Wade shrugged, giving the impression that it

was of little interest to her and that she was merely trying to make polite conversation.

'Oh, no reason. Only it costs money to keep and train horses—we know that, don't we, Simon? To do so, one must be reasonably wealthy.'

Nancy stared at her, her expression tightening at the unexpectedness of this conversation. There was something different in Miss Wade's manner towards her which was beginning to unsettle her, and she wondered at its cause. Mr Wade came to her rescue.

'I say, Elizabeth—that's a bit rude. The financial affairs of Mrs Adams's father hardly concern you.'

'Please, Mr Wade—let your sister finish,' Nancy said, remaining calm, eyeing Miss Wade steadily.

'Oh—I know it's none of my business,' Miss Wade continued in honeyed tones. 'It's just that I find it rather curious—and strange—that someone from a well-off background should find the need to do such menial work as you do—although perhaps your husband did not leave you well provided for.'

'Enough, Elizabeth. Whatever Mrs Adams's circumstances happen to be, they are her concern. Excuse my sister, Mrs Adams. She is too outspoken.'

Something shifted inside Nancy. She lifted her chin in that way she had of showing her defiance, of giving quiet rein to her anger. 'Please don't concern yourself, Mr Wade—although I would prefer to keep my husband out of any discourse.' She looked at Miss

Wade. 'On the contrary, I do not consider the work I do menial. In fact, I enjoy my work. It is rewarding in many ways.' She gave no sign to Miss Wade that she was disconcerted or intimidated by her. She would not give her the satisfaction. But she was wondering what could have prompted this sudden interest in her affairs. She had no intention of staying to find out.

Getting to her feet, she smiled tightly at them both. 'Please excuse me. I have things to do. No doubt we will meet later.'

'Mrs Adams. Wait.'

Nancy turned, surprised that Miss Wade had followed her. 'What is it?'

'Why are you here, Mrs Adams?'

'Because I was invited—and because I wanted to meet Lady Blackwell. We have much in common.'

Miss Wade's eyebrows rose as she stared at her, her red lips twisting scornfully. 'Namely her grandson. I don't know what you have in mind where Dominic is concerned, but whatever it is, you'd do better to forget it.'

'I beg your pardon?' Nancy stared at her coldly. 'Would you mind telling me what you mean by that?'

Miss Wade returned her stare, her eyes shining ruthlessly. 'That no matter how much you throw yourself at him, you'll never succeed in getting him to look at you.'

'Do not suppose that I would encourage him to do

so.' Nancy laughed, delighting, as she always did, in the ridiculous. 'Dear me, Miss Wade. What on earth has got into you?'

'Righteous anger, if you must know,' Miss Wade flared, clearly infuriated by Nancy's calm manner, 'which means that I have just cause. So don't deceive yourself into believing Dominic is interested just because he speaks to you. He's being polite, nothing more. Why,' she scoffed, 'he'd laugh you right out of bed.'

'I doubt it, since such a thing is unlikely to happen,' Nancy responded, refusing to be intimidated by such cutting remarks. Nancy did not consider herself plain in the slightest. In fact, attired in her own finery, she was certain she could give Elizabeth a run for her money any day. 'You're being quite absurd, Miss Wade. You're letting your imagination run away with you to the point where you are in danger of becoming hysterical.'

'Oh, I don't think so. I've seen the way you look at him. I've waited a long time for him to propose to me. I won't see that time wasted. I don't intend to stand by and watch a nobody like you jeopardise my plans.'

The anger and bitterness seeping out of Miss Wade was so palpable that Nancy could almost feel it. 'You may be assured that I have no intention of doing any such thing.'

'Then we understand each other. You will stay away from him?' Miss Wade queried.

'I'm sorry to be a fly in the ointment, Miss Wade, but that's going to be difficult, since at this present time we inhabit the same house,' Nancy answered flatly. 'But I'm sure if you want him so much then nothing will stand in your way.' She looked at Miss Wade and calmly pointed out, 'But the matter between the two of you is not absolutely settled, is it? First you have to make him want to marry you.'

'And I will,' Miss Wade continued emphatically. 'I will do everything in my power to bring that about.'

Nancy gazed somewhat pityingly at her. 'If that is what will make you happy, then I see nothing wrong with it. But don't overestimate your ability to manipulate him. I would not equate Dominic Blackwell with the other gentlemen in Society. I have known him just a short time, but I already know he is nothing like them.'

'How can you, a woman who spends her time looking after destitute children, possibly know anything about gentlemen of breeding?'

'Don't be deceived by what I do, Miss Wade. Such things are not beyond my sphere,' Nancy said pointedly. 'Now, if you're through with your insults, I have better things to do.'

Having nothing but contempt for Miss Wade's paltry attack, seeing nothing in it but ignorance and malice, refusing to be hurt by her cruel barbs, Nancy shoved them to the back of her mind.

That evening, Nancy chose to wear a brocade emerald green gown with narrow paler green stripes. With the help of one of Lady Osborne's maids, they had managed to dress her hair, pinning it high on her head and teasing the ends into long ringlets to hang over one shoulder. A single ruby drop nestled at her throat, its colour finding an echo in the tones of her hair.

She closely inspected her image in the dressing table mirror, considering her features. The face that stared back at her was an attractive face, the features delicate, the eyes appealing. Her thoughts turned to Lord Blackwell and how her feelings towards him were changing the more she saw of him. She told herself she must remain resolute and not succumb to the man's charms on any account. And yet, she thought on a softer note when she remembered the tenderness that had warmed his eyes when they'd parted earlier, this would not be easy. Getting to know him was her first real encounter with the intimacy and power of an overwhelming attraction between a man and a woman, of desire that melted the bones and inflamed the flesh and caused all coherent thoughts to flee. Her long-ago feelings for Thomas simply paled in comparison.

Hearing guests arriving, she quickly pulled herself

up sharply. This was not the time for girlish fancies
and longings. She'd had enough of that with Thomas,
and it had got her precisely nowhere. With a hardness
of purpose born of necessity, she gave her mind over
to how best she might get through the rest of her stay
and how to prepare the battle lines now she knew Miss
Wade was one of the guests.

When she was ready, she surveyed her appearance
in the cheval mirror and saw her radiance reflected.
Not since Georgina's wedding had she worn anything as glamorous as the gown she now wore. She
felt transformed by its magnificence, and experienced
a sensuous pleasure in its softness. It was bold and
quite dramatic and extremely daring, its form-fitting
bodice cut low, and the fullness of the skirt empha-
sising her tiny waist and falling in luxurious shining
folds to her slippered feet.

Content with her appearance, she removed the lid of
a scent spray and sprayed the perfume. The scent was
subtle and tantalising, suggesting a rose-filled garden
under a hot summer sun. Satisfied that she could do
no more, she glided from the room with all the natural elegance of a lady. Before going downstairs, she
went to the nursery to see if Lady Jane was ready,
only to find her seated before the fire with a sleeping
Rose in her arms.

'I won't be joining you, Mrs Adams. Rose is still
fractious, and I don't like to leave her.'

'I'm sure her nurse will inform you should the need arise, Lady Jane.'

Lady Jane bit her lip, settling further back in the chair. 'I know, but to be honest, Mrs Adams, I have no desire to socialise. I prefer to stay here.'

Nancy sat opposite her. 'If you're sure.'

'I am. Make my excuses to Dominic, will you? He'll understand. I've already told Grandmama I won't be joining you—but you must make the most of it, Mrs Adams. Everyone here knows of Grandmama's constant need for funds for her various charities, which could prove beneficial to you.'

Nancy smiled slightly. 'I am also here to raise funds, Lady Jane, and I'm looking forward to getting to know your grandmother. She's a lovely lady.'

'Yes, she is, and I love her dearly. I don't get the chance to come here as often as I would like. Mama and Grandmama don't get on, you see—which I suppose is because she married Dominic's father shortly after his mama died. Apparently, at the time, Grandmama made no secret of the fact that she never thought Mama was good enough. But that's another story, and nothing will change the way things are now.'

Reluctant to leave the cosy warmth of the nursery, Nancy stayed with Lady Jane a while before leaving her to go downstairs. It could not be put off any longer.

Chapter Nine

Dominic was by his grandmother's side to greet her eminent visitors with charm and self-assurance. One after another, the carriages came slowly up the avenue of trees, lit up from the basement to the roof for the occasion by lights flaring cheerfully in the darkness. Only the most eminent of the local gentry had been invited, so that the guests felt themselves to be highly privileged and would therefore be more likely to donate to Lady Blackwell's various charities. It was clear, early as it was, that the event would be a success.

Later, when Mrs Adams appeared on the stairs, Dominic heard not a word of the conversation he was having with one of his neighbours. For the first time in his life, he was rendered speechless as his eyes fastened on the young widow in her fashionable gown and with a sophisticated coiffure. As she descended the wide flight of stairs, she possessed the grace and beauty of a Grecian goddess and the regal bearing of a queen. In the shifting blur of people, colour and flashing jewels that moved in front of his eyes, her presence affected everyone assembled like a rare sunburst.

He strode towards the stairs to meet her. When she reached the bottom step, he took her hand. There was a twinkle in his eyes, and a slow, appreciative smile worked its way across his face as his gaze leisurely roamed over her body in an unspoken compliment.

'You look entrancing,' he said in a quiet voice. 'I'm delighted you were able to join us—if somewhat tardily.'

'I'm sorry. Am I late?' The look she gave him was one of unadulterated innocence.

'You know you are. What were you trying to do? Make a grand entrance?'

'What? Me? Really, Lord Blackwell, I think you know me better than that by now,' she murmured.

He glanced down at her with a hooded gaze. 'No, I don't. But I would like to.'

She smiled impishly. 'I think you know me well enough.'

Laughing softly, he took her arm. 'My name is Dominic. Enough of the formality—Nancy—if you agree for me to address you by your given name.'

'Of course, you have my permission—Dominic.'

'Now we've got that out of the way, come and meet some of my grandmother's guests before you embarrass us both.'

'You, my lord? Embarrassed? Never. And why didn't you tell me Miss Wade and her brother had been invited?'

'I didn't invite them. They invited themselves at the last minute when they found out I was coming to Berkshire.'

'You could have told me at Paddington—before I got on the train.'

'What? And have you running back to that institute of yours? Not a bit of it. It's your company that is important to me until you have to leave.'

With a natural grace and a serene smile on her lips, Nancy felt an odd sensation of unreality as Dominic introduced her to the other guests. As they passed through sumptuously furnished rooms, the sheer magnitude and beauty of the house seemed overwhelming and utterly breathtaking. Her own home, Aspenthorpe, was a fine example of a stately home, but it fell somewhat short of what she now saw. The house shone with the brilliance of hundreds of candles. Mirrors glowed with refracted light from the crystal and diamonds strewn around the bare throats of women. An army of exquisitely attired footmen in midnight blue and gold moved among the guests, bearing silver trays balancing sparkling glasses of champagne.

As she walked beside Dominic, glancing at the assembled guests, she suddenly found herself the object of dozens of pairs of eyes. It was as though she stood in a blazing light as people turned towards her. Every male and female, young and old, seemed to focus on her, some staring frankly, while others looked at her with a more restrained curiosity.

When Dominic was satisfied that he had introduced her to most of those present, he drew her aside.

'I thought Jane would be with you.'

'I'm afraid not. I went to the nursery before I came down. She's not yet ready to be among so many people. She prefers to remain in the nursery with Rose.'

He nodded. 'I can understand that. I'll go up and see her later.'

'I passed the dining room earlier. Your grandmother has laid on a spread fit for a king.'

'No guest has ever left my grandmother's table with anything less than complete satisfaction.'

Nancy looked to where Lady Blackwell stood surrounded by friends. She dominated the room in her wide skirts of beaded silver brocade, with her white hair piled precariously high on her head. 'She is very generous.'

He grinned. 'Generous—yes, but most of the guests will be lighter in their pockets when they have donated to her charities, and the more they imbibe, the more they donate.'

Nancy laughed. 'I like her more by the minute. She's a lady after my own heart.'

* * *

Blind to the satisfied way his grandmother was observing them, Dominic's manner was proud as he calmly presented Nancy to his grandmother's house-guests—a polite, friendly gathering of some of the more sedate members of London's elite who had travelled to Berkshire. They were men and women whose names Nancy would never remember.

Taking her aside, Dominic placed a glass of wine in her hand. She sipped it gratefully, meeting his eyes over the rim.

'I'm going up to see Jane,' he said quietly. 'I can't pretend I'm not concerned about her.'

'Are you any closer to finding out the name of Rose's father?'

He nodded. 'I have. I've written to the family. I hope to hear from them shortly.'

For the rest of the evening, Dominic found his eyes drawn to Nancy like a magnet. She lit up the room simply by being present, and as she interacted with the guests, it was clear she was experienced in social repartee. She became a lively, amiable, laughing, beautiful young woman in possession of a natural wit and intelligence. He had never imagined she could sparkle as she did, and when Simon made a beeline for her, staying close to her throughout the evening, it made him uneasy. He was not at all pleased at the effect she was having on the American.

* * *

The huge table in the splendid dining room was laden with a magnificent array of food on silver plates. Lady Blackwell had provided for her distinguished friends in the lavish manner for which she was renowned. There was a wide selection of roast meats, fresh fish, puddings and fresh fruit, all manner of pies and several fine cheeses. All this was to be washed down with bottles of wine and sherry, claret and port and brandy and many more intoxicating drinks to suit every kind of palate.

More guests who lived in the locality were arriving by the minute. Sherry was served in the drawing room, where everyone seemed to know everyone else.

Feeling a need to be by herself for a moment, Nancy found her way to the library, where she breathed a sigh of relief. A fire burned in the hearth, and around the impressive room, books in the hundreds were shelved on the walls. She was perusing them, finding several of interest she would like to take a better look at, when someone walked in. She felt a sinking feeling in the pit of her stomach when she recognised Simon Wade. He had clung to her side for most of the evening, and one of the reasons she had entered the library was to escape his unwanted attentions.

She caught her breath as he sauntered towards her. He was good-looking, all right, no question about it, but fortunately she knew him for what he was and was completely immune to his kind of potent sexual allure.

When he reached her, she managed to give him a cool, indifferent glance. Propping his shoulder against the bookshelves, he folded his arms across his chest, looking very pleased with himself.

'Well, well, Mrs Adams, so this is where you escaped to,' he drawled, studying her at close range with open male interest. His seductive, smoky eyes appraised her, and a lazy smile curved his mouth. 'I was hoping to find you alone. You know, you bear no resemblance to the woman I was introduced to at Dominic's house in London.'

Nancy raised one eyebrow at him and regarded him frostily. 'Is that so? I am surprised you can remember since I wasn't looking my best.'

'I saw through all that—and I shall endeavour to see a good deal more of you while we are here.'

'You are too forward by far, Mr Wade. I think I am right to be wary of you. You look like a scoundrel to me.'

'And you would know what a scoundrel looks like, would you, Mrs Adams?'

She raised her eyes to his. 'Oh, yes, Mr Wade. I have come across men like you before and always stay well clear. Now, will you please go away. Lord Blackwell has some interesting books I would like to take a look at.'

He grinned, not to be deterred. 'I am a very persistent fellow, Mrs Adams.' His voice was pleasant, almost playful, but there was nevertheless a steely edge to it. 'I am a good-natured, gregarious sort of person, and you are a beautiful young woman, an acquaintance of my good friend. If I can make your life a little more cheerful while we are both here for the weekend, then why should I not endeavour to do so?'

'Why not indeed?' Nancy uttered drily. 'I am a working woman, Mr Wade, with an institute of needy children to take care of. Lady Blackwell is involved in the same kind of work I do, and I am here to discuss my work with her. We might be of help to each other. It is obvious to me that you have a way with women— with everybody, come to that, even Lord Blackwell himself—but my instinct tells me you will do me no good. Do you flirt with every woman you meet?'

His eyes twinkled mischievously. 'Only the ones that take my fancy. I find you quite a challenge. Did anyone ever tell you that you have wonderful eyes?'

'Not recently.'

At that moment, Dominic came in, looking most displeased to find Mr Wade propped against his bookshelves, gazing at her upturned face.

'What are you doing in here, Simon? I thought you would be in the billiard room, knowing your fondness for the game.'

'I saw Mrs Adams come in here, so I took it upon

myself to get to know her better. Always was the impetuous sort. You must have seen the effect her presence has had on all those here tonight. I have no doubt she is already ruffling a few feathers and causing quite a stir.'

'Is it because of my looks and being a stranger that I will cause a stir—or because I was with you, sir?' Nancy retorted dryly, with a delicate, knowing lift to her brows.

Mr Wade laughed outright, showing teeth as white and strong as those of a wild animal. 'You read me too well, dear lady—my reputation must have gone before me,' he said, the gleam in his eyes suggesting an intimacy she didn't like, and a salacious, lazy smile curling his full lips. 'It is not merely a stir I would like to cause with you, but an outright scandal.'

Dominic rolled his eyes and looked at Nancy. 'Please excuse my friend's behaviour. I think the wine must have gone to his head.'

'I suspect a scandal would not concern him, only the making of one,' she said calmly, having already formed her own judgement of Simon Wade. She had seen the spontaneous smiles he bestowed on the women within his sphere having the desired effect, for their lips twitched and melted into smiles, which they hid behind fluttering fans that spoke a language all of their own.

'You read my friend only too well, Mrs Adams,'

Dominic said, bestowing an annoyed look on Simon. 'I came here to find you, Simon. I think Elizabeth is looking for you—something about a walk in the garden before it is too dark to see anything.'

Mr Wade shrugged himself away from the bookshelves. 'In which case she who commands must be obeyed,' he uttered grudgingly.

Without another word, he sauntered to the door and went out. Not until the door had closed did Dominic look at her. 'So why are you in here when there's a party going on beyond the library door?'

'I could ask you the same.'

'If you must know, when I saw you come in here with Simon hot on your heels, I thought you might want rescuing.'

'Then I should thank you. He is somewhat overbearing. Is he always so exuberant and easy with his charms?'

'Always. Wherever he goes, it's the same story. In New York, his popularity is quite sensational—which, unfortunately for his friends, has a stimulating effect on him. *Fatigue* is a word he is not familiar with. He is extremely wealthy, his passion being horses and enjoying the high life in New York. He was right about you. In the space of a few hours, you have endeared yourself to every one of Grandmother's guests—especially the gentlemen. As soon as you appeared on the stairs tonight, you slayed the lot of them. Allow me to congratulate you.' A lazy, devastating smile passed over his features, his eyes doing a low sweep of her body so that Nancy could almost feel him disrobing her. 'It appears the engaging young widow I first knew has become a beautiful woman of exotic beauty.'

Nancy had seen and felt the unwanted admiration directed at her. She found it tiresome. 'Please don't exaggerate.' She moved closer to the fire to hide her confusion, aware of the magnetic charm he was exuding.

'I don't. No doubt they will all become poets overnight—especially Simon—and express their adoration for this bright new star in their midst.'

'Really?' She smiled, her eyes slanted and quietly teasing, feeling the treacherous warmth seep through her. 'And will you pen one yourself, my lord?'

He grinned. 'My dear Nancy,' he said softly. 'Haven't you collected enough hearts without wanting mine, too?'

She turned away, surprised by how different her name sounded when spoken by him. She was suddenly tired of this light banter that meant nothing to either of them. 'Please stop it. I do not like being spoken to like this. I have done nothing to deserve it and will go to my room if you continue to do so. I do not particularly like Mr Wade. Having had an insight into his character, I have no wish to know more. His manner and way of speaking to me, I find repugnant in every degree. It is enough to tell me that he does not possess any of the virtues that constitute a gentleman.'

'I apologise,' Dominic said on a more serious note. 'Simon does tend to make a fool of himself on occasion—usually when he's had too much to drink. But you cannot escape the fact that you have made quite an impression on him. I hope he doesn't become too much of a nuisance while you are here—or when you get back to London, for that matter.'

'I'm sure you're quite mistaken,' Nancy said, trying to make light of what he was implying. 'The moment he gets to London and some other female catches his eye, he will have forgotten all about the ordinary and uninteresting Mrs Adams.'

Something flared in Dominic's intense gaze, and he managed a faintly crooked smile, his eyes lingering on the soft contours of her mouth, 'That is not how others see you. There is certainly nothing ordinary or uninteresting about you. Take my word for it,' he said softly.

Hot colour flooded Nancy's face, and she felt suddenly bemused. Dominic was looking at her penetratingly, as though he were trying to discover what she was thinking.

'I—I was speaking to Miss Wade earlier,' Nancy said tentatively. 'She made no secret of the fact that she was surprised to see me here. You told me there was nothing between you. And yet she implied that the two of you are…close, and that it is only a matter of time before you make her an offer.'

Dominic frowned. 'Did she?' He sighed, placing his hands on her shoulders and turning her to face him. 'What I told you before is the truth. I have no intention of asking Elizabeth to be my wife. I confess there was a time when I might have dallied with the idea, but it went no further than that. She is rather…unpredictable and sometimes unkind. Yes, she is wealthy, and I don't deny that at this present time, my finances could do with a boost of capital, but I am not so mercenary as to offer marriage to a woman for that reason alone.'

'Are you telling me you aren't in love with her?'

'No, I am not,' he said gently, moving closer to her. 'I never was, and I never will be. I'm sorry if she is giving you a hard time, but you really shouldn't worry about her. She can be extremely vexing at times.' He paused, frowning thoughtfully, and then he told her, 'I shouldn't have said that. She has many attributes to her credit. Elizabeth is beautiful and vivacious. She is also fun to be with and popular with everyone—and I am not unaware that she has aspirations where I am concerned. I am not blind to her overtures.'

'Then—why do you not respond?' Nancy asked impulsively, realising too late that it was the height of bad manners to ask a gentleman such a personal, intimate question, but it had tripped off her tongue before she could stop it.

He grinned. 'Because I have a well-developed instinct for self-preservation.' After a brief pause, he continued. 'And then I met you. When I marry,' he said, his smile fading, his voice softening and his eyes shining down at her with a caressing, purposeful light, 'I want my wife to have more than women like Elizabeth can give me. I want her to be the most special woman of all.'

The slow curve of his firm lips and the sparkle in his translucent eyes that followed his statement combined to sap the strength from Nancy's limbs to a disarming degree. She didn't know what it was, but there was an inflection in his voice and a warmth that seemed to suggest he was talking about her, as if he had already made up his mind that she was the one special woman he wanted. She lowered her eyes, much too conscious of the magnetism of the man and the uneven beat of her heart. She flushed with confusion—and regret, for her common sense raged, and she knew she could not allow herself to consider he might ask her to be his wife. She tried to shake off the effect he was beginning to have on her. She moved to step past him in the direction of the door, but his hand shot out, capturing her elbow.

'You're not leaving?'

'I think I must.'

'No, you're not. You are going to stay here and have a glass of wine with me.' Striding to a sideboard, he poured two glasses of red wine from a decanter and handed one to her. She took it reluctantly.

'You're neglecting your guests, Dominic. Don't you think it's time you returned to them?'

'They're my grandmother's guests, not mine.'

'But it is your house.'

'I won't be missed. Besides, I'd much rather stay in here with you.'

'You shouldn't say such things. You seem to forget what it is I do and that I have no time for—for any of this.'

Dominic sighed. 'Forget? How can I forget when you remind me of it whenever we find ourselves together? Not always by word, I admit, but by your manner.'

'I am sorry. I don't mean to. But—for the time being, it has to be this way. You do understand, don't you?'

'Do I have a choice? You are an extremely fascinating woman. You intrigue me.'

'And you are a man of the world. I am a working woman, and by speaking to me like this, you are making it very difficult for me. It is all so sudden, Dominic. I think it's time you returned to the others,' she said quickly, putting down her glass of untouched wine. 'It's been a long day. If you don't mind, I'll retire to my room.'

'If you must,' he said, coming to stand beside her,

then moving with her towards the door. Before she could disappear into the hall, he lightly caught her arm and turned her to face him. Nancy was not small, but he was taller by at least five or six inches, and she had to look up at him. 'Tomorrow morning, some of the guests are riding out—through the park and towards the village. I know how well you ride. I thought you might like to accompany us.'

'Why—I—yes, yes of course I would.'

He nodded and stepped back.

With her hand on the partly open door, Nancy paused and turned and looked at him. 'I forgot to mention it but—I—I believe I met your son earlier.'

He nodded. 'Mark, yes. He told me.'

'He's a lovely boy and does you credit. He resembles you greatly. Good night, Dominic.'

'Good night, Nancy.'

Following her out of the library, Dominic watched her cross the hall and climb the stairs. She might wish to appear supremely indifferent to him, but there was an irresistible element of sexual attraction between them that could not be denied forever. Every time he saw her, he saw some new expression on her face that made her even more attractive to him. He had been honest when he'd told her she intrigued and fascinated him, for she was beginning to affect him in a way no other woman had, to stimulate him in a way he had not experienced since before his tragic marriage to Sophia.

His feelings for this unassuming woman were indeed serious. A strong yearning to hold her, a yearning that almost overwhelmed him with physical need, seized him. But what now? What did it mean? That he had stayed single long enough?

An amused smile touched the corners of his mouth at the thoughts that were filling his mind, of the shock that would explode upon Society if he did marry Nancy. He smiled inwardly. It would be worth marrying her just for the reaction—not that he cared a damn what anybody else thought.

Nancy didn't go to bed right away. She was tense and restless and didn't feel much like sleeping. When all the guests had either retired for the night or departed for their homes and the great house was quiet, she left her room and silently made her way down to the kitchens, where she poured herself a glass of milk.

In no mood for returning to her room, she wandered into the music room, which had long French windows overlooking the gardens. The curtains had not been drawn, and the room was lit by the silvery light of the moon.

Closing the door softly behind her, she placed her glass of milk on the top of the grand piano and raised the lid, idly letting her fingers trail over the ivory keys.

Unable to resist the urge to play and without an audience, she sat on the piano stool and automatically began to play a Chopin nocturne. She played softly so as not to disturb the slumbering household, closing her eyes and becoming immersed in the music, the notes coming to her like crystal-clear drops of water. Immediately she began to relax, the music releasing her from some deep, unconscious anxiety.

She played with a degree of emotion which seemed to carry her away—far beyond the walls of the room. It was a feeling almost beyond her control. She did not hear the door open and Dominic enter the room, closing it softly behind him. She was only aware of his presence when he stood behind her. Sensing she was about to stop playing, he moved to stand beside the piano, resting his arms on its top and looking at her closely.

'No—don't stop. I would like to listen.'

'I hope you don't mind me being in here. I couldn't sleep.'

'Not at all. No one plays the piano anymore. Feel free to wander the house at will.'

Nancy continued playing, no longer afraid to look at him, of meeting his eyes. The expression in them was unforgettable. He was looking at her with such a passionate intensity which, combined with the music, began to awaken all her senses, making her conscious of only this one moment seemingly suspended in time.

It was as if it had become entwined with the music, as though everything that had gone before and everything that was to come were irrelevant. Dominic was looking at her as no man had ever looked at her before, and she had never felt drawn to any man as she was to him.

When the last notes of the nocturne faded and died away, she let her hands fall into her lap. There was complete silence inside the room. Both were reluctant to break the magic of the moment which had held them in thrall. The intensity of Dominic's eyes held Nancy spellbound, weaving an invisible cord about her from which there was no escape—from which she had no desire to escape, until at last he smiled.

'That was beautiful. You play the piano well. Another of your many accomplishments. You really are a talented woman.'

'Thank you.' Getting up from the stool, she reached for her milk. 'I'll bid you good-night. I'm looking forward to the ride into the village before I have to catch the train back to London.'

'Can't I persuade you to stay another night?'

She shook her head. 'I really do have to get back.'

He nodded, going to stand by the French windows and looking out over the sloping lawns, bathed in the moon's silvery sheen. 'Are you trying to elude me, by any chance?'

Taken aback by the suddenness of his question,

Nancy moved a little towards him, his tall, clear-cut profile etched against the light. It was true. She was trying to avoid being alone with him, but she could not say so.

'I was not aware that I was. Why on earth should I?'

'Perhaps you are afraid.'

'Afraid? Afraid of what?' she asked in a voice that strove to sound natural, but succeeded in only exposing her nervousness and uncertainty.

'Afraid to face up to your feelings.'

He turned to her, his gaze compelling, and there was a moment's silence in which Nancy's heart began beating in a quite unpredictable manner.

'When you played the piano just now, were you aware of how much you told me in that music? You expressed to me how you felt—and I understood because I, too, feel the same. They are feelings we have both tried to suppress. But I ask myself, how much longer can we continue to do so?'

His voice reached out to Nancy and held her, but she turned from him, unable to continue looking into those hypnotic eyes.

'How much longer do we have to fence with words? And how much longer are you going to pretend you feel nothing?'

The air between them was charged with tension. Nancy shivered suddenly. He noticed immediately.

'Are you cold?'

She shook her head. How could she tell him it was because he encroached too closely, that he aroused such a tempest inside her that she was indeed afraid—afraid of herself, and that she might lose control over her body and emotions completely.

'Then can you tell me that I am wrong?'

His voice died away into the silence of the room as he waited for her answer. Still he did not touch her, but he was just behind her, so close she could feel his warm breath on her neck.

She shook her head slowly. 'No,' she whispered, her voice trembling slightly. 'No—you are not wrong.'

'I know you are dedicated to your work—but does that mean you have to exclude your feelings?'

'Yes. When it affects what I do.'

Very gently, Dominic placed his hands on her shoulders and turned her round to face him. 'Would it? Don't you think it's about time you had something for yourself? I've wanted you from the moment I first saw you—and I believe you know it.'

He was standing very close. Nancy could smell his skin and the faint aroma of his cologne. His presence held her like a magnet. She swallowed hard, shaking her head in a vain attempt to resist. 'No—'

'Yes,' he insisted, his voice seductive and ever so persuasive as he lowered his head, his eyes gleaming with a sensual luminosity as they focused on her quiv-

Helen Dickson   211

ering, parted lips, 'just like I have known all along that you feel exactly the same way about me.'

His voice was low, with a husky rasp, and his eyes held Nancy's captive, gleaming in the dim light. The effect of his warmly intimate expression made her heart turn over. His lips merely brushed hers lightly, but the touch sent a wave of happiness through her. He continued to make a line of trailing kisses from her mouth down to the soft flesh of her throat. She arched her long white neck to receive them, closing her eyes, her thick, dark lashes resting on her cheeks, fluttering like butterflies' wings.

'We—we shouldn't be doing this,' Nancy protested weakly, breathlessly, without the will to resist—nor did she want to.

'Yes, we can. I am a widower. You are a widow. There is no reason why we have to deny how we feel,' he murmured, continuing to kiss every inch of her beautiful, fine-boned face. 'I've been very patient— wanting to give you time. But I think that time has just run out.' So saying, he wrapped his arms around her and covered her mouth with his own. Her lips parted beneath his to receive his kiss, willingly, passionately. His potent virility was acting like a drug to her senses. Sensations of unexpected pleasure washed over her. She realised it was no longer possible to put a stop to what she had so dangerously begun—and did she really want to? The answer was clear—no, she didn't.

Between his kisses, Dominic paused to murmur passionate endearments. Nancy closed her eyes and melted against him, allowing herself to be carried away on this overwhelming wave of passion, experiencing a joy which temporarily effaced everything. They became lost in the torrent of the passion. Nancy groaned, raising her hands, slipping her fingers into his thick, dark hair, gripping it fiercely to bring his mouth more closely to her own. What was happening to her? She had never felt quite like this, but she still recognised the emotion. It was happiness, such as she'd not felt in a long time, and never with such warmth, such intensity.

Their kisses were deep and urgent, as if each one might be their last. Dominic caressed her, sliding his long, determined fingers, as light as thistledown, down her spine and over the gentle curve of her buttocks. They seemed to burn her flesh beneath the material of her dress, the sensation causing a spark to flicker and flare within her, racing through her veins like liquid fire, filling her with a craving for love like she had never experienced it before.

Chapter Ten

An eternity later, Dominic lifted his head. Nancy reluctantly surfaced from the glorious Eden where he had sent her, her face suffused with languor and passion, her eyes luminous, dark and velvety. She sighed. She offered no resistance, just a calm contentment of acceptance.

'So, Nancy—I was right in my suspicions.'

'Why—what do you mean?'

'Beneath that cool exterior you present to the world, you are like a smouldering volcano.' He smiled, his eyes warmly devouring her upturned face. 'I cannot wait to witness the eruption.'

'I'm afraid you'll have to,' she whispered, pulling back slightly within the intimate circle of his arms, seeing the tenderness filling his eyes. 'Although I have never been likened to a smouldering volcano. This is all so unexpected.'

'Is it?' he pressed.

She sighed. 'No, not really. But I do need time

to think, to put everything into perspective. I never meant this to happen. I have tried so hard to avoid it.'

'I don't think it's what either of us planned, but it was inevitable—feeling as we do. You must have known, being in this kind of situation before—with your husband.'

'Yes—I mean no,' she said hesitantly, lowering her eyes.

'Are you saying you did not love him?' His eyes became serious, probing and questioning.

'I—I am not saying that, exactly,' she murmured softly.

'I hear more feeling in those few words than you realise. It makes me curious as to your background. I realise that I know almost nothing about you whatsoever. Have you ever been in love—if not with your husband, then someone else?'

Nancy's expression became wistful. 'No—at least, not in the sense you mean. But you have,' she dared to say with frank curiosity, smiling—the kind of smile that warmed and lit up her lovely eyes, the kind of smile that elicited confidence and demanded a response. 'You were married. You must have been in love with your wife.'

Instead of closing up, of guarding his privacy, as Nancy had expected, Dominic settled his steady gaze on her thoughtfully, becoming rather grim. From his expression, she sensed that it had been a turbulent relationship, but the pain she'd seen suddenly vanished, and his features were already perfectly composed when he looked at her.

'I thought I was in love. I admit it.' He hesitated, and for a moment, Nancy thought he wasn't going to say more. When he did, his voice was quiet, hesitant, almost as if he was testing his ability to talk about it, making her already regret having mentioned his wife. 'Love can make fools of us all. It blinds one to someone's shortcomings and warps one's judgement. I was young and naive, taken in by the first beautiful face I saw. I was only twenty-one years old at the time I met Sophia. She was a little older. Unfortunately, things did not turn out as I'd hoped. I admit, however, that I saw the warning signs before we married.'

'Then why did you not heed them?'

Still holding her close, he looked down at her. 'I never could resist a challenge—especially when the gauntlet has been thrown down by a woman as beautiful as Sophia.'

'Even though you might get burnt? As you evidently were.'

He nodded. 'Even then.'

'Did you love your wife very much?'

'I thought I did—in fact, for a time, she was the centre of my existence. Yet she did not reach my mind or touch me spiritually. I made a mistake—but I had to experience living with her to realise it. I well re-

member my ecstasy, the wonder of it. I also remember
the doubt, the bewilderment that came after, followed
by the pain and torment the knowledge of the truth
brought me when she was disloyal—and the brutality
and the struggle for self-preservation that came when
she left me and our son for someone else.'

He fell silent, and his eyes fastened on something
over her shoulder, but Nancy, glancing sideways at
him, thought he did not see it. As she watched him, a
faint frown seemed to slide over his face like a dark
shadow, and she regretted having mentioned his wife.

'I'm sorry. I hope you didn't mind me mentioning
your wife. My mother always accused me of talking
too much when I'm excited. How did she die?'

He nodded. 'She wasn't here at the time. Apparently it was sudden. According to the physicians who
treated her, it was some kind of growth on her brain.'

'I'm sorry. That must have been a very difficult
time for you.'

'It was. Mark was still an infant—too young to understand. Later, it was difficult telling him what had
happened, but he dealt with it better than I hoped.'

'Children can be very resilient. I—I apologise if
my question upset you.'

He stared at her for a moment, her wealth of hair
flowing over her shoulders glowing like the dancing
flame in the single lamp on the piano, shining with an
inner light. Then he shrugged and smiled, the moment

of melancholy having passed. He settled his gaze on her face. 'It all happened a long time ago. I have no reason to hide anything. It is better to speak of such things than keep them hidden.'

'And you were not in a hurry to remarry?'

'No. I have an heir, so perhaps you can understand why I was content to remain as I was for a while, to go my own way and to enjoy being pursued by those who desire to be the next Countess Osborne.'

'And always careful to elude capture,' said Nancy softly.

'I am always open to persuasion—should the right woman come along.'

He spoke quietly, and Nancy saw his eyes held more seriousness than his voice, which told her his marriage still affected him more than he would have her or anyone else know. There was a host of questions she wanted to ask him about his wife. She was curious to know more about the nature of her betrayal. However, not wishing to probe further into what was obviously an extremely sensitive matter, she declined to press.

He gathered her close, planting a kiss on her lips. 'I have talked a great deal about myself, and as yet I know very little about you. Who are you really, Nancy Adams?' he asked softly. 'And why do I have this peculiar feeling that you are the one who is being evasive?'

'Because I am. It's best this way,' she answered,

averting her eyes, beginning to feel uncomfortable beneath his much too penetrating, enquiring gaze, feeling the atmosphere changing between them to one of warm, vibrant intimacy once more.

'You are an unusual woman, Nancy. I find your company both pleasurable and enlightening.'

'Thank you, although I suspect it's because you prefer the company of an intelligent woman—a woman who is a conversationalist rather than one who has nothing to say but yes and no.'

'I do,' he laughed, his eyes twinkling. 'But there are those whose belief is that a man is better pleased when a good dinner is placed before him than when his wife spouts Italian or Greek. I have to say that you are more intelligent than most women of my acquaintance, and if you are not careful, you will have me thinking I should fall for a woman's mind—but her physical attributes cannot be ignored,' he murmured, his gaze languidly sweeping over her face, his eyes settling on the gentle mounds of her breasts beneath the fabric of her gown, measuring, lingering, a slow smile curving his lips.

The soft sincerity of his voice, the tone of it, rippled over Nancy's skin and took her breath away. Behind the words, she detected an irresistible force, coercing, seducing, and she was drawn to it once more, wanting to experience the passion of moments ago.

'But enough of that,' Dominic said. 'It is you who

interests me just now.' His arms tightened around her, drawing her close until her body moulded against his, finding her lips once more and kissing her long and deep. She clung to him like ivy clings to a tree, his long, lean body giving her a promise of pleasure such as she had never imagined.

'I want you,' he whispered, his mouth against hers. 'I want you with me always. Fate decreed our paths should cross that night you helped Jane, when I saw you leaving the house with Rose in your arms. Ever since then, I have wanted you. Being near you and not being able to touch you for fear you might take flight have nearly driven me insane. What is there to think about?'

Nancy gazed wonderingly into his eyes, seeing in them the truth of his words. She had discovered that in being with him, in being kissed by him, what it was like to be violently attracted to a man without necessarily loving him, and she was finally prepared to accept it. Heat scorched through her body when she met his smouldering eyes, which studied her, feature by feature, as though he could not gaze upon her enough.

'And I want you, too—very much,' she whispered, her words uncomplicated by thought. 'It is something I have been aware of for a while, but I didn't want to think about it. I thought I was in love once. I was mistaken. I'm afraid of myself now. It was simple delusion, and I don't know if I can trust my judgement anymore. I got everything wrong. What we feel is real—but don't you see that this changes everything between us?' She was suddenly afraid that because of what she had kept from him, was still keeping from him—her name and her pretend widowhood—she could be in danger of losing his respect.

Dominic's eyes hardened suddenly, but he did not release his hold on her. 'No, I don't see. What are you trying to say?'

'That—that it will affect my work—everything I have set out to do. You know it takes all my time,' she prevaricated, not yet ready to disclose her real identity or the fact that there never had been a husband.

Perhaps she was reading too much into what Dominic wanted. He hadn't asked her to be his wife, and hadn't she told herself since the day Thomas had spurned her that she didn't want a husband? She had gone to too much trouble to achieve her independence to throw it all away on the first man to come along who attracted her. But she had come to care for Dominic Blackwell deeply, so nothing was going to be simple. If her independence did not mean so much to her, then the barriers that separated them were not too formidable for them to surmount, but would he ever forgive her deception for pretending to be someone else? Should she tell him? If she wasn't an experienced widow, as he thought, would he even still want her?

'You must understand that I have worked hard to achieve my independence. I—I cannot abandon it now.'

'I understand how you must feel, but I am not asking you to abandon anything, so why speak of it now?' Again he held her close. 'Oh, Nancy,' he said against her hair. 'You possess such innocence. Sometimes you are as transparent as day, and yet at others, you are as dark and mysterious as night—with a confidence and wisdom way beyond your years. What are we going to do? I cannot let you go.'

As he held her within his arms, Nancy's heart almost ceased to beat. She stared at him, filled with indecision. He had succeeded in awakening inside her emotions and desires which had left her wanting more. Gazing into his eyes, she was like a poor, helpless rabbit caught in a snare. His words went through her like a flame.

Dominic took her chin between his fingers and raised her head so he could look into her eyes. 'Well, Nancy? What have you to say?'

He finally released her, breaking the slender, fragile thread that had held them together a moment before—fragile yet invisibly binding, for Nancy would never be able to forget. Sliding her arms up his chest and about his neck, she drew his face once more down to hers, her lips warm and moist as they tenderly caressed his own.

'This is too important a matter to be fully discussed tonight,' she murmured evasively. 'I think we should wait and see what tomorrow brings.'

'And tonight?'

A mischievous smile played on her lips. 'After to-night, we will know if we are compatible. Maybe what we feel is all a fantasy, and we are about to make a terrible mistake.'

'There is no denying that there is chemistry between us.'

'However strong it is, maybe it will turn out to be self-deception and disappear in a puff of smoke.'

'And maybe it is of the kind that lasts—and then what will we do?' he said.

'Neither of us can answer that just now. After to-night, we will see.'

Taking her hand, he pressed it gently. 'I think we should continue this conversation in more comfortable surroundings, don't you, Nancy?' he said. 'Come. Let us retire to your bedroom, where neither conscience, my wife, nor your husband will intrude tonight.'

Together they went into the hall and up the stairs.

Neither of them were aware, as they walked towards Nancy's room, of the vengeful watching eyes from the slightly open door at the end of the landing. Only when the two of them had disappeared inside did Elizabeth Wade quietly close the door.

Nancy's room was filled with a warm, cosy intimacy. She paused in the centre of the room. Dominic came to stand behind her. The curtains had not been drawn, and the starlight and the moonlight entering through the windows bathed the room in a soft silver glow.

When she turned to face him, sensing her unease, Dominic smiled into her soft, anxious amber eyes. 'Try to relax. You really have nothing to fear.'

Never had he met a woman who had such a stranglehold on his emotions. Initially he'd believed it might be because he hadn't been amorously involved with a woman in a while, but the more he thought about it, the more he realised that it was she, herself, whom he wanted. Not only did he want her, he wanted her to want him as well, to banish all thoughts of her dead husband from her mind.

This worried him, because he did not intend becoming trapped in the kind of relationship he'd had with Sophia, his beautiful, unscrupulous wife, the kind of relationship he had thought was perfect, only to have his love and desire used against him like a treacherous weapon in her hands. Her betrayal and desertion of him and Mark had almost destroyed him, and he could not forget. Not since that time had any woman succeeded in coming close to touching his emotions. He used them to satisfy his needs and then forgot them, casting them aside in the same callous manner as his wife had cast him aside.

But from the first encounter with Nancy Adams, his instincts had told him she was not like anyone else. She had become the supreme object of his desire, and her sensuality somehow seemed more potent now in the demureness of her emerald-green gown.

Nancy stood quite still, waiting for what would happen, expectant, hopeful. Dominic towered over her, his physical presence rendering her weak.

'This,' he said, 'is the moment I've been thinking of since I first saw you.'

His hands stroked her shoulders, and she could feel the warmth of his breath on her flesh as he lowered his head and placed his lips on the scented hollow of her neck, where a pulse fluttered beneath her skin. She closed her eyes and melted back into his arms as they wrapped themselves around her, tightening around her waist until her body was moulded against his. Slowly she turned and faced him. In his eyes, which looked down at her face, tilted up to his, were all the things he wanted to say yet remained unspoken.

Slowly he lowered his head and covered her mouth with his own. Her lips warmed under his, parted and softened, her breath sighing through. After a time, which seemed like an eternity, he raised his head just a little.

'Are you sure about this, Nancy?' he murmured, his lips close to hers. 'Are you certain this is what you want?'

'Yes,' she whispered. 'Oh, yes.' Slipping her arms around his neck, she pulled his face down to hers. It was too late to turn back now—much too late, and she didn't want to. She wanted more than his kisses, and she felt in him the same need—urgent—demanding to be satisfied. But he must not suspect her inexperience, her innocence.

Taking her hand, he led her to the bed, where they managed to remove her dress and anything else that would get in the way of their lovemaking. She heard his quick intake of breath as her body was slowly revealed to him, his eyes fastening hungrily on her naked beauty. Her skin was white and cream, and he was clearly bewitched by it, helpless to resist temptation. Quickly he divested himself of his clothes, and when they stood naked, facing each other, there was no shame or modesty. Dominic looked at her with such awe that a delicate blush suffused her skin. Drawing her down onto the bed, he at last took her into his arms.

Pulling her close, he kissed her flesh with expert lips, causing a multitude of sensations to explode inside her. The texture of his skin next to hers was smooth and warm. He was so sure of himself, his hands subtly experienced, caressing, exploring, arousing her to the pitch where passion becomes irresistible.

His kisses were long, and those, too, were wonderfully skilled. The unfamiliarity of them made Nancy gasp, causing a natural hunger to stir deep within her body. Nothing existed but this man and his sensual mouth claiming hers in kisses of such tenderness. Nancy felt all her hesitation disintegrate as she returned his kisses with all her innocent, unselfish ardour, feeling his hands moulding her close. Quivers coursed through her as his lips left hers and took possession of her breast. Never would she have suspected that the feel of a man's lips on such a secret part of her body could create such incredible pleasure. She arched her neck while he kissed her throat, feeling like an escaped bird which had been caged too long as she finally allowed herself the freedom of abandonment.

Hungrily he caressed the slender outline of her body, touching her here, caressing and kissing her there, so that no part of her escaped his attention, her sighs and moans feeding his ardour, fuelling his passion. She moved sensually as his hands slid lower to search and caress her womanhood. Nancy's instinct at such an intimate invasion was to object, to thrust him away, but he filled her with such exquisite promise as he continued to stroke, to arouse her, that she moved her hips instinctively against him, pressing, arching herself closer, as if an unknown force was compelling her.

Dominic's breath quickened against her throat as he began to move to a primitive and powerful rhythm, showing her a desperate need that seemed to Nancy to become a torment inside, the restraint he had shown so far vanishing in his desire to possess her. She moaned, her hands tangled in his hair, her back arching in helpless surrender. Aware of his arousal, she moved of her own accord beneath him, urging him on. They came together almost instantly and with a violence so unexpected that Dominic did not see the tears that sprang to her eyes or the pain that crossed her face as she turned her head away—but the few seconds of discomfort were lost in what came after.

As he moved inside her, Nancy felt something wild and primitive growing, something so wonderful that her consciousness receded as he powerfully drove them both to unparalleled agonies of desire, and just as she thought she must cry out, ask him to stop, the sheer pleasure of being with him took her over. Their need for each other overwhelmed them, and Nancy's body, released at last from its long-held virginity, became insatiable, wanting, needing more. Her mind and all her anxieties seemed to dissolve so that she was aware of him and only him as he controlled all her senses. She seemed to be hurtling through space where there was no past, no future, no responsibilities, only this moment.

When they finally lay spent, their bodies entwined, the hot climactic world that had held them in its grip began to subside. Nancy's hair spilled over them both like a silken sheet, and Dominic lifted it off her face.

When Nancy opened her eyes, it felt like she was

awaking from a deep sleep. Dominic was lying on his side, looking at her in wonder, his face strangely calm and his dark head supported on one fist, the waving locks of his hair drooping over his moist brow. He kissed her lightly, lovingly, and she stretched languidly like a kitten, moving her body into the curve of his and closing her eyes.

'Don't imagine you're going to sleep,' Dominic breathed huskily, nuzzling her ear. 'I'm not done with you yet.'

Her lips curving in a soft smile, Nancy looked up at him. She was sure her eyes were glowing with pleasure and her skin, like Dominic's own, was damp with a sheen of moisture. She sighed, feeling neither shame nor guilt. Raising her hand and combing her fingers through his hair, she grasped a handful and pulled his head down to hers, reaching for his mouth with her own, and her body began to move against his with bewitching invitation.

Again they made love, but now slowly, intently, and with a tenderness which was beyond anything she could have imagined. Amazed by her own sensuality, she allowed Dominic to guide her, his lovemaking sending her to another place for a second time. Her body arched against the man who held her, moved with her, firmly, gently, carrying her to unexpected delights, until, in a state of complete exhaustion, she slept.

* * *

Dominic was the first to wake. Nancy's body was glowing and warm from their lovemaking. He thought how heartbreakingly lovely she was—a picture of intoxicating sensuality. She was beautiful, dignified and ladylike in her demeanour, but beneath the façade of serenity and gentleness, she was sensual and provocative. When he had made love to her, they had been sexually attuned to each other, and she had satisfied him completely in a way no other woman had before—not even Sophia.

He got out of bed to retrieve his clothes. Returning to the bed to pull the covers over Nancy's sleeping form, his eyes were drawn to the sheet they had been lying on, and he froze. His stomach sank when he saw the bloodied stain, hidden until then by their bodies and the night. Mutely he stared at the telltale mark as the truth hit him. He was looking at the stark evidence of her innocence.

Nancy had been a virgin—but how could that be? His senses reeling, he asked himself why had she lied to him. For what reason. What was she hiding? She was not what she seemed, after all. After his turbulent marriage to Sophia where she'd repeatedly deceived him, he would have none of that. Without disturbing her, he swiftly dressed and left the room, his features as hard and forbidding as a granite sculpture, his eyes as brittle as glass.

* * *

When Nancy awoke, she stretched and raised her sleepy eyelids, disappointed not to find Dominic still beside her, although she supposed he couldn't be seen exiting her room. Her body grew hot with embarrassment when she remembered what had occurred between them in the dark hours of the night, finding it curious that she should feel no sense of shame or regret at what she had done. She sighed, stretching languorously, feeling sexually awakened, and free of ignorance and anxiety.

She wanted to shout her bliss to the world. Instead, because she had only allowed herself this one night, she would have to cultivate her secrecy, but she would be haunted by the sense that she would never again know such passion, such ecstasy. The fact that her future could not be shared with the man who had awakened her body to such divine, sweet torment, and that her happiness wasn't destined to last, didn't seem to matter just then. It wasn't until later that she would be forced to face the enormity of what she had done.

Remembering that she was to join the party on the ride through the park to the nearby village and looking forward to it, she scrambled out of bed. After her ablutions, she donned the dress that would be most suitable for the ride and the journey back to London mid-afternoon. Leaving her room to partake of some breakfast before going to the stables, she kept her eyes open for Dominic, disappointed when he failed to materialise.

When she arrived at the stables, the yard was a hive of colourful activity, the atmosphere jovial and relaxed as people milled around and mounted Dominic's splendid horses. Miss Wade and her brother were already mounted and ready for the off. Miss Wade looked extremely fetching in a ruby-red riding dress with a matching hat cocked at an impudent angle. Nancy was relieved when they did not approach her, but she was curious as to why Miss Wade threw her a look of such cold hostility that she could feel its icy blast from across the full length of the yard.

As people began to ride out, and with Dominic still nowhere in sight, her attention was caught by a horse with its noble head leaning over a door to one of the stalls.

'Is this horse to remain behind?' she asked one of the stable hands.

'Aye, miss. He's a spirited mount. His Lordship told us not to saddle him up.'

Feeling sorry for the animal, Nancy moved towards him. He whickered, stretching out his nose and shaking his mane vigorously.

'Poor thing,' she whispered, removing her glove and rubbing his velvety nose affectionately. 'What an infuriating tyrant your master is. How awful for you to have to stay behind when all your friends are riding out without you.'

'Not so much a tyrant as a responsible host,' a voice said behind her. 'He's one of my most prized horses—a peppery beast at the best of times. He would throw anyone he doesn't know straight out of the saddle.'

Nancy turned to Dominic, a light flush mantling her cheeks when she remembered the previous night. How attractive he was, she thought, with his darkly handsome face and the breeze lightly ruffling his hair. He was resplendent in an impeccably tailored dark brown riding coat, his snug-fitting riding breeches disappearing into highly polished tan riding boots.

Nancy's lips broke into a soft smile, inviting him to smile back at her, but Dominic failed to notice. The smile froze on her lips when she saw his ice-cold expression as he moved closer to her, causing her to shrink before his disdain. His face as he stood looking down at her was fixedly calm, and yet alight with contempt.

Instinctively she stepped away from him, feeling something inside her curl up and die when she met his eyes, unable to see anything of her tender lover of the night.

Utterly bewildered and unable to understand what had happened to turn him into this cold, dispassionate stranger, she said, 'Dominic? Please tell me what is wrong?'

'Not here.' Taking her elbow, he led her to a quiet corner of the yard. Thankfully most of the guests had left, and the stable hands and grooms were busy cleaning out the stalls.

'Last night. I had not expected to be your first lover. Why did you not tell me you were a virgin?' he demanded quietly but harshly.

Nothing Nancy could say would counteract the truth that she had been discovered. In not revealing her true identity, she had clearly roused his temper to a pitch she could never have imagined. She chastised herself harshly for having made such an irretrievable, appalling error.

'How—how do you know?' she asked hesitantly.

'The bloodied sheets tell their own tale, Nancy. How naive could you be to think I wouldn't find out?'

Nancy could feel the anger uncoiling inside him, the fury of a man betrayed, deceived, and knew she deserved it, but instinctively she pushed back regardless. 'I see. I'm sorry, Dominic, but I fail to see why being a virgin should make you so angry.'

'Can you not? Had I known, I would never have touched you.'

'But why? Why does it matter to you so much?'

'You are supposed to be a widow, for heaven's sake. I don't know what game you think you're playing, but I am not in the habit of deflowering innocent virgins. Are you telling me that the man you were married to did not touch you, Mrs Adams—or is it something else? I really have no idea who you are.'

Not enjoying the way his questioning was becoming more like an interrogation, Nancy raised her head and met his gaze squarely. 'Perhaps it would be better if we kept it that way.'

'Was there ever a husband?' he pressed.

'No,' she said without hesitation. 'But I have my reasons for the subterfuge—one being that I wanted to open the institute on my own merit, without bringing any unwanted attention to my father or my family. Another is that as a single woman, I would not have been taken seriously, which was the reason I decided to forge ahead as a widow. I would be grateful for your discretion on the matter.'

'As you wish. Under the circumstances, it is probably best I know nothing more about you,' he said, his face hardening into an expressionless mask, his eyes probing hers like dagger thrusts. 'You lied to me—although if you think I feel flattered that you gave me that which you have clearly denied the fictitious Mr Adams, or any other man, then you are sorely mistaken.'

His eyes glittered with a fire that burned Nancy raw, his words flicking over her like a whiplash. She wanted to shout who her father was, but, reluctant to reveal her identity in the face of such cruel condemnation, she refused to discuss her present circumstances with Dominic.

However, she couldn't bear them to part on such bad terms. 'I realise what you must think of me, but it is not what you imagine. I wasn't trying to trap you so I could become the next Countess Osborne. I assure you that not for one moment did I have marriage to you in mind. For reasons of my own, I abhor the idea of entering into such an alliance with any man. As for being a liar, you are right. I haven't told you the truth.'

'Indeed, you haven't. Last night I believed you to be a widow—a woman experienced in lovemaking. I'm still finding it hard to believe the alluring temptress who offered herself to me so willingly was a virgin. I am at a loss to know why you would throw away your virtue on a man who has offered you nothing in return for it and never will. No doubt you can justify your reasons to yourself, but your conduct tells me all I need to know about your moral standards,' he said, his eyes flicking over her with cynical contempt.

Nancy gasped, her cheeks burning as she felt anger flare up inside her caused by his insult, his injustice. How could he say such terrible things to her? Her anger gave way to uncontrollable wrath.

'How dare you?' she flared. 'How dare you hand down judgement on me when your own behaviour is just as reprehensible? You were only too keen to sleep with me out of wedlock. Are you telling me your character is irreproachable?'

'I do dare,' he replied, his voice scathing, his cold eyes impaling hers. 'You gave me no indication that you were a proper young lady who expected the highest standards of gentlemanly behaviour from me. Any decent, well-bred young woman would have rather endured hell-fire and damnation than do what you have done. I dare say that unless you can find a man and persuade him to make an honest woman of you, you will go down the same sordid road as countless women before you.'

'I imagine I'll become exactly the kind of woman whose company you enjoy so much, then,' retorted Nancy with heavy sarcasm.

'If you like,' he cut back, 'but I don't feel I have to justify to you what I do. Now I have initiated you in the skills of lovemaking, you should be very well-qualified to please the next unsuspecting male who comes along.'

'So! You really think that of me, do you, Dominic? That as soon as the next man begins paying me attention, I will be unable to resist seducing him?'

'Why not?' His mouth curled. 'You were eager enough to yield to me when I held you in my arms.'

Nancy sighed, suddenly feeling ancient. 'That was because it was you that I wanted, Dominic. Several years ago, something happened to me. It was a life-changing moment, and after that I made up my mind not to marry. I have not been romantically involved with any man since that day—until now, which, since you have made your feelings plain where I am concerned, I have sincere cause to regret. After meeting you, it didn't take long for me to realise that we have something in common. Like me, you prefer to make your own choices. I owe nobody a living. I am my own woman, free to do what I choose. After losing my virtue to you, nothing has changed. When I decided to pass myself off as a widow, I did not see it as a crime but more of a convenience, and where your sister is concerned, I agreed to take her child—as I have for countless desperate women since I opened the institute. So you see, I don't understand what I have done to make you treat me quite so despicably.'

'And if there is a child?'

Nancy stared at him. She had briefly thought of that, that there might be a child from their union. She could think of nothing more wonderful than to give birth to his child. But she would not have it raised in a household where there was no love between its parents.

'There may not be a child,' she replied carefully. 'If there does happen to be one, then we will discuss the matter again. I have the means to take care of a child myself, but you have my word I would not deprive you of seeing it.'

Dominic looked at her in astonishment. 'What are you saying? That I should set aside my own child? To my knowledge, I have never fathered an illegitimate child, and I have no intention of ever doing so.'

Nancy's body stiffened. 'So it is your conscience that is bothering you. Dominic, please listen to what I am saying. I doubt there will be a child. If there is, we will deal with it then. I will accept your support for any child we might have. Otherwise I want nothing from you. Do not feel yourself to be under any obligation.'

Dominic's jaw tightened, and his eyes burned furiously down into hers. 'I don't. My obligation would be to the child—should there be one. I could put some money in trust until a later date—but I would despise myself if I did not try to do better than that. I would insist that any child of mine must be spared the stain of illegitimacy. I will not disown a child of my blood.'

'The only way you could do that is to marry me, Dominic. But I would refuse, of course. Have you not listened to a word I said? Now please stop this. There may be no child, so this argument is moot.'

Her stubbornness seemed to provoke Dominic's eyes to blaze with renewed fury. 'If there is, you will never endure the disgrace and humiliation when it becomes public knowledge. The scandal will be intolerable. I am sorry that it has come to this. I admit that I behaved in a manner of which I am sincerely ashamed and regretful.'

His cutting tone and the injustice of his words increased Nancy's anger. But it was the way he retained his arrogant superiority that was hard for her to take. 'You? Ashamed? Regretful? Are you quite sure you know the meaning of those words?' she scoffed. Drawing herself up proudly, she showed him that she could be just as hard and cold. He would never know how much he had hurt her, that indeed her heart was breaking. Moving further away from him, she half turned. 'If you don't mind, I will return to the house. To save you further embarrassment, I will plead a headache and keep to my room. I will leave as planned for London later this afternoon.'

Without further ado, she made her way back to the house, but not before she had glimpsed Miss Wade across the yard seated gracefully atop her horse, no doubt still waiting for Dominic. Nancy ignored her. Elizabeth Wade was welcome to Lord Dominic Blackwell. Without glancing back, Nancy went on her way. She was engulfed with so many conflicting emotions, she had never been so confused in her life.

Something had happened to her that she had not bargained for. She had never for one moment imagined making love could be like that, and she could not deny that she was attracted to Dominic in a way that astounded her. His cruel words and his attitude just now had hurt her deeply, and it would be a long time, if ever, before she recovered from the pain of it. She had fallen into a trap of her own making, for, once again, she was unable to walk away from a man with her emotions intact.

Chapter Eleven

Arriving back at the house, Nancy was disappointed when a footman came to inform her that due to a derailment on the train line to London, all trains had been cancelled. The line would be back in working order the following day. She was determined to keep out of Dominic's way for the rest of the day. Mid-afternoon found her sauntering in the garden with his grandmother. They talked about their individual charities and were in agreement that they might be able to help each other in the future.

Seating themselves in a small arbour, they watched as several guests came out of the house to admire the gardens. Nancy's gaze settled on Dominic across the broad expanse of lawn. Returning from the ride, he had made no move to approach her. In fact, it was as if she were not there. He was with Miss Wade, who had her arm hooked possessively through his. She let her eyes dwell on him. She so wanted to see that look in his eyes that she had seen in the dark hours of the previous night.

As she continued to observe him, never had a man looked so attractive or so distant, and never had her heart called out so strongly to anyone. She tried to pull her wits together, all too aware of his grandmother studying her with curiosity.

'You know Miss Wade, do you, Mrs Adams?'

'Yes—yes, I do. We were introduced in London. Miss Wade and her brother attended one of the fêtes we put on to raise funds.'

Lady Blackwell sighed, shaking her head as her eyes followed her grandson and the woman next to him as they paused to speak to other guests. 'She is attractive, I suppose.'

'Yes—yes she is.'

'She has both youth and beauty, and from what I've learned about her, she has excellent connections and wealth—and a certain fashionable notoriety. What more could a man desire in a woman?' There was a wry note to her voice, and she spoke as if she were speaking to herself.

Continuing to watch the pair, in answer to Lady Blackwell's comment, Nancy thought that money and property were always useful commodities. But then, as the only daughter of an American millionaire, Elizabeth Wade had all that. Yet would she be as desirable if she wasn't dressed by only the finest couturiers and wallowing in luxury? Of course she was as attractive as any of her contemporaries, but, Nancy wondered, was it her money that preceded her wherever she went? Was it money that triggered all those sideways covert glances, the conversations that faltered when she approached?

'Miss Wade's father is very rich,' Lady Blackwell said. 'I believe he made his money in industry and other commodities—and armaments, a business which has flourished because of that dreadful war in Crimea. Miss Wade's father and Dominic have shared business interests. Some would say Miss Wade is a good catch, but for some reason, rich American girls are not accepted by the New York elite.'

'I understand Miss Wade is to accompany her brother to France shortly. I am sure someone—either here or in France—will snap her up.'

'That could well be. It would seem that American girls' outspokenness and independent spirits are characteristics that Europeans find charming. Miss Wade's father is ambitious, a man who wants only the best for his daughter—a title, which is why he has sent her to England with her brother, to be seen and admired like a precious gem, a gem destined for a coronet. At least. Dominic could provide him with that should he decide to offer for her. I can only hope my grandson thinks long and hard about it before he commits himself. I'm concerned about him doing the right thing.'

'I'm sure he will,' Nancy said stiffly.

'If I were a betting woman, I'd wager Dominic isn't in love with Miss Wade.'

'Not everyone who marries is in love,' Nancy said quietly. 'Men and women often have their marriages arranged by their parents. Some are of the opinion that love and marriage are two separate things.'

Lady Blackwell studied her closely. 'And what is your opinion, Mrs Adams?'

'That those who express that opinion must be sadly cynical people. What other reason is there to marry?'

'Well, children is a good place to start.'

Nancy gave her companion a look of feigned astonishment. 'Oh? I did not realise one needed a marriage ceremony to beget children.'

Lady Blackwell chuckled. 'What a wicked observation, Mrs Adams. In fact, some would say you are quite shocking.'

'Wicked, maybe, but also sensible.'

The other woman's smile disappeared. 'You are a wonderful revelation, Mrs Adams, and I shall look forward to further conversations with you in the future. You must visit me again when I'm not entertaining.'

A look of understanding passed between them. 'Thank you.'

'I understand that due to difficulties on the train line, you are to leave in the morning.'

'Yes—quite early, in fact. I had intended being here

for just the one night.' She smiled. 'It means I have more time to partake of your generous hospitality. If I don't see you before I leave, I would like to thank you for the kindness you have shown me.'

Nancy entered the house. Pleading a headache, she requested her dinner to be sent to her room.

She didn't see Jane come out of the drawing room. The hall table was strewn with a selection of magazines and newspapers for the guests' perusal. Selecting a few, she tucked them under her arm and went up to the nursery.

Dominic was alarmed on seeing Jane's distress when he entered the nursery. She was in a state of shock. Her face was ashen, her eyes dark and troubled.

'Jane? What is it? Has something happened—the baby...'

She shook her head. 'Rose is fine. It—it's something else.' Producing a magazine, she handed it to Dominic. 'Read it. I don't know what to make of it.'

Dominic gave her a puzzled look, for her eyes and her voice were full of something he did not care for. Whatever it was she wanted him to see had truly upset her. At first his brain was numb, for all his senses told him that something was badly wrong, that what he was about to see was not pleasant. He took the magazine from her. 'What is this?'

'Look at it, Dominic. After you've read it and seen

for yourself who—who Mrs Adams really is—I'm sure you will be as shocked as I am.'

Slowly Dominic lowered his gaze and stared at the picture. It was of a wedding party, a Society wedding. Looking closer at the faces, he came upon one that was familiar. At first he thought he was mistaken, but on taking a closer look, he saw it was Nancy. It must have been taken at her sister's wedding. 'I don't understand.'

'You will when you've read her real name beneath the picture.'

Dominic read, digesting it slowly, unable to believe what he was seeing. He'd thought he'd already felt hurt enough by Nancy's deception, but it seemed he was wrong.

There was an appalled silence as he stared wordlessly at the picture. Jane waited until he held the magazine away from him. Seeing her brother's roiling emotions, she went to him, for in that instant it was obvious he had been felled by a crippling blow.

'It—it would appear,' said Jane, her voice low and intense, 'that Mrs Adams has deceived us all. What could have been her purpose, I wonder? It says her name is Nancy Ryland, Dominic. You do know what this means, don't you? She—she is David's sister. There must be an explanation for her subterfuge, although she wouldn't have known, would she? As far as I'm aware, she doesn't know the identity of Rose's father—unless you told her.'

'I haven't told her,' he said, his voice not quite sounding like his own.

'And her married name is Adams, so how would I have known to connect the two?'

There was no expression on Dominic's face, but the turmoil, in his eyes and the marble severity of his face would leave no one in any doubt as to the depth of his feelings. 'Nancy isn't a widow, Jane. There never was a husband. She decided on the subterfuge when she opened her institute, thinking people would take her more seriously as a married woman—or a widow, as it turns out.'

'I am so dreadfully sorry about all this, Dominic. I realise how painful it must be for you—as it is for me to have all those wounds of losing David reopened. You must let Nancy explain.'

'Don't try and defend her, Jane,' he said instantly. 'I was taken in by her—as were you, which just goes to prove that she's a better actress than either of us realised. She clearly has an artful tongue, and her powers of persuasion are quite remarkable.'

'I do not believe she has done anything for vindictive reasons. She has no idea her brother and I...that Rose is her niece. David is her brother, and he's recently died. She will have suffered as much as I. She is not Sophia, Dominic. You must give her the chance to explain.'

'As far as I am concerned, there is nothing to explain. It is there in black and white. She has betrayed my trust—and to think I thought I was halfway to falling in love with her.' When he heard Jane's gasp of surprise, he fixed her with a hard stare, breathing hard. He swallowed painfully. 'Yes, my feelings for her were that strong, Jane. I was prepared to make her my wife. But that is over now—for how could love endure such an unforgivable deception?' He strode towards the door.

'Where are you going?'

'To see to our guests. I've absented myself too long as it is.'

When the guests had retired to their rooms, his eyes heavy with fatigue and the effects of too much whisky, Dominic went outside. Thinking of Nancy, he felt his stomach quiver and his breathing become laboured in his chest. From the moment Jane had presented him with that damned magazine, he had been fraught with a mixture of different emotions and had suffered an agony of torment, having to fight against the desire to go to Nancy immediately, to confront her with the truth.

The pain and anger of her deceit began to burn inside him. It grew and grew with such force that he could hardly contain it. The very thought that he'd trusted the wrong woman again almost drove him mad. He paused and leaned against a wall, a towering presence in the garden, the light from the moon throwing monstrous shadows on the ground. On seeing Nancy emerge from the house, shoving himself away from the wall, he smiled, a crooked, mocking smile, although his expression remained hard and unyielding. He had no intention of allowing her to see how close he'd come to offering for her and how badly she'd hurt him, but there was something that she had to know.

Deciding to take a stroll about the garden before going to bed, Nancy slipped outside. The moonlight was bright. Seeing a man in the distance and recognising Dominic, she felt her heart stir with a mixture of delight and apprehension. She walked towards him, feeling totally unprepared for what faced her.

Something in his gaze made her pause irresolutely. His hair drooped over his brow, and he looked at her unsteadily. Had he not seen her, she might have retraced her steps, but it was too late. She paused and looked at him, disturbed by his manner.

'Come closer,' he commanded, his tone terse and impersonal, with no smile or word of affection.

With a fluttering heart, Nancy hesitated, for even though she'd seen him angry before, the man she now faced was a stranger to her. She thought she glimpsed pain in his eyes before he veiled them, and her heart clenched.

'I'm sorry if my presence offends you. Since I was informed of the incident on the train line, I have tried to keep out of your way. Had I known you were out here, I would have remained indoors. Is—is something wrong?' she asked tentatively.

'Since you ask—yes. Something is very wrong, Mrs Adams—or should I say Miss Ryland? Nancy Ryland, that is.' His voice was quiet, each word enunciated carefully, and the eyes that met hers were like steel.

Surprise left Nancy speechless, for it was the last thing she had expected him to say. How did he know? Still—perhaps it was better that her true identity was out in the open. 'How did you find out?'

'There are pictures in a magazine Jane was looking through. Is it true? You are a Ryland?'

'Yes,' she replied, unable to see the sense in denying it. 'Sir John Ryland is my father. I see I need not pretend any longer.'

'Pretend? Pretending is a child's game. Deceit is a woman's,' he said heavily. 'Why did you not tell me who you were? Why did you allow me to believe you were just ordinary Mrs Adams, when all the time you were the daughter of Sir John Ryland, one of the wealthiest men in the kingdom? I am awaiting your explanation—if you have one to offer.'

'It was for precisely that reason,' Nancy explained. 'I have told you that I wanted to make my own way on my own merit—not because of who I happen to be. I wanted to be successful when I opened the orphanage and considered it essential that I take on my own identity—which happens to be my mother's maiden name. The name Ryland is too well-known in the business world.'

'How very commendable,' Dominic drawled, his lips twisting with sarcasm.

The tension between them was increasing. Nancy stared at him, for beneath his words, she could feel strong emotions fighting their way to the surface. She had not told him her true identity, but she was beginning to suspect his behaviour wasn't due to this.

'Is there something else that's bothering you, Dominic? Something that has nothing to do with me concealing my identity?'

Slowly, without taking his eyes off hers, Dominic drew himself up to his full height so that he towered above her, his body taut. His next words were to shatter her completely.

'It concerns your brother—David Ryland.'

Nancy stared at him, bewildered. Suddenly she felt chilled to the marrow. 'David? But—I don't understand. What are you saying? What has my brother to do with any of this? We have still heard nothing from the war office, so we have to assume he is dead.'

Dominic's face was set hard. 'Your brother is the father of my sister's child. He seduced my seventeen-year-old sister and got her with child. Now do you understand why I feel the way I do about the Ryland name?'

'Jane has told you this?' she asked quietly.

'Yes.'

As Dominic threw the cruel truth at her, she wondered if he even realised just what it would do to her. 'No,' she whispered, shivering with the aftermath of shock and shaking her head in abject despair, reaching out her hand and steadying herself on the wall to keep herself from falling. 'What you say cannot be true. You are mistaken. You have to be mistaken.'

'It is the truth,' he said flatly.

'I will not believe it,' she cried in desperation, scalding tears beginning to run unchecked down her ashen cheeks, the pain so great she could hardly speak. 'David would not have done anything so dishonourable. He wouldn't.' Her tears now were for the cherished, untarnished memories of her adored brother that had given her such comfort ever since she'd heard the terrible news.

Turning away, she shook her head as if trying to deny the truth of what Dominic had told her. This could not be happening. How could it be? David and Jane? How had they even met? There had been no secrets between her and David. That was how close they had been. Now she didn't know what to think.

'I cannot believe it of David,' she said quietly. 'He would never…'

'How staunchly you defend him,' Dominic said bitterly.

'Yes,' she flared, turning to face him. 'I do defend him, because I knew him and loved him dearly. For heaven's sake, he was my brother. I have every faith that he is innocent. He was a good man and incapable of what you accuse him of.'

'I am not accusing him. I am merely stating a fact. I admire your loyalty to your brother, but it is obviously somewhat misplaced. Jane would not lie.'

Nancy stood away from him, straight and erect—as if carved from stone. 'She—she knows? She knows that David was my brother?' He nodded.

She was quivering, visibly struggling against what Dominic had told her. The light fell softly on her face, which was like a tragic mask. 'I adored David like no other,' she said, a sudden vision of her brother, of his proud and handsome face, vivid in her mind's eye. 'Have you any idea what it's like to believe he's dead? The dreadful images that have tormented me as to how he might have met his death—hearing the horrendous stories of the total carnage on the battlefields of Crimea… It devastated my whole family. And now you tell me this. How could you be so cruel—so heartless?'

'I would have thought you'd prefer to know the truth rather than live a lie,' Dominic said evenly. 'And you seem all too ready to forget that he also ruined Jane's life.'

They stayed silent for a moment, not speaking, the awful truth and what it meant to them both now stretching between them. The ordeal was proving too much for Nancy. She turned from Dominic's hard gaze and walked away from him. She stopped and looked back at him one last time, her heart breaking.

'If what you say is true, then I am sorry—so sorry for Jane, for if she loved David as much as we all did, then her suffering must be great indeed. She will take comfort in her child, and your support is what she needs now. I will speak to my parents, who will be deeply affected by this news and will want to see Rose. She is their granddaughter, after all. Have you contacted them?'

'I have written, yes.'

'Then I must see them as a matter of urgency. What is clear to me is that, because of who I am, my presence now offends you. Under the circumstances, I understand that it would be impossible for me to see you again. I will leave first thing in the morning. Goodbye, Dominic.'

Chapter Twelve

When Nancy reached the sanctuary of her room, she finally allowed her defences to crumble. Engulfed in a well of misery and loneliness, she sank onto the bed, her shoulders slumped. The euphoria of the previous night had been torn to shreds. In order to have Dominic to herself, for him to make love to her, she had sacrificed her virtue, and despite her always having thought that she could take a lover with impunity, his rejection of her afterwards had left her with a mass of shame. To add to all that, Dominic had called her a scheming deceiver—and now she had the added burden of the knowledge that David was the father of Jane's child. Dominic had written to her parents. They would be broken by the news. She must go to them.

In the garden, motionless, Dominic watched Nancy walk away. What he had disclosed to her had hurt her deeply. When he had first seen her with Jane's baby in her arms, he had thought then that she'd looked familiar. Try as he might, he had been unable to remember where he had seen her before. Now he knew.

She was the stricken, jilted bride he had seen on the day eight years ago when he had been visiting his friend Hugh Sutherland in Oxfordshire.

Despite himself, pity swelled his heart, causing the rage and hurt that had possessed him to finally relax its grip somewhat. His heart ached as he watched her disappear into the house. From the moment they had met, an overwhelming attraction had drawn them together, and now fate had stepped in and separated them in the most cruel manner. But even if he could forgive her deception after what Sophia had done to him, there could be no kind of relationship, no future, for them after what he had learned about her and her family standing between them like some eternal obstacle.

And yet how could he forget the love and passion Nancy had aroused in him? She had bewitched him utterly and then broken his fragile trust, and he would have to live with that for all time.

Nancy awoke with a heavy feeling of sadness, knowing she must leave for the train station as soon as she was ready. The house was quiet as she descended the stairs, with no sign of Dominic. She sighed, telling herself that this was probably a blessing. It was best that she left without either of them inflicting further pain on the other. Besides, she had to see her parents as soon as possible, although she'd have to go back to London first.

She came across Jane in the hall.

'Jane!'

'You are leaving.'

'Yes, Jane, I am.'

'Without saying goodbye to me?'

'I'm sorry. I just didn't feel like facing anyone this morning.'

'I didn't think you would, which is why I have come to see you before you left. Here,' she said, handing Nancy the telltale magazine. 'You might like to look at this on the train.'

'Thank you, Jane. I haven't seen it yet.'

'I appealed to Dominic to try and persuade you to remain a while longer, but he said your mind was made up and that you have to get back. He—he told me about you—why you did what you did, pretending to be a widow. I saw in the magazine that you're David's sister. I couldn't believe it at first. It—it's an incredible coincidence.'

'I couldn't believe it at first either.'

'For what it's worth, I'm sorry,' Jane said gently. 'It must be as difficult for you as it is for me. Please believe me when I say that I loved David with all my heart. Have you seen Dominic this morning?'

'No. I doubt he would want to see me anyway.'

'He'll come round eventually—when he's thought about it. Why didn't you tell me who you are?'

'There was no reason to. I didn't know David was Rose's father.'

'Will you be going home—to Oxfordshire?'

'Yes. I have to see my parents. Apparently Dominic has already written to them telling them about you and David. They found it incredibly difficult coming to terms with his loss. They have already lost one son, and to lose David as well was just—just so awful.'

'Do—do you think they would want to see me and Rose?'

'Yes, yes, Jane, I do. If they could see Rose, despite the circumstances of her birth, I am sure she would be a great comfort to them.'

'Would you be agreeable to that?'

'Yes, of course I would. They are her grandparents, after all, and she is a part of David. I'm not sure what Dominic would think though. He seems so upset just now.'

'Give him time. But what of you, Nancy? You and Dominic have become—close. In fact, I would say he is more than halfway to being in love with you—and I suspect that his feelings are reciprocated.' When Nancy gave her a wary look, she smiled. 'I'd have to be blind not to see how it is between the two of you.'

Nancy nodded, swallowing hard. 'I—I can't speak

for Dominic, Jane, but I really don't think he loves me. And, well—no matter how I feel about him, the closeness that we shared for so brief a time is over.'

'Don't say that, Nancy. I am sure the matter will be resolved in time. This has come as a surprise to all of us.'

'It has. But who would have thought when I came for Rose that day that she was David's child—my niece.' She swallowed a small sob and walked to the door. 'I have to go now. The train won't wait. Goodbye, Jane.'

She was glad to find the carriage already waiting for her. Jane followed her out of the house and watched her depart. As Nancy climbed inside, her heart cried silently, wishing she could have seen Dominic one more time, for him to hold her and tell her that everything would be all right between them. Before he had known her true identity, she had vaguely wondered if it was possible to determine a way that a life with Dominic and her work could go hand in hand. But in one day, she had lost one of those things and kept the other.

None of it was his doing. He was not the one who had deceived her. He had been honest about his intentions from the start. She was the guilty one. Shock over the whole horrendous affair had rendered her temporarily numb, but she knew it would soon give way to real suffering.

* * *

From a vantage point close to the house, Dominic watched Nancy climb into the carriage. All manner of thoughts raced through his mind—suspicions and questions which would have to remain unanswered. For one agonising moment before she took her seat, he thought she was going to turn and look at him. His gaze brushed over the flush in her cheeks, the smooth, high line of her brow—the stubborn tilt of her chin. The manner in which her bodice clung to her breasts, outlining their round, firm shape until he swore he could feel their softness once more filling his palms. This was ridiculous. How could he want her so badly? He had made love to her for one night only, and usually, for him, once was enough. Then why was this occasion so different? Why did he feel so devastated about her leaving? He almost couldn't believe he was losing her.

Ever since Sophia's betrayal, followed by her death, he had struggled to trust anyone, least of all a woman. He'd never wanted to be that vulnerable again, so he'd rigidly kept his feelings in check, suppressing all the pain and fear that had raged within him at the time. It was a lesson he'd refused to forget, a mistake he'd vowed never to repeat. He had sworn never to give one woman such power over him again. Admittedly he'd got more than he'd bargained for when he'd made love to Nancy Ryland.

He'd done nothing but think of her all night, and his anger had finally burnt itself out, leaving him feeling hollow. Tempted to call her back, he almost weakened, but then he thought of her faceless brother and how he had treated his sister, and it was like having a bucket of cold water poured over him. Pain tore through him—not the crippling pain from a wound, but the kind you could not see, the kind that had no location.

The betrayal and humiliation heaped on him by his dead wife came flooding back once again. Rationally, he knew Nancy had had nothing to do with any of that, but how could he make her a part of his life when every time he looked at her, he would remember her brother?

But, he thought, his mood softening when his thoughts drifted back to how it had felt to hold her in his arms, to make love to her, and how much pleasure they had derived from each other, it was impossible to deny that she had become a part of him. How could he live without her? But he would have to learn to.

Not until she was on the train did Nancy open the magazine Jane had given her. The pages were filled with pictures and news of last month's Society events.

She turned the pages until she came to the one she was looking for. Her mouth went dry and she went cold all over when at last she saw her face staring out at her from between the pages, along with those of her parents and Georgina and her husband in their wedding finery. She groaned inwardly, for she should have known that a publication reporting such a prestigious wedding would be sure to turn up at Osborne House.

Since the introduction of photography in Britain, the medium had gained public recognition and was growing rapidly. Her father found it interesting. It combined his love of art and science, and he'd been pleased with the photographs of Georgina's wedding he had commissioned from a photographic studio in Oxford.

She didn't imagine Dominic read ladies' magazines, but his grandmother and several of the guests would have liked to look through them. As it turned out, it had been Jane.

Thinking of Jane and little Rose, she was dreading going to see her parents to talk to them about David, but it was something she had to do.

Distraction from his volatile feelings for Nancy might have come in the form of Elizabeth, if Dominic had been that way inclined. But entering his rooms the night after Nancy's departure, nothing could have surprised him more than to see Elizabeth stretched out on his bed, a cloud of dark brown hair spread out on the pillow, nothing but a silk dressing gown covering her naked form.

'Elizabeth? What on earth…?'

Her eyelashes fluttered and she smiled up at him, stretching languorously like a cat in the sun, unashamed of her scant attire and making no effort to cover her naked legs. Dominic was utterly incredulous.

'Elizabeth,' he repeated sharply once he'd recovered from the initial shock of seeing her lying on his bed. 'Kindly explain what you are doing in my bedroom.'

Resting her head on her hand, she looked up at his thunderous face, pouting her soft lips, making a pretence of being hurt. 'Really, Dominic! If I'd had any hope that you might be pleased to see me, your tone of voice would have taught me otherwise.'

'That is beside the point. I come to my room and find you on my bed, and you are surprised when I ask you to explain yourself?'

'Come now, Dominic. I'm to depart for France when we return to London tomorrow. I couldn't leave things as they are between us without letting you know how I feel about you. To be with you was the only reason I came all this way with Simon.'

'Really? I don't recall ever asking you to do that. My recollections are that you accompanied Simon because you wanted to see Europe.'

'And to be with you.'

'And that is the reason you have entered a gentleman's bedroom uninvited?'

'Why, I thought that was what you wanted too.' She

smiled softly, boldly undeterred by his sharp manner. 'And I'm still here. Why don't you join me?'

'Don't look like that, Elizabeth,' Dominic snapped frustratedly when he saw her simpering smile and the calculating enticement in her look. 'I have no intention of ravishing you now or in the future. Ever.'

'Why not, Dominic? Is it that you don't find me attractive?'

Dominic gave her a hard look, his mouth tightening as he stared down at her, at the pink mouth and long-lashed green eyes. He found it strange that he got no pleasure from perusing her almost naked form. The only emotion she was capable of rousing in him was revulsion.

'You are a beautiful woman, Elizabeth, and you know it. But you shouldn't be here. Please leave.'

'But I want you, Dominic—indeed, I do believe I am in love with you—and I can't bear to think I might lose you,' she said, trying to put the softness back into her voice and school her features into a tender look, but it didn't work on Dominic. He'd already seen beneath her mask.

'If that is what you think, then you only deceive yourself,' he told her coolly. 'Not once have I given you reason to believe you are anything more than an acquaintance, but I always knew you were available— too ready to grasp everything I could give you.'

'That is not true. I have everything I need—and everything else I want I can have,' she pouted.

'Not quite, Elizabeth. You don't have the title of countess—and I am not prepared to give you that. It is what you want. Admit it.'

'Yes—if you must know,' she admitted hotly. 'Which I imagine is what Nancy Adams also has her eyes on. I know what occurred between the two of you the other night. I saw you go into her room together.'

Dominic shuddered. The thought of being joined in holy wedlock to Elizabeth was one that froze him to the marrow. In spite of recent events, he was well aware that Elizabeth lacked Nancy's goodness, her humour and fresh and lively wit, and she didn't look at him with two adorable amber eyes, and smile that wonderful smile at him.

'Leave Nancy's name out of this,' he ground out.

Flinging herself off the bed, Elizabeth stood before him with her hands clenched by her sides and her face so contorted with rage that she was almost ugly. Dominic could see that she finally realised all was lost.

'Oh, I will, but not before I've had my say. I am not unaware of her need for funds to run her precious institute. You slept together. Could it possibly be because it was in payment for her services—the kind you give to a whore?'

Dominic's anger was so powerful in that moment that he had to clench his hands by his sides to prevent them from reaching out and throttling her. 'Whatever happened between Nancy and me was not some meaningless encounter with a woman of the streets.'

'Ha! So—the truth hurts,' she cried. 'Your oh-so-pious Nancy Adams certainly showed her true colours that night, did she not? Little wonder she wanted no one to know about her sordid coupling with you, or why she left in such a hurry.'

The bluntness of Elizabeth's statement jarred every one of Dominic's nerves. 'And you have a warped definition of how a well-bred young woman should behave. Nancy could give *you* lessons in the art of being a lady. Dear Lord, how you must hate her.'

'Yes, I do hate her. I hated her the first time I laid eyes on her—with her hoity-toity manner and boasting a superiority of mind that was positively sickening.'

'Enough, Elizabeth,' he said, gritting his teeth. 'I've asked you to leave. Return to your room before one of the servants comes in.'

'You'll be sorry for this, Dominic, I'll see to that. What do you think will happen when it gets out what sort of woman she really is? Her precious institute will suffer when the scandalmongers get hold of her indiscretion. She will be damned as a shameless wanton, unfit company for unsullied young ladies, unfit to mingle in Polite Society.'

Dominic watched her turn and walk to the door, but he did not miss the flare of temper in her eyes. In a silky, menacing voice, he said, 'If it is your intention to blacken Nancy's name and cause her any unnecessary suffering, then I advise you to reconsider. There will be no scandal. If you so much as breathe one word that will bring disgrace to her, I swear you will have cause to regret it.' These words were spoken in such a lethal voice, it left Elizabeth in no doubt that he meant it. 'Is that clear enough for you?'

Elizabeth drew herself up with nervous hauteur. 'You can't threaten me.'

'No?' he inquired silkily. 'I meant every word. One thing you should know about me, Elizabeth, is that I'm a very determined man, and if any harm comes to Nancy or anyone else I care about by your hand, I'll destroy you. Believe me when I tell you that you don't want me for an enemy.'

He watched her turn away from him and open the door. His next words halted her. 'Remember that you also have much to lose. Your father is an extremely upright, moral man, and if he learns how you set out to entrap me into wedlock—and the disgraceful methods you used to do it—he'll not be lenient with you.'

With a bitter, defeated look, Elizabeth turned and went out.

As the days went by, try as he might, Dominic could not banish Nancy from his thoughts. She had a way of getting under his skin and insinuating herself into his mind that troubled him. She was certainly physically appealing, with a face and body that drugged him. But he was also drawn to her in other ways, with her intelligence, sharpness of mind and a clever wit that he greatly admired, making her entertaining company and interesting to be with. It would be virtually impossible for him to forget her.

Chapter Thirteen

After informing Betty at the institute that she had to visit her parents and making sure everything would be taken care of in her absence, Nancy left for Oxfordshire. She hadn't told her parents she was coming, so they were surprised to see her.

Mary, who was down from Leeds for a few weeks, had taken her two girls to visit friends and was expected back shortly, so Nancy wanted to take the opportunity to speak now. A look of unease passed between her parents, and they both seemed to grow much older as they faced their daughter. Nancy stood by the fire, too restless and uneasy to sit down. She lost no time in telling them of her reason for coming. Pale and visibly shaken, they listened as she told them about David, of his romantic affair with Lady Jane Blackwell, and that a child, a little girl called Rose, was the result.

'We already know that, Nancy,' her father said heavily. 'Lord Blackwell wrote to inform us. I've yet to respond to his letter, but in truth, we are still in shock. We cannot believe it of David. You know Lord Blackwell?'

'Yes, I do. He told me he had written informing you of the situation.'

'What is to be done?' her mother asked shakily. 'We will have to face him at some point.'

'Yes, you will. Rose is your grandchild. It is only natural you would want to see her. I have, and she is utterly adorable. You will also like Jane. She is goodness personified, and I know she would like to meet you both, too.'

'We would both like to meet her,' her father said. 'How did you come to know Lord Blackwell?'

'I—I happened to meet Lady Jane when Rose was born. Her mother can be rather ill-natured and could not agree to her daughter keeping the child, which was when she approached me. It broke Jane's heart when I took Rose away. I hated doing it. Lord Blackwell came to the institute and took her back to his sister. We have seen each other since then on occasion.'

'Does he know who you are—that you are my daughter?' her father asked.

'He does now, although I didn't tell him when we met. He—He thought I was a widow.'

'How did he take the news about David?'

'It's no good pretending he took it well. He was extremely angry. I am certain he will want to see you.'

Her father nodded. 'And we would like to meet him.' He gave her mother a look that Nancy couldn't interpret. 'In fact, Nancy, only this morning, we've finally had news about David.'

'Yes,' her mother said, leaning forward, a trembling smile playing on her lips. 'We should have told you immediately, but we wanted to hear about Rose first. He is alive, Nancy—David is alive—still somewhere in the Crimea in a field hospital—but he is alive after all.'

Nancy stared at her. 'Alive? David is alive?' She could not believe it. Tears sprang to her eyes. This was indeed the best news. 'Goodness me—after all this time. That is—wonderful news. Oh,' she gasped. Going to her mother and taking her hand, she knelt on the carpet in front of them both. 'But why have we not heard anything before now? After all this time, I—I thought he was…'

Her mother squeezed her hand, brushing Nancy's tears away. 'We all did. We had given up hope. We just received a letter from the hospital where he is. You and David were always so special to each other, I know. But this is the news we have all waited for— what we've prayed for.'

'But—how is he? Is he well? Is he badly wounded?'

'We know he was wounded but not how serious his wounds were. We do know he is finally recovering. It appears he has been unconscious for some time, and no one knew his identity. He must have finally come round and told them who he is.'

'Poor David. Have you been informed when he will be coming home?'

'Soon, we hope. We will ask James to meet him in Southampton.'

Nancy sat back on her heels. 'Jane must be told immediately. She has suffered grievously. And Georgina—and James. Do they know yet?'

'No. We will send them a telegram today,' her mother said quietly. 'But tell me more about Lord Blackwell.'

'There is nothing to add, really. I went to stay at Osborne House in Berkshire on Lord Blackwell's invitation last weekend. There were lots of people there. His grandmother was holding an open house. She is also involved in many charities and an avid fundraiser. She's a very interesting lady.'

'And Lord Blackwell?' her father asked, watching her closely. 'What kind of man is he?'

'He—he is an honourable man—a businessman like yourself. He is a widower. His wife died several years ago, leaving him with a son, Mark.'

Hearing a catch in her voice, her father reached out and raised her chin, looking into her eyes. The sadness she felt was there for him to see. At that moment, she bore no resemblance to the independent young woman who had left Aspenthorpe to devote all her time and energy to destitute children.

'Will you be returning to Osborne House?'

She shook her head miserably. 'No,' she whispered. 'I will write to Jane, but as for her brother… When he knew who I was, he did not take it well.' Unable to keep her tears in check a minute longer, she wept. 'Oh, Father, I do believe he hates me now.' Her father lifted her up and folded her in his arms and tenderly stroked her hair, rocking her as he used to when she was a child as she sobbed against his chest.

'Hush, Nancy. You must not upset yourself so,' he murmured gently. 'I am sure Lord Blackwell was angry, and I can understand why—considering the circumstances. In his eyes, his sister has been taken advantage of. To discover that she has borne a child out of wedlock is bad enough—but to find out you are the sister of the man who fathered that child must have come as a terrible blow. I don't wonder he is angry.'

'And when people are angry, they often say things they don't mean,' her mother said comfortingly. 'He'll calm down—you'll see—when David comes home and the storm blows itself out.'

'No,' Nancy mumbled. 'You don't know him. And it's not all about David and Jane.'

Releasing herself from her father's arms, she looked at them both. 'I'm sorry. I'm making a fool of myself. I'll go to my room and write to him. It's only right that he tells Jane about David in case she's overcome by the news—although I shudder to think what her mother will make of it.'

'Why do you say that, Nancy?' her father asked.

'The Dowager Countess is a formidable woman. She belongs to an age where good breeding still matters more than wealth. She is Lord Blackwell's stepmother, and they do not see eye to eye—especially where Lady Jane is concerned. Of course, Lord Blackwell adores his sister.' Getting to her feet, she wiped her wet cheeks with her handkerchief. 'I shudder to think how he will react when David comes home.'

When Dominic saw Aspenthorpe at the end of a tree-lined drive, he was unprepared. It was an impressive red brick mansion, the handmade bricks having mellowed over the years to a silvery pink. Built in perfect symmetry, it stood in harmony against a backdrop of well-cultivated farmland. He found himself drawn to it. He liked it—liked its warmth, its suggestion of inner peace.

Dominic had made enquiries about Sir John Ryland—what kind of man he was. What he'd learned was encouraging. As a hard-headed businessman, he was highly respected by those he had dealings with. Those who knew him personally also spoke well of him.

When the carriage drew up in front of the house,

Dominic stepped down. He would make up his own mind when he met the man whose son had compromised his sister.

The acres surrounding Aspenthorpe were a patchwork of fields and hedgerows and winding country lanes. The weather was warm and sunny when Nancy and Mary with her two young girls and three energetic terriers walked along the familiar paths, as the sisters had done on countless occasions since childhood. They headed to their favourite destination—the waterfall, which cascaded in a short fall over the shiny rocks.

They paused on the narrow stone bridge to indulge in a pastime which they so enjoyed in their own childhood. The children threw twigs off one side of the bridge into the crystal-clear water below and ran to the other side in glee and excited anticipation to see whose would be the first to come floating through. Often the twigs became stuck between the rocks under the bridge, and the whole performance had to be enacted again.

It was a lovely occasion, with Nancy enjoying being with her family once more, having decided to stay on for a while, the atmosphere lightened by the expected homecoming of David, although they still had not been told the nature of his wounds.

It was a happy group that returned to the house,

going to the drawing room, which immediately became a cacophony of noise from child and dog alike.

Nancy followed them inside, her cheeks flushed from her walk, her eyes shining brightly and her lips parted in a broad smile as she laughed at something funny one of the girls had just said to her—until she became aware of the still figure sitting in a chair. He rose when he saw her, his penetrating eyes meeting hers, and her heart leaped. Thrown off balance, she stared at him uncomprehendingly. Immediately the smile froze on her lips, although her heart was overflowing with gladness, and it was all she could do to stop herself from casting herself into his arms.

There was a silence in the room as everyone became aware of the presence of this terribly handsome, if somewhat aloof, gentleman. Polite introductions were made, after which Mary ushered the protesting children and dogs from the room, leaving Dominic and Nancy alone.

Dominic moved closer to Nancy, who had not altered her position since entering the room. He seemed at ease, as though it was the most natural thing in the world that he should be there. But knowing what it was that had brought him to Aspenthorpe, she couldn't believe he was quite so calm inside. Greeting him now, with a proper degree of casualness, was much more difficult than she had expected when she still remembered their bitter parting in Berkshire so clearly over a week ago.

Despite herself, a wave of happiness swept over her as she was able to look again on those features buried so deep in her heart. His face was drawn, his mouth now held in a tight line, and she was conscious of a curious feeling of tenderness at the sight of the stray lock of hair that insisted on falling over his brow.

However, his blank countenance told her that, whatever she had hoped, he had not forgiven her for her deception, nor could he ever forget who she was. There was to be no reconciliation. There would be no further embraces or past differences forgotten. There was no welcoming smile, nothing at that moment to indicate he still cared for her. Managing to subdue her disappointment, she pulled herself together.

'Hello, Dominic,' she heard herself say. 'How are you?' She knew it was a stupid, inadequate thing to say, but she had to say something, and with her heart beating so fast she could almost hear it, she couldn't think of anything else.

'Hello, Nancy,' Dominic replied, realising in that moment just how much he had missed her. It was the first time he had seen her behaving so carefree and casual, and he thought how much it suited her. How lovely and vibrant she looked, with her hair all mussed up and her skin aglow from her walk. When she lifted her eyes to his and he saw the quiet yielding in their depths, it nearly sent him to his knees. He wanted to lose himself in her eyes, to pull her into his arms and unburden his heart. He wanted nothing else in the world but to make love to her right now.

Knowing how important her work at the institute was to her, he had not been prepared to see her at Aspenthorpe. Since he had last seen her in Berkshire, he had been plagued with so many conflicting emotions where she was concerned, becoming lost in a turmoil of contradiction and insoluble dilemma.

Under the circumstances, it was only right that he saw her parents. He had arrived at Aspenthorpe unexpectedly. He had chosen to delay his arrival for a week or so, thinking Nancy would have already returned to London after visiting her parents. He did not trust himself to see her, for it would surely shatter his every vestige of reason and resistance. He had not been prepared for the surge of gladness that had almost unmanned him when she had walked into the room.

As he moved towards her and his eyes studied her, Nancy could see that, despite the harshness of his features, there was something about his expression that told her he was pleased to see her. She thought there might even be a flickering of admiration in his eyes, which filled her with a wonderful elation.

But it was gone almost as soon as it had appeared, for when he stood before her, his eyes remained fixed on hers without even the whisper of a smile to soften his expression.

'You are well, Nancy?'

'Yes—very well, Dominic—and worry not. I can already confirm to you that there is no child, in case you were still wondering. I know neither of us wanted anything to complicate matters more than they already are.' She'd been shocked by the strength of her own disappointment that she'd not even have a child to remember him by.

'No, of course not.' An expression, too quick for her to decipher, flashed in his eyes. 'I am here to see your parents. I apologise for turning up unexpectedly.'

'I'm sorry they were not here to receive you. They are visiting neighbours but will be back soon. Your sister is well—and your grandmother?'

'Perfectly. Jane has remained in Berkshire. Grandmother likes having her.'

'I can understand that. The country air will be good for Jane and Rose. I enjoyed meeting your grandmother.'

'And she you. She was impressed with your work at the institute. She's already speaking of taking the train to London to pay you a visit—to see for herself what it is you do at your institute.'

'I admire the work she does. She would be more than welcome if she were to visit.'

'You must know why I am here. After what transpired when you were in Berkshire, when it was revealed to me that David was your brother, I could not let the matter lie and just ignore it.'

A flash of anger in Dominic's eyes told Nancy he was still coming to terms with the unfortunate circumstances concerning Jane, but there was nothing she could do about that now. For her parents' sake, she must remain calm.

'That is not what any of us want. I know how hurt you must feel. So do my parents. They have also suffered greatly.'

'What are you trying to say?'

'They have both been badly shaken by recent events. I would appreciate it if you do not upset them further.'

'I have not come here to do that. I am not insensitive to what they must have suffered—and I respect your attempts to do all you can to alleviate their distress. None of this is their fault, and it is unfortunate that your brother is no longer here to explain his actions. But for my sister's sake, it is imperative that the matter is dealt with properly.'

Nancy was confused. 'Of course. I couldn't agree more—only, did you not receive my letter about David?'

He shook his head. 'No. No doubt it will be waiting for me when I return to London.'

'Well, as you know, we all thought David was dead. However, my parents received notification several days ago that he is alive after all. He—he is wounded, in a field hospital in Sevastopol.'

While Dominic took a moment to digest this information, his expression remained blank. 'I see. This changes things. Your parents, along with you and your siblings, must be incredibly relieved.'

Nancy lowered her eyes, unable to look into his, which were still expressionless. 'Absolutely. It's what we have wished for all along. We don't know yet when he will be shipped back home, but I have no doubt my father will contact you when he arrives.'

'I would appreciate that. We must await his arrival before deciding what is to be done—what is best for my sister and Rose.'

'Yes, I agree.'

'Are you to return to London shortly?'

'Yes—in a few days. My sister Mary is here with her children. I haven't seen them since Georgina's wedding, so I thought I'd delay going back to the institute.'

Dominic's manner softened a little. 'Despite what has occurred between us, I do wish you every success in your work, knowing how important it is to you.'

'Yes, it is.' She turned from him. 'I think I can hear

my parents' return. I'll go and tell them you are here. We don't want you to miss your train.' She moved towards the door, where she paused, the pain of parting from him almost too much to bear. 'Tell me, Dominic,' she said, turning to face him, unaware that her whole heart was in her eyes. 'Have you made up your mind to dislike me all your life? I know I deceived you and broke your trust, but could you ever learn to forgive me?'

Her words, quiet yet spoken with such impact, caused Dominic to stand quite still and look at her. His face was taut with emotion, and within his eyes, something moved and glowed a little. Her own eyes, locked with his, suddenly welled with unshed tears.

Dominic strode towards her, his hand half reaching out to her. He withdrew it as if wanting to touch her but too afraid to do so. 'Dislike? Despite what you did, I don't dislike you, Nancy. You know what my feelings are. I think I made them plain to you that night in the music room when I found you playing Chopin on the piano. The memory of that night will remain with me always.'

'But you have no wish to refresh the memory?'

'Stop it, Nancy,' he said hoarsely. 'I admit that my arms ache to hold you—but you must see that our reality prevents us from becoming further involved with each other. Dear Lord, I miss you, but we can't go back. Both of us know that.'

The tears spilled over Nancy's lashes as she turned resolutely away from him, but she experienced a feeling of absolute joy in knowing he still cared for her. 'Then you must forget you ever met me. As things have turned out, it is inevitable that we will meet on occasion because of your sister and my brother.'

She didn't turn and look back as she left him, but it seemed as if her heart would break. She blinked back her tears, refusing to give in to anguish. No doubt time, determination and hard work would help her, for she must keep her sights fixed on her future. He had told her that they couldn't go back, and yet he had said he missed her.

Apparently not enough.

Dominic stood there for a long time after Nancy had gone, feeling the chill of her leaving. Never in all his life had he felt as wretched as he did at that moment. When he had entered the room, the sight of her had almost knocked him off his feet. His gaze had swept over her face with its clear skin, slightly tilted warm amber eyes, and full soft lips that positively invited a man to kiss them. Tendrils of her auburn hair drifted like whispered secrets against the curve of her cheek, precisely where he should have liked to place his lips. Desire had poured through him. She had a body that was created for a man's hands, a body that could drive a man demented with desire.

Recollecting himself, he had forced his gaze away, dragging his thoughts from the joy of her, from the memories of their light banter on the day they had shared the picnic on the heath, the way she had looked on the night they had made love, her face aglow with anticipation of what was to happen next. He thought of the way she had melted against him and kissed him with what he now knew has been an innocent but instinctive passion, how warm she had felt in his arms, wonderful and loving. She was nothing like Sophia, but that didn't matter anymore.

Breathing deeply, he moved to the window overlooking the immaculate gardens to await Sir John Ryland and his wife.

Sir John and his wife were surprised by Dominic's sudden arrival at Aspenthorpe. Despite their apprehension that all might not go well, and that it could be disastrous for any future relationship, they were happy he had come, and the matter concerning his sister and their son could be discussed. Sir John would have liked James to be present, but he was away on business.

Nancy sat in on the meeting. She did not add or detract from what was said but listened intently. Sir John insisted that David would do the right thing by Lady Jane and offer to marry her, but until he came home, there was nothing that could be done.

Dominic's emotions were mixed. Before he had come to Aspenthorpe, he hadn't been completely sure what he was going to say to Sir John and Lady Ryland. But knowing now that David Ryland had not been killed in battle after all, his common sense prevailed over his pride. This provided him with the best chance to save the situation for Jane's and Rose's sake, and it would be folly on his part to refuse it.

When he got up to depart, Lady Ryland asked him to stay for dinner, an offer he politely declined. As he was leaving the room, he paused, his eyes meeting Nancy's for a long, silent moment. That was all. He did not speak to her again.

Nancy would probably never get over Dominic. She knew that now. Whatever illusions she might have had where he was concerned were gone. But she missed him horribly. Time did nothing to lessen her heartache, and the part of her he had awoken had shrivelled and died. The days she could cope with, for she had things to do to keep her mind occupied, but the nights were agony.

She had returned to the institute to await news that David was on his way home.

She was surprised and extremely delighted when Dominic's grandmother arrived at the institute, looking as elegant and dignified as ever. Nancy welcomed her warmly,

'It's good to see you again, Mrs Adams—or should I call you Miss Ryland now?' she said with a mischievous twinkle in her eyes.

Nancy laughed lightly. 'I can see you have been talking to your grandson, Lady Blackwell—and I would be happy for you to call me Nancy. There never was a Mr Adams, as you know. When I was setting up my project, I passed myself off as a widow because I thought I would be taken more seriously, and to protect my father from what might be difficult questions about my work.'

'I can understand that.'

'I hope Lady Jane is well. I am sure your grandson will have told her by now that David—my brother—is still alive and will be coming home shortly.'

'Yes, and I must say I am delighted as well. Jane welcomed the news, of course. She was ecstatic and is impatient to see him. What a coincidence that the father of her child is your brother, and what a relief it must be for you and your family, knowing that he is safe.'

'It is indeed.'

'I have thought of you often since you left Berkshire. When Dominic informed me that Jane's mother was to visit Paris for several weeks, I thought it would be a good time to come to town and pay you a visit.'

'I'm glad you've come,' Nancy said, all the old

warmth she had felt for the older woman shining through.

Nancy was more than happy to show her around and introduce her to some of the workers who took care of the children. Afterwards they had a delightful lunch in Nancy's rooms.

'It is my intention to expand,' Nancy said when Lady Blackwell questioned her about educating the children. 'I'm already looking for premises. A volunteer tutor gives up his time when he is able, but some of the children are with us for a long period, and it is not enough.'

'After what I have seen today, I will do what I can to fund your very worthwhile cause.'

Nancy smiled. 'Funds are always welcome, Lady Blackwell.'

'Dominic tells me he also saw you when he visited your parents. How did he seem to you?'

'Oh—he was polite and courteous…'

'And as unforgiving and unyielding as ever, I'm sure,' Lady Blackwell muttered disgruntledly. She fell silent, taking a sip of her tea before looking uneasily at Nancy. 'Forgive me if I appear to be speaking out of turn, but Jane has told me how it is between the two of you. Has he told you anything about Sophia—his wife?'

'Yes, although I—I think he feels uncomfortable speaking about her.'

Lady Osborne nodded, her eyes filling with pain. 'Yes, I'm afraid he does. His life was made quite wretched when they were married. It is a subject he always avoids talking about, but since that time, he has regarded women as both dispensable and replaceable. He is my grandson and I love him dearly, but I feel I must warn you that if you are drawn into an affair with him, have a care—because when a woman becomes possessive of him, as they invariably do, he quickly becomes unobtainable. His liberty is too important to him at present. I would not wish to see you get hurt.'

'I appreciate your concern, but I am no woolly-headed milksop to be so blinded by a man's handsome looks not to recognise a gentleman's intentions, and to know when to step back.'

Lady Blackwell smiled graciously and looked at Nancy with a strangely reflective smile. 'I thought so too at your age. When my husband died, I'm afraid I was very easily tempted by a handsome face. I had a dreadful habit of stepping forward instead of back. It is my dearest wish to see my grandson find a suitable wife—and a mother for Mark.'

Nancy could understand how difficult Dominic's marriage had been. Perhaps in time some of his bitterness and lack of trust in women would be eased. How she hoped so. She flinched at the notion that she had contributed to his pain by not revealing her true identity to him. Lady Blackwell had certainly given her something to think about.

Chapter Fourteen

At last David was coming home. Nancy went to Waterloo Station to meet him. James had gone down to Southampton to meet him off the ship. From Waterloo, they were to go directly to Aspenthorpe.

The reunion with David was an emotional one, a mixture of relief and joyful tears. Nancy flung herself into his arms. He was too moved for speech. For a long moment, brother and sister clung together. After what seemed like an eternity, they pulled away, and Nancy looked at him and smiled, her eyes moist with tears.

'Welcome home, David. Thank God you're back safe,' she whispered, gazing anxiously into his pain-filled eyes. They were bloodshot, his lids heavy, stark evidence of his lack of sleep on the long voyage from the Crimea.

'We are going directly to Aspenthorpe, David,' James said. 'The whole family will be there to welcome you home.'

As they boarded the train, Nancy sent up a silent

prayer of thanksgiving that her beloved brother was now safe and reasonably well. He had been severely injured in battle. Following an injury to his head, he had been rendered unconscious for some weeks, and then when he had finally awoken, he'd initially not re-called who he was. He had also been shot in his right leg, which had become infected. He now walked with a limp, and he still struggled with the pain.

On the journey, Nancy had gently broken the news of all that had occurred since he'd left. On learning that he had fathered a daughter with Jane, David had wept tears of remorse that he had left her to shoulder such an enormous responsibility on her own.

All his siblings were waiting at Aspenthorpe to greet him, crying out with relief and happiness to see him home, with Lady Ryland fussing round him like a mother hen, but as the days passed, he could not con-ceal the fact from Nancy that that he was dreading the moment when he would have to face Lord Blackwell.

Dominic lost no time in going there once he heard David was home. By the time he reached Aspen-thorpe, having had time to assess the situation more clearly and sensibly, his feelings over what the man had done to his sister had abated somewhat. He was wise enough to know that if anything at all was to be salvaged from the mess, and he could reach an un-derstanding with Sir John Ryland and his son, anger and recriminations would serve no purpose. But he could not overlook the fact that his sister's reputation had possibly been ruined beyond all saving.

'Lord Blackwell,' the butler intoned in a serious voice. From where she stood beside her parents and James, Nancy saw how her brother paled visibly as the illustrious, proud and powerful Earl of Osborne entered the room, as if David were expecting to see an executioner bearing an axe against the man who had compromised his sister.

At Dominic's entrance, Nancy's parents and James rose to their feet. Polite exchanges were made. Dominic reached out and accepted James's outstretched hand, and everyone resumed their seats. Nancy's heart turned over when she gazed at him. He looked remarkably impressive sitting across from her parents. She sat motionless, letting her eyes feast on him, allowing herself the luxury of studying his face, feeling the same wonderful, bone-melting excitement stirring inside her that she did whenever she looked at him.

She watched him closely, hoping for a warm glance or a smile, even, but his eyes were fixed on David, whose dark chestnut curls were brushed neatly back from his boyishly handsome face. He knew he had no alternative but to throw himself upon Lord Blackwell's mercy and pray that by doing so, he would not forbid him to see Jane. In that warm, elegantly furnished room, all reality seemed to have been suspended, leaving David to hang in the numbing vacuum of his own uncertainty.

Nancy had been dreading this moment when she would have to confront Dominic and see what she knew would surely be contempt written all over his features. But she was wrong. This aloof man might not be the smiling, considerate man she had come to know, but her heart soared when his gaze finally settled on her and his granite features softened and his eyes warmed, as if he realised how difficult his meeting with her beloved brother was for her.

The tension in the room was palpable as polite conversation was made, until Dominic turned his attention to David.

'I understand that you were injured in the Crimea. You are recovered, I hope.'

'I am better than I was, sir,' David said. 'I still suffer from the bullet I took in my leg, but it is finally healing.'

'I'm glad to hear it.'

'Having sustained such severe injuries, David won't be returning to his regiment,' Sir John explained. 'He is to join James in running the family business.'

Dominic nodded. 'That's probably for the best.'

Clearing his throat, David said, 'H-how is Jane?' Perched on the edge of his seat, he was unable to keep the nervousness out of his voice as he raised the matter that was uppermost on all their minds.

Dominic looked at him directly. 'My sister is in Berkshire. It's the best place for her at this time. She is well, and Rose is thriving. Your past conduct where she is concerned was reprehensible—it went way beyond the bounds of propriety. Even her mother had no idea what was going on between the two of you until Jane told her she was with child. The responsibility for this whole unacceptable affair rests on your shoulders. You took an innocent young woman of good breeding and ruined her. I have a moral code, just like everybody else, and you have breached that code. What have you to say for yourself?'

David met his gaze steadily. 'I—I was a fool, I know, a self-indulgent fool, but meeting Jane blinded me to all else. Please accept my deepest and sincerest apologies for any upset I have caused—to your family and especially to Jane. If it is agreeable to you, I would like to marry her as soon as it can be arranged. I assure you that my love for your sister is profound. I loved her from the moment I set eyes on her. I will make her happy and be a good father to our child. I admit that in the past, I have done things I am not proud of, but I will never betray Jane's love.'

Nancy knew her brother spoke from the heart. Since he had returned home and been told of the birth of his daughter, he had been badly shaken and had agonised repeatedly over how much Jane might have suffered without him and also over the disapproval of Lord Blackwell, more so than he had his father's reaction over his act of recklessness, which had been severe.

'Be assured, Lord Blackwell,' Sir John said, 'that my son will do what is right by your sister.'

'I'm a reasonable man, Sir John, and I am not so foolish as to deny your son's access to my sister—and their daughter. But you must understand that whatever is decided also has to be approved by Jane's mother— who is in Paris just now.' He looked at David. 'The last thing she will want is a public scandal, so I do not think you will meet any opposition from that quarter—but not until she has had her say will I agree to this. I will warn you in advance that the Dowager Countess's entire life has been religiously and scrupulously dedicated to the precepts of convention, so you must prepare yourself for the sharp end of her tongue. In the meantime, I think you should go to Osbourne House to see my sister and meet your daughter. I'll be going there myself soon. It might be as well for you to accompany me.'

'Yes, of course,' David said gratefully.

'You must go to London with Nancy first, David,' his mother said, 'and stay at our house in Belgravia. Lord Blackwell can contact you there. When do you plan to return to the institute, Nancy?'

'In two days, the day before Mary and Georgina are due to leave.'

'I intend to leave for Berkshire within the week, so I will let you know the details,' Dominic said, getting to his feet.

'Would you care to stay for dinner, Lord Blackwell?' Nancy's mother asked hopefully.

He smiled but shook his head. 'Thank you, but I have to get back to London. It's convenient that my good friend Hugh Sutherland lives close by—you will know him, Sir John.' Sir John nodded. 'I called on him earlier, and he kindly offered me the use of his carriage to come here and take me back to the station.' After bidding everyone farewell, he turned to Nancy. 'Would you see me out?'

Nancy nodded and led him into the hall and out to the waiting carriage.

'Thank you for coming, Dominic,' she said. 'I sincerely hope everything can be sorted out now that David's home.'

He nodded. 'So do I. The fact that he ruined my sister aside, he seems to be a pleasant young man who genuinely loves Jane.'

'He is. I am sure Jane and David will be extremely happy if you and your stepmother agree to them marrying. I would hate to think of Rose growing up with the stigma of illegitimacy.'

'I won't let that happen. I'll have a word with Constance and make her see that marriage to your brother is the most sensible thing. But what of you, Nancy?'

'Me? Why—nothing is changed where I am concerned. I will carry on doing what I enjoy doing. Your grandmother called on me before I came home. It was lovely to see her. She was impressed with the institute.'

'I know. She told me. She is still in London—catching up with a few friends. I will go back to Berkshire with her when she is ready, which is why I suggested your brother accompany me there as well.'

How Nancy wished she could go with them, that he would invite her to do so. Ever since she had last seen him, she had wanted him to come to her, waited for him to change towards her, as he surely must now David was marrying Jane, she told herself hopefully. They could not go on wanting each other yet moving in opposite directions. Only her memory of the night they had shared made her think that if it had been like that once between them, then perhaps it could be so again. And so she would continue to wait, to want him, while humiliation and pain at his continued rejection smouldered inside her.

'When we last parted, I told you that I miss you— that my arms ache to hold you. I was not lying, Nancy. When you left and I had time to consider everything that had happened—how much you and your family must have suffered over the loss of your brother—

I was ashamed of my behaviour. Regardless of how hurt I felt, I wanted to come after you to beg your forgiveness, to tell you how sorry I was for everything I had said. In my arrogance and pride, I have been stupid and unfeeling in my treatment of you. I cannot forget you—nor do I want to. Can you put me from your mind?'

She shook her head. 'No. How could I?' she murmured, which was the truth.

'Then I ask you to keep thinking of me, and when this business between Jane and your brother is resolved, perhaps things can be different.'

'What has happened to Miss Wade and her brother? Are they still in London?'

He shook his head. 'No. They left for France when they left Berkshire—but not before Elizabeth and I...' He fell silent, fresh anger searing through him when he recalled that unpleasant scene in his bedroom.

'Why? What happened?'

'There was a scene. Angry words were exchanged. She had aspirations towards me which I could not fulfil. My rejection of her did not go down well. She threatened to expose you because of the night we spent together—to make things difficult for you in London.'

Nancy was horrified. 'That is dreadful. Do I need to worry?'

'No, thank God. I know her father would make sure

all her freedom was curbed if he knew what she'd done, and she backed down.'

'That's a relief.' For a fragile moment before he looked away, Nancy thought she saw weariness and a terrible pain in his eyes. Without thinking, she reached out and touched his arm. 'I know how vindictive she can be. But she has gone, thank goodness, and I refuse to think about her any further.'

'I intend to do the same—although it would be interesting to see what the French make of her.' He gazed down at her, warmth now in his eyes. 'It is you I want, Nancy. You I want to spend my life with. I will be back as soon as things are settled between Jane and David.'

Nancy was encouraged by his words, spoken softly and with sincerity, but how she wished he had included the word *love*. She pushed away that tiny kernel of doubt when, thoughtfully, he reached out his hand and touched her loosened hair falling about her shoulders. Nancy was the first to break the silence between them, looking at Dominic wide-eyed and uncertain, relieved to see his mood had lightened. His gaze took on the sheer male beauty of him, of his darkly handsome face and the saturnine twist to his firm lips. In all her life, she had never known a man quite like him.

'Are you quite sure you wouldn't like to stay for dinner?' she asked coaxingly.

Shaking his head, he turned to the waiting carriage. 'I have to leave.' Turning back to her, he placed a finger under her chin. He searched the depths of her amber eyes for a moment, and then he sighed. 'None of this has been easy for you, Nancy, and for that I'm sorry. When I get back to London, I'll catch up with you at the institute.'

The tenderness of his words invited silence, wrapping itself around them, which was as well, for there were so many things each wanted to say but could not—not now, when it seemed as though a slender thread of something deep was beginning to grow between them.

'Yes,' she murmured, 'I—I'll wait.'

And then he was gone, leaving Nancy to watch the departing carriage disappear along the drive.

Leaning his head back on the upholstery, Dominic closed his eyes and expelled a long breath, trying to bring his thoughts under control. When Sophia had died, he had persuaded himself that he would never fall in love again, that he would have the strength of character to withstand such a debilitating emotion, but then he had met Nancy.

He thought he knew her, her emotions and how her mind worked, but this new Nancy, a Nancy who seemed perfectly at home in serene, rural domesticity, evoked his surprise. His mind flew back to the woman he had first met and, yes, fallen in love with, when she had been living her life far removed from the restrictions that governed everyone else in their sphere. He remembered the moment they had both been instantly aware of how attracted they were to each other. He remembered the thrill of excitement he had experienced when they had made love. Even when he'd discovered her real identity, which had driven a wedge between them he'd thought would always remain, not once had he failed to admire the vibrancy and liveliness of her spirit.

Having had time since their parting to consider their situation seriously, he regretted not having spent more time with her in recent weeks. The situation with her brother and their busy lives had not given them the chance to get to know each other and to develop a better, closer relationship and understanding.

It occurred to him that he had been condemning Nancy for Sophia's sins. Deciding to keep her at arm's length had been based on nothing substantial, only his own fear of trusting and loving again. He could quite understand why she had decided to pass herself off as a widow. Her father was an important man, a very successful businessman, and she did not want to encroach on his privacy. And where her brother was concerned, she had been as surprised as he'd been to discover his relationship with Jane.

The meeting with David Ryland had gone better than Dominic had expected. What he had seen was a polite young man not lacking in respect who genuinely loved his sister. It was more than he could ever have hoped for.

Returning to London and missing Dominic more than she had thought possible, Nancy threw herself into her work. Betty, the only person who knew her true identity, did her best to dispel her mood of melancholy, telling her that it was unnatural for a young woman of her standing to put all her energies into her work and not to enjoy any of the entertainments and amusements that could be had in London. Nancy knew she was right. It was ages since she had visited the theatre or any of the other fashionable haunts.

Feeling more at ease now David was happily ensconced in Berkshire with Jane and Rose, Nancy, Betty and Amy took a hackney carriage to the Cremorne pleasure gardens in Chelsea by the side of the River Thames. It was a place of informality, where extravagance and pleasure were fashionable. Cremorne, along with Vauxhall and Ranelagh, had been established as one of London's favourite resorts. Its walkways and dark paths leading from lamp-lit alleyways, with so many intricate twists and turns, made it an ideal place for flirtation, assignation and intrigue, where ladies of the town loitered in the shadows and many a stolen kiss was to be had. There were sideshows and supper boxes, even a circus and a small theatre.

The three of them, joined by Amy's young man, sauntered along the paths, taking in the amusements. An orchestra was playing, and a pagoda was brilliantly lit with hundreds of coloured lamps and was surrounded by a circular platform for dancing.

Nancy was feeling relaxed and just about to get some refreshment when suddenly she saw Dominic coming towards her, lean and immaculate in a black evening suit. Unable to believe that her joy could be so great, she stopped while Betty, believing she was still following her, carried on walking. Nancy continued to stare at Dominic in shocked surprise, at a complete loss for words as he approached. It would appear their meeting was not as much a surprise to him as it was to her. How she had missed him, and now they were face-to-face. All she could do was gaze at him as he approached, feeling painfully self-conscious, not knowing what to say and waiting for him to speak.

Back in London after travelling to Berkshire with David Ryland, secure in the knowledge that when Constance came back from France, a wedding would soon follow, and feeling in a strangely mellow mood after a good meal and a glass or two of fine wine, Dominic had been eager to see Nancy. He had left the house only to be told when he reached the institute that she had gone to the Cremorne Gardens. Disappointed that he had to delay the moment of seeing her, he went there in the hope of finding her.

He mingled among the crowds that always flocked to Cremorne. Everyone was there—double-chinned politicians, lauded writers, artists, actresses, courtesans—all resplendent in shimmering silks and satins, the women's dresses cut low to reveal smooth, bare shoulders. He was content to watch as people strolled, chatting and laughing, with expectancy on their faces as they thought of the good food, good wine and pleasant music to be listened to and enjoyed.

That was when he saw Nancy. His eyes roamed involuntarily over the length of her body, for she was dressed in a silk, full-skirted gown the same colour as her auburn hair, with a spray of orchids on her shoulder. There was a rather wistful air of melancholy about her that, besides giving her an alluring quality, also made him feel instantly protective towards her.

'Hello, Nancy. You look exquisite.'

'Thank you. How are you, Dominic?'

'Very well. I've just arrived back from Berkshire after seeing your brother reunited with Jane—and trying to talk my neighbour into selling me one of his horses.'

'And did you manage to do that—purchase his horse?'

'No, but he's thinking about it.' He fell silent, looking at her closely, for the first time in his life horses being the last thing he wanted to talk about.

'How was David when you left—and Jane?'

'Very well—and impatient to make their union official. Although they'll have to wait until Jane's mother gets back from France.'

'I've no doubt David will be writing to tell me all about it. I didn't expect to see you here.'

'I wanted to see you. I called at the institute. I was told this was where I could find you,' he said, side-stepping a boisterous group of young people with a disapproving scowl on his face.

Nancy smiled. 'So you came here to find me—but I suspect you don't like the pleasure gardens very much, do you?'

'Pleasure gardens are not my favourite places,' he replied softly. 'I prefer somewhere with a quieter, more intimate atmosphere.' He looked at her tenderly. 'I've missed you, Nancy—very much, in fact. Look, would you like to join me for a drink—if your friends don't mind, that is? I can find us a box where it's less crowded.'

'Yes,' she replied almost shyly. 'I'd like that. I'll just go and tell Betty. Otherwise she will wonder where I am.'

Dominic watched her speak to Betty at the refreshment stall. Ignoring the inquiring, humorous glances thrown his way from her friends, he turned to look for a place that was more private. When they were settled and wine was brought and poured by a waiter, he looked across at her, thinking how poised she looked, how elegant.

The light in their supper box was muted, and when he gazed at her, her eyes were large and dark in her lovely face. Her hand, slender and white, was resting on the table, toying with the stem of her wine glass.

'It is evident that you are quite at home mixing with people in Society, Nancy.'

'Considering my father mixes with all manner of people in his business, coroneted lords and ladies of Society included, I'm very used to it.'

'Your friends seem in a happy mood. Is it an occasion that brings you here tonight?'

'No, not at all. Betty thinks I work too hard and persuaded me to come along.'

'She's right. You do work too hard. You deserve time off to enjoy the pleasures of life on occasion.'

'I like working. Is your grandmother in London?'

'No. She's back in Berkshire. She did mention contacting you to make a donation to your institute.'

'I welcome it—especially now I'm thinking of expanding—which will take all my time in the next few years. I'm already looking for suitable premises.'

Dominic tensed when she said this. 'You are thinking of opening another orphanage?'

'I'm not sure about that—perhaps I will, but at present I'm considering opening a school for the older children.'

'It will leave you little time for yourself.' Dominic leaned back in his chair with his long fingers entwined in front of him. He was studying her closely, trying to stay calm and relaxed, but he was waiting for more than an answer to his question.

'I will have plenty of help. I will to bring in more workers and someone to teach the children, but I am certain it can be achieved.' She smiled. 'It won't be all work. My mother and sisters will see to that, as they intend to make good use of the house in London to be closer to the entertainments in town. Discovering David is alive has given everyone a new lease on life.'

'And marriage?' Dominic asked, watching closely for her reaction.

Taken unawares by his question and feeling awkward beneath his scrutiny, Nancy averted her eyes. 'I—I haven't given it much thought.'

'You did—at one time. I have a confession to make. Perhaps I should have mentioned it before.'

'Oh? And what is that?'

'Several years ago, I happened to have been visiting Hugh. He was accompanying me to the station when we became caught up in a wedding—your wedding, to be precise.'

Nancy paled. 'I see. It—it was a long time ago.'

'Yes, but it was definitely you I saw that day.'

'Where were you? Outside the church?'

'Yes. I don't think the groom had turned up.'

'You're right,' she said sharply, sitting up straight. 'His name was Thomas Marsden. He jilted me for someone else—and he didn't have the decency to tell me. He simply left me at the altar.'

'He hurt you badly, I can see that.'

'He humiliated me—embarrassed me. I was terribly angry and swore I would never let another man do that to me again. That was when I decided to make my own way in life, unencumbered by a husband. I was fortunate that my grandmother had left me a legacy that enabled me to open the institute to do some good for others—for children who really have nothing at all. I swore I was done with love and marriage—and I've kept my promise to myself. That way life is more straightforward. It suits me.'

'I can understand that,' he said quietly.

Her eyes shot to his, remembering what he had told her about his wife when she had been at Osborne House. 'Of course you can. I remember you telling me your wife was unfaithful to you—which must have affected you deeply.'

He nodded slowly. 'Yes, it did. And it was just as hurtful as being let down at the altar. I also had a child to protect after Sophia left us.'

Resting her arms on the table, Nancy looked at him tenderly, her discomfort of a moment earlier having vanished. 'Tell me more about her, Dominic. What was she like?'

'You have every right to ask me about her, and I will tell you. It's just that I've grown out of the habit of speaking about her. In fact—' he sighed, reaching out and taking her hand '—I rarely speak about her to anyone.'

'Not even to your son?'

'No. It's wrong of me, I know, but I cannot bring myself to.' He fell silent, looking ahead, wrestling with his troubled thoughts.

'Please don't feel you have to explain anything to me, Dominic.'

'I want to. It's time I did. It's just that it's difficult to know where to begin.'

'At the beginning is as good a place as any,' Nancy prompted gently. 'Was she fair—dark? What?'

'Her colouring was dark, and she was very attractive. She was an only child, and hopelessly spoiled by her parents, who were wealthy landowners. She was utterly beautiful but completely selfish, and I should never have married her,' he said quietly.

'Why? Why do you say that? You must have loved her.'

'At the time, I suppose I did, which made me blind to her flaws. Marriage between us was what our families wanted—they were well acquainted—but the marriage began to fail almost from the start, and even more so when Mark was born.'

'But—why?'

His expression became grim. 'Things were as bad as they could possibly get. She was not maternal and didn't want to conceive, wanting to preserve her figure and her beauty. She didn't want Mark. She could hardly bear to look at him. I could suffer her rebuffs, her slights and her coldness, but her lack of love for our son was beyond endurance.'

Thinking of her own close family, she was sad to think a mother could not love her own child, although of course, in her line of work, she came across that phenomenon regularly.

'Sophia was a woman of enormous vivacity, never knowing what it was like not to have what she wanted—and she wanted me to flaunt her like one of her useless possessions. She never was a happy, loving wife. At one time I did contemplate her request for a divorce, which I eventually decided against. The Blackwells are old-fashioned, their ways and traditions steeped in the past. Family and honour mean everything. It was instilled into me from an early age. But there were so many rows and recriminations because I refused to live permanently in town that life became almost unbearable at Osborne House.

'Sophia began to spend most of her time in London. Every time she took a new lover, she made sure I knew about it. Unable to accept the situation any longer—or to withstand the disgrace she was determined to inflict on me—I was on the point of relenting and telling her she could have the divorce. Unfortunately, she died before this could be implemented. The sordidness of the whole affair almost destroyed me.'

'I am so sorry.'

'Yes—well—that's how it was. Perhaps now you will understand why I find it difficult speaking of her.'

Nancy squeezed his hand, sighing sadly. 'You must not let what happened fester and destroy your future as it has done the past. It is over. It is done. You must try and put it behind you—along with the misery she caused you. When Tom jilted me on our wedding day, I swore I would never marry again. And I meant it then. I found solace and determination to succeed in my work—and then I met you, and suddenly my world was turned upside down.' Dominic searched her eyes with a mixture of such gentleness and gravity that a stirring of emotion swelled in her chest. Reaching out, he touched her face as though trying to convince himself she was real.

'What a wonderful woman you are, Nancy Ryland. You are everything Sophia was not. She was vicious and ugly in her deceit, with no thought for anyone other than herself. I don't deserve you.'

'Yes, you do.'

'Ever since you left Berkshire, I have suffered a living hell.' His voice sounded harsh as it forged from his chest. He placed a finger beneath her chin, gazing at her lovely features. 'I deserve your contempt for everything I said to you after our night together when you gifted me with your virginity. You have no idea how I regretted my cruel words and actions. I wouldn't blame you if you were still angry with me. I feel quite wretched about the way I behaved towards you. It was unforgiveable—but I sincerely hope you can find it in your heart to do so and allow me to put things right. My conduct and disregard for your feelings were inexcusable. I apologise most humbly, Nancy.'

Nancy gave him a little smile, feeling herself melting at the tenderness she saw in his expression. An aching lump began to swell in her throat. 'It's been a difficult time for me too. I understand why you felt as you did—and how angry you were after you discovered I wasn't who I'd said I was. In your shoes, I would have felt the same. I should have told you before we made love.'

He rose suddenly when the music from the orchestra became low and sentimental, taking the glass from her fingers and setting it aside. 'Come. Enough doom and gloom for one night. Let's dance—as least that way I'll be able to hold you, which is what I've longed to do since that night we shared your bed. The floor isn't as crowded as it was.'

Taking her hand, he led her out onto the dance floor, drawing her to him, his hand coming to rest firmly against her waist. Nancy sighed and melted against him, giving herself entirely to the magic of the music and the joy of being in his arms.

He danced well as he guided her slowly around the floor, his eyes fixed intently on hers, the music and his closeness filling her with warmth. The wealth of emotions his nearness induced in her almost overwhelmed her, and she wondered if he could feel the beating of her heart.

Time seemed meaningless, and Nancy was aware of nothing in the world except this man and this moment. Neither wanted the music to end. After the first dance, they danced a second and then a third, neither of them speaking, grateful to the conductor for not changing the tempo of the music. Gradually Dominic's hand drew her closer, and he placed his cheek against her hair.

With her head resting on his shoulder and her eyes closed, Nancy caught the familiar smell of cologne and enjoyed the hardness of his body pressed close to hers as they moved in unison, completely attuned to each other.

It could have been a day, a month or a year later when the music stopped. Lifting her head, Nancy opened her eyes and saw his head poised over hers. There was no need for words as they stood in their enchanted circle of light and looked into each other's eyes, aware of nothing and no one but each other. But then Betty was beside them, breaking into the magic of the moment. Unconsciously, still holding Dominic's hand, Nancy turned and looked at her.

'I'm sorry to interrupt, Nancy, but we're leaving. We have an early start in the morning. Are you coming with us?'

'Er—I—I suppose so. Betty—Amy, you will remember Lord Blackwell. You will have seen him at the institute.'

Amy stared at him boldly and smiled broadly. 'Yes, I remember you, Lord Blackwell. We met at the summer fête. Me and my friend were in a spot of bother over spraying champagne all over the place. Do you remember, my lord?'

He laughed, his white teeth gleaming in the subdued lighting. 'I doubt I shall ever forget it, Miss—'

'Robinson—but Amy will do.' She smiled, clearly charmed by him.

'Well, Nancy, are you coming with us?' Betty asked again.

Feeling Dominic gently squeeze her hand, she thought it was his way of telling her not to go, and she was just as reluctant to part from him now.

'No, Betty. Actually, I think I'll stay.'

'How will you get back?'

'I'll see she gets back safely,' said Dominic.

Amy's eyes danced mischievously from one to the other. 'Yes, I'm sure you will. Come along, Betty. We'd better get a hackney.'

The music was starting up again as Nancy turned back to Dominic, and they danced some more. When it ended and they drew apart, she smiled up at him.

'Shall we sit down?' he asked softly.

She shook her head.

'Wouldn't you like some more wine—or champagne?'

'No. I think I've drunk enough for one evening.'

'Would you like to leave?'

'Yes. I think I'd like that.'

The night was cool now, the lamps casting a yellow glow along the paths. Outside the gardens, they took a hackney to the institute. Pulling up outside the building, Dominic climbed out and assisted her, moving towards the short flight of steps leading up to the door. He stopped suddenly, and she looked up at him. The lines of his face were etched like granite in the starlight.

'Can I offer you a drink—coffee—or something stronger?'

Dominic looked at her for a long time before answering. His eyes, almost as black as his sleek hair in the darkness, were intently studying her face, bathed in the soft, silvery glow from the moon.

'That's not what I want, Nancy. I think we know

that, don't we? If you let me inside, we both know what will happen. Is it what you want, too?'

Poised and still, there was more eloquence in Nancy's silence than any words she could have uttered. Her head told her to go inside alone, but her heart was telling her something else. She knew she was going to listen to her heart, for she was certain she was destined to love this man. She was aware that what they were about to embark on was a dangerous folly, but what she felt for him was too strong to resist any longer—too strong, too compelling for either of them to resist.

Lowering her eyes, Nancy opened the door and went inside.

Not wanting the strong, dangerous current of attraction that had been flowing between them all evening to be broken—or perhaps it was his own desire, his own desperate need to possess this woman he had desired and now loved—Dominic hesitated for a moment, then dismissed the hackney and followed her inside.

With just the cry of an infant to be heard from the nether regions of the institute, Nancy led the way up the stairs to her rooms. With the door closed, Dominic came to stand behind her. They did not light the lamps, for there was enough starlight entering through the windows for them to see.

Nancy stood quite still, waiting for what would happen, expectant, hopeful. Dominic's hands stroked her shoulders, and she could feel the warmth of his breath on her flesh as he lowered his head and placed his lips in the warm, scented hollow of her neck where a pulse fluttered beneath her skin.

Her senses soared as they undressed swiftly, and he drew her down onto the bed. She was soon swept along on long shuddering waves of pleasure which overwhelmed her to such an extent that it became almost unbearable. She arched her spine and pressed her breasts to his bare chest, feeling the urgency in his hard, lean body.

At last she yielded her body to his. They became like two vines wrapped around each other—united in an indulgence of love and pleasure until, at last, there was the ultimate, wonderful release.

On waking, Dominic quietly looked down at Nancy, his heart contracting with longing and pain on seeing how lovely she looked, bathed in the early morning glow. She was still sleeping, her sweet, curving form curled up among the tangled bedclothes, her head cushioned on her cap of thick auburn hair. Her lips were moist and slightly parted, through which she breathed softly. One long, slender leg was stretched out, incredibly perfect.

The sheer intensity of his feelings seemed to resonate throughout the room. After a while, seeming to sense his gaze on her face, she opened her eyes. The quiet, unblinking way she had of looking at a person reminded him of some ancient mystic—as though she could see a good deal farther than most people. Her face was calm and full of tenderness. It was also looking at him with an expression that made him lower his head without conscious thought. The kiss he placed on her lips was brief and tender, yet as remarkable in its impact as though they had just plighted their troth.

'What are you thinking?' she murmured, placing a like kiss on his cheek.

'That I want you with me, Nancy—always. You see, my darling, when you left me at Osborne House, I was the most wretched of men. The plain and simple truth is that I missed you. I was miserable without you, and I realised just how much you have come to mean to me—how much I care for you. This night means so much to me. You gave me all of yourself and held nothing back. I won't lose you now I've found you again. These past years, I've felt as if my soul were missing. You have helped me put myself back together. I love you, Nancy. Deeply. And I know you love me, too. I can feel it when I hold you in my arms.'

Nancy sighed, feeling her heart soar with hope at

his tender expression. She had never seen his eyes so full of love. 'Yes, I admit it. I do love you, Dominic. I love you as much as it is possible for a woman to love a man.'

'We are bound, you and I, and nothing is going to part us. If you will have me, we will be married very soon. I promise.'

'I would like that,' Nancy whispered, her eyes shining with happiness, 'but there is so much to sort out, so much we will have to discuss.'

'As my wife, you will no longer continue living at the institute. You do know that, don't you?'

'Yes, of course I do. It's just...'

He sighed, his arm tightening around her. 'What? What is it that is so important it takes precedence over my making love to you?'

'The institute—and the school I want to open.'

'Ah!'

'The children are such an important part of my life. Betty will oversee the administration—she is more than capable—but you won't stop me continuing to do what I can, will you?'

'Would it matter if I did?'

'Of course it would. I want you to approve of everything I do.'

'I will not object. I'll even put some money into the venture when you find a new premises for a school.

We will look together, if you like, so you don't have to worry.'

Nancy tilted her head and looked at him, caught up by the emotions she could not conceal. 'Thank you, Dominic. That means a great deal—but you do know that above all else, you are the most important thing in the world to me.'

His arm tightened, and he bent his head and lightly kissed her lips. 'Bless you for saying that. You're always so practical, my love. I will never stand in your way, but at this present time, my mind is on productivity of a different kind—a process that might be in motion already, don't forget.'

With a pink flush spreading over her cheeks, she laughed lightly. 'If we do have a child together, a little brother or sister for Mark, then I will be the happiest of women. But you really won't mind if I continue with my work?'

'I have no objections. I am by no means prejudiced against females with brains. Since we met, you have taught me something new, that there is no substitute for a clear-sighted, intelligent woman.'

'And I know you want more children,' Nancy whispered, her flush deepening, an answering sparkle lighting her eyes. 'As I do.'

Grinning wickedly, he cupped her face between his hands, brushing his thumbs over her smooth cheeks. 'I do, and I intend to spend every night of our marriage in the pleasurable occupation of siring our offspring. Mark will be an amazing big brother to them all. I'm terribly selfish, my love, and I want us to be married without delay. What do you say?'

'That I am so happy I could die.'

He grinned, placing a kiss on her brow. 'Don't you dare. I can't get married without you,' he teased, gathering her to him.

They dozed and made love again, leisurely now, their skin warm and moist, glistening with perspiration, until they were gloriously fulfilled. It was wonderful. It felt so right between them. Finally they slept, their bodies entwined once more.

Bright sunshine spilled through the window and over the bed. Nancy awoke and stretched in blissful lassitude, feeling like a flower opening to the sun's warmth. She opened her eyes, remembering the previous night, and she was filled with blazing happiness.

She turned, expecting to see Dominic still lying there beside her, but the bed was empty. Remembering he had told her he would leave early to avoid causing gossip, she snuggled into the hollow made by his body, feeling again the touch of him, and her body tingled anew. She breathed deeply of the smell of his cologne, which still lingered on the sheets, knowing they would find incredible joy in their future together.

Epilogue

Dominic and Nancy travelled to Osborne House. Dominic wanted her to spend some time with Mark before the wedding, getting to know him better. It wasn't difficult to love him. She spent a great deal of time with him, which was no great chore for he was a delightful child, with an open and friendly nature, and she derived immense pleasure from his company. She was always ready to join in his games and accompany him to the lake to fish. Full of enthusiasm, he never tired of showing her some new aspect of the house and gardens.

The happiest times were when Dominic accompanied them. When he was working, he always kept a watchful eye on them from his study window. She realised that he was closely following their exchanges and watching them attentively, speculatively. He did not withhold from commenting.

'I congratulate you. You have made a conquest. Mark has taken to you better than I cared to hope. I can see he's found a true friend in you, Nancy. You are fortunate. He doesn't take to people easily. He's told me how much he likes you.'

'I have become extremely fond of him too. It would be impossible not to. He's such a delightful boy.'

'Yes, he is. He's a great joy to me.'

'I can understand how you feel, for I feel it too.'

He looked at her intently. 'I love how you find such pleasure in his company.'

'I honestly do. When we are married, I intend spending a great deal of time with him.'

'I would like that. Mark's best interests have been paramount to all else since he was born—and still are,' he said, his look becoming one of preoccupation and complete absorption as he glanced up the stairs, where his son had just disappeared. 'I hated leaving him when I went to New York. I've made a point of seeing more of him since I came back. That's how it will be from now on, and with you as his mama—' his eyes warmed when he looked at her '—everything will be perfect.'

Things became frenetic as preparations got underway for Dominic and Nancy's wedding. Everyone was highly delighted that Nancy was to wed at last, and no matter how much her mother disapproved of her determination to carry on with her work at the institute, Nancy was adamant that she was not about to give it up. She was also deeply touched that Dominic was behind her in this.

When the day for the wedding arrived, it had a distinct aura of unreality. In the church—the same church in which Nancy was to have married Thomas Marsden—aglow with candlelight and perfumed with lavish blooms, among a sea of smiling family, close friends, a select few from the institute and a pastor waiting with a marriage book open in his hands, on her father's arm and with Mary and Georgina in attendance, it was with a quiet joy that Nancy walked down the aisle to be joined in holy matrimony with Dominic.

From where he stood beside Hugh Sutherland, unable to contain his desire to look upon his bride, Dominic turned. With enraptured eyes he watched the auburn-haired beauty holding a spray of white lilies move slowly towards him down the aisle. She was ethereal and magnificent in her grace, sunlight slanting through the windows drenching her in her ivory satin bridal gown in its silver light. It heightened his carnal hunger to have the joyful knowledge that she would soon belong solely to him.

Stepping out, he waited for her in watchful silence. Something like terror stirred his heart. *Dear Lord*, he prayed, *make me cherish and protect her all the days of my life, and give her the joy and happiness she de-*

serves. Reaching out, he took her hand, his long fingers closing firmly over hers. She responded to his smile, and in that moment of complete accord, their marriage to each other seemed right. She looked up into his eyes, and the love and devotion he saw in those liquid depths almost sent him to his knees. Side by side they faced the pastor to speak their vows, unaware of Nancy's mother dabbing away her tears of happiness and Dominic's grandmother looking proudly on.

When they were pronounced man and wife, Dominic bent his head and gently kissed his bride on the lips, unable to believe this wonderful creature belonged to him at last.

David and Jane exchanged glances as though there was some delightful conspiracy between them. Perhaps memories of their own wedding shortly after David's return from the Crimea had been resurrected by this happy day.

The wedding breakfast held at Aspenthorpe Hall was a truly opulent and impressive affair, with course after course of exquisite, mouth-watering dishes served with all the pomp and splendour expected of Sir John Ryland.

Dominic leaned close to his wife, the sweet, elusive fragrance of her setting his senses alive. 'You look exquisite,' he murmured. 'What are you thinking?'

She turned her head and looked at him, her face lively and bright. 'About us—and all this,' she said quietly, gazing around at everyone gathered together for this joyous occasion. 'I never believed it possible that this could happen.'

Looking to where his grandmother sat close to Constance, he smiled and turned back to his wife. 'Well, there's another good thing to come out of this.'

'And that is?'

'Constance has condescended to brave my grandmother's presence. Now the ice is broken, it will be interesting to see what will come of it. They will never be friends, but I suspect that for Jane's sake, an unspoken truce has been declared between them. She might even decide to pay us a visit in Berkshire.'

'I hope she does. I hate unpleasantness.'

Later, when the musicians struck up and began to play the first dance, Dominic proudly led his wife into the centre of the floor. Gazing down into her upturned face, he whirled her around to the delight of everyone, their bodies falling gracefully into the rhythm of the music.

They were the only couple dancing, the others being content to watch and admire. The desire that leapt between the groom and his wife was like nothing they had witnessed before. They watched transfixed as Dominic's long fingers splayed across the small of his bride's back. All the while he was looking at her, and she at him, as if there was no one else present, and everyone was bewitched by the mystery that seemed to be behind the highly charged communication of their eyes.

When other couples drifted onto the floor, Dominic danced his wife through the open French doors onto the terrace.

Nancy smiled up at her handsome husband when he took her in his arms. 'Do you know that I have loved you for so long, ever since the first time you took me in your arms.'

'Bless you, Nancy,' he said with a raw ache in his voice, bending his head and kissing her lips tenderly, all the love that had been accumulating over the years since Sophia's betrayal in that kiss. 'The connection between us has been there from the start, too strong for us to deny. You are a beautiful and truly wonderful woman, Nancy Blackwell.'

'And am I to believe you love me for my beauty alone?' she teased gently.

His features became solemn. 'No. I am not so shallow that I would have let your beauty alone make me love you. You have a multitude of other assets that I admire and love. You are a rare being, Nancy. You are everything I dreamed a woman, a wife—and one day a mother—could be. And more.'

Nancy tilted her head up to his and saw he was perfectly serious. 'That is a compliment indeed, Dominic. Thank you.'

* * * * *

If you enjoyed this story, you'll love more of
Helen Dickson's great historical romances

His Unlikely Countess
Penniless Until the Earl's Proposal
'Her Duke Under the Mistletoe'
in *Regency Reunions at Christmas*
The Earl's Wager for a Lady

And why not pick up her
Cranford Estate Siblings miniseries

Lord Lancaster Courts a Scandal
Too Scandalous for the Earl
Scandalously Bound to the Gentleman

MILLS & BOON®

Coming next month

THE DUKE'S MEDDLESOME MATCHMAKER
Emily E K Murdoch

Book 1 in The Unconventional Oliver Sisters trilogy

'You are not my client,' said the proposal planner slowly.

Henry turned back to Miss Oliver. 'Absolutely not,' he said firmly.

She examined him for a moment, and heat grew in his chest at the attention. Not because it was her, naturally. He would have felt discomforted if it had been anyone.

'Well,' said Miss Oliver finally. 'Well. That changes things.'

'So you'll stay?' Henry said eagerly. He wouldn't be the one to ruin things for Charles. After all, it had been the one thing their father had asked of him, on his deathbed, Henry's years of medical training still not enough to keep the man he loved alive.

Look after your brother, whatever you do.

The proposal planner stepped down from the dog cart—which he had to assume was a good sign.

'My brother is a good man,' Henry snapped, trying to ignore the heat roaring through his body as she stepped closer. 'I want him to be happy.'

'Even if you think I am some sort of charlatan,' Miss Oliver said, halting before him and gazing up at him through long eyelashes.

Henry swallowed. Charlatan? Yes, that was one word for her. It wouldn't be particularly accurate. *Beauty*. That was more accurate. *Temptress*, for it was tempting to lean down and taste—

He stiffly stepped back, half wondering how he'd managed to get himself into such a situation. *Honestly, man. Pull yourself together!*

Miss Oliver was examining him closely. 'It appears most difficult to please you, Mr. Paisley.'

God in His heaven… 'All I am asking is that you fulfil your agreement with my brother,' was all he could manage. 'He is the only family I have left.'

Something flickered in Miss Oliver's gaze. 'I'll stay,' she said shortly, walking around for her trunk.

Henry almost tripped over his own feet to get out and retrieve it for her. It was the least he could do.

'Good,' he said, handing her the heavy thing. *What did she have in there?* 'I'm glad you're staying.'

'I'm not staying for you!' Miss Oliver bristled. 'I—I am already fatigued by avoiding your displeasure.'

They stood there for a heartbeat, glaring at each other, until Miss Oliver snorted, turned around and stamped over to the inn.

Henry watched her go. *Well!* That would be the last time he'd ever be tempted by Miss Oliver!

Continue reading

THE DUKE'S MEDDLESOME MATCHMAKER
Emily E K Murdoch

Available next month
millsandboon.co.uk

COMING SOON!

We really hope you enjoyed reading this book.
If you're looking for more romance
be sure to head to the shops when
new books are available on

Thursday 15th January

To see which titles are coming soon, please visit
millsandboon.co.uk/nextmonth

FOUR BRAND NEW BOOKS FROM
MILLS & BOON MODERN

Indulge in desire, drama, and breathtaking romance – where passion knows no bounds!

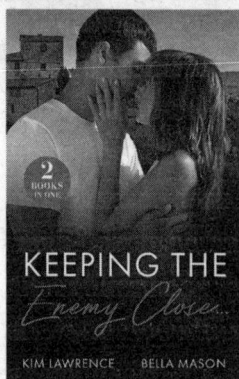

OUT NOW

Eight Modern stories published every month, find them all at:

millsandboon.co.uk

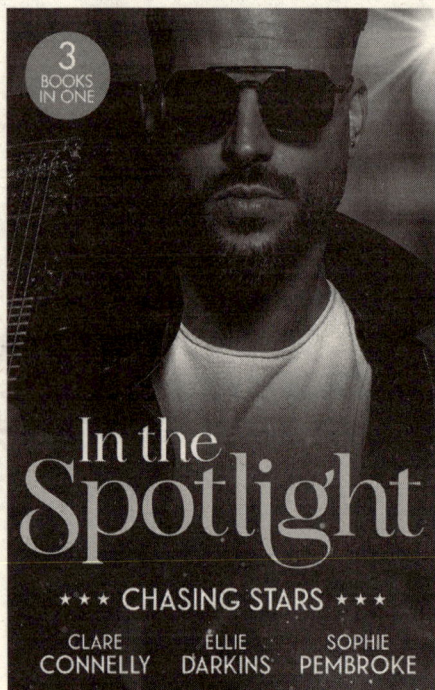

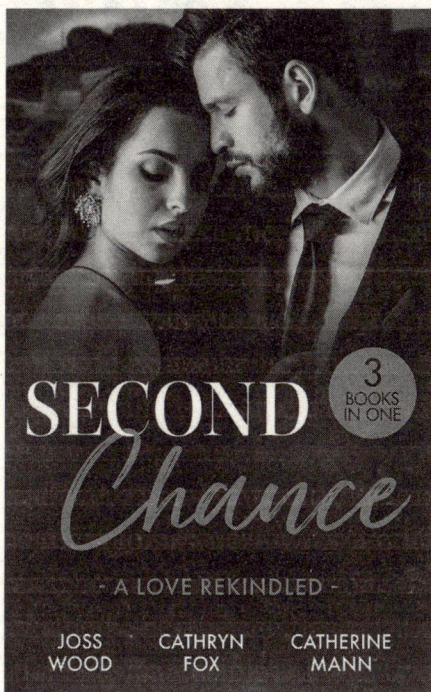

LET'S TALK

Romance

For exclusive extracts, competitions and special offers, find us online:

f MillsandBoon

X @MillsandBoon

◯ @MillsandBoonUK

♪ @MillsandBoonUK

Get in touch on 01413 063 232